Exodus Missed

J. D. Marcey

Literary Wanderlust | Denver, Colorado

Published in the United States by Literary Wanderlust LLC, Denver, Colorado. www.LiteraryWanderlust.com

ISBN print: 978-1-956615-60-9
ISBN digital: 978-1-956615-61-6

Dedication

For Wayd

Chapter 1

What Just Happened?

The scream of the perimeter alarm jolted Jinn from a fitful sleep. She lurched forward, throwing her arms up in defense before her mind slowly caught up with her. Her eyes narrowed as she tried to clear her confusion. The phone next to her vibrated. Out of habit, she picked it up, and Pseudo's concerned face popped into view.

"Jinn—you good?" Pseudo asked, magnified eyes darting around the screen.

"Yeah, I think," Jinn grumbled and reached over to silence the alarm. She rubbed her eyes as Pseudo tried to work out what had caused it to trip.

"You were asleep?" Pseudo asked.

"Yeah." Jinn rubbed her eyes. The adrenaline began to wane, and her limbs were heavy as she climbed from bed. Balancing the phone precariously on the cluttered table, she sifted through the piles of books and research papers in search of some wearable clothes. A pair of leggings was balled up in the corner. She shook them out and pulled them on.

"Outside sensor was tripped," Pseudo offered, his sharp voice cutting through Jinn's fog.

Her eyebrow quirked in irritation at a new hole worn into the sleeve of her favorite shirt, a sheer black rayon emblazoned with the cover of Mary Shelley's *Frankenstein*. The single bedroom opened onto a common area, which was somewhat less disorganized. She padded by her threadbare couch and checked her reflection in the dusty television screen. Her eye caught on a sliver of light coming from beneath the front door where the foundation had started to sag. Jinn worried how many more storm seasons it would take before the structure gave up and she'd have to move again.

She tiptoed through her kitchen—mostly empty except for flasks, beakers, measuring equipment, and notes, all meticulously organized in stark contrast with the rest of the house.

"Check the windows first—" Pseudo admonished as Jinn reached for the handle of the back door.

"I'm fine, Pseudo," Jinn snapped at him. She winced at her own face staring back at her from the bottom corner of the screen. Her short black hair was standing straight at all angles, and her olive skin was pale and blotchy due to the slept-in makeup that was supposed to highlight her green eyes. She looked half-dead. Of course, Pseudo didn't notice.

She pulled open the door and swept her gaze through her back garden. Her greenhouse, set up with specialized LED lights to quicken photosynthesis, would need to be taken down and brought inside before the fall storms, but at least today was clear.

"Turn your cam. All I see is your chin," Pseudo said with irritation.

Jinn growled at him for interrupting her thoughts before tapping the screen.

"Nothing's out here," Jinn said.

"Lab?" Pseudo asked.

"Different system, Pseudo," Jinn said.

"Oh yeah," Pseudo said sheepishly.

Jinn glanced over toward the lab. If someone was looking to rob her, that would be the better choice. She manufactured her own proteins using genetically modified mushrooms.

"I see something—" Pseudo shouted through the screen "—in the greenhouse."

Jinn turned and saw movement just on the other side of the entrance.

"It's small," she said aloud. "must be a foraging animal or something, maybe a deer?"

"A deer? When's the last time you saw a deer in Atlanta?" Pseudo scoffed.

"Fine, a dog or something." Jinn snorted.

"Careful," Pseudo hissed as Jinn approached the greenhouse. Jinn put her hand on the door's lever and paused, taking in a breath.

She swung the door open and gasped when she was met by the wide and terrified eyes of a small child. The boy could not have been more than three years old, and he was filthy. His curly dark-blond hair was matted around his head. His skin was pale where he wasn't caked in dirt, and he was holding a mostly ripe tomato that he had been eating like an apple. The juice was running down his face and across his little distended belly. She could smell the soil in his diaper. This child had obviously been alone for a while.

"What? What is it? A dog?" Pseudo was shouting from the phone. "Jinn? You there? Say something."

"I'm fine, Pseudo," Jinn said, keeping her voice light and even. "It's just Sebastian—must've been hungry."

"The kid from down the street?" Pseudo asked.

"Yeah," Jinn said, kneeling down next to the child. "What's his mother gotten into now?"

"Damn." Pseudo shook his head. "Poor kid."

"Talk later, Pseudo," Jinn said to the screen. "I'm gonna try and find Maddie."

"Okay," Pseudo answered. "I'll reset security. G'luck."

Jinn tapped the phone to end the video and reached her hand out toward Sebastian. Her heart ached for the toddler.

"Mommy not wake up," little Sebastian whimpered, protectively pulling his mangled tomato close. Jinn's skin prickled with anger. Maddie wasn't a terrible person. When she was in her right mind, she was kind and funny, but she was addicted to *source*, something that Jinn was all too familiar with. She had never seen anyone around that she believed could be Sebastian's father, and his mother was so hung up on blitzing source that she barely existed for the child at all. This was not the first time Sebastian had come to her in search of something to eat. Jinn had tried to help Maddie with food, but as addicts do, she refused—fully believing she had her life under control. As awful as it was, there wasn't anything Jinn could do but give the poor child something to eat when he came around.

"C'mon," Jinn said, reaching for Sebastian's little hand. It was sticky. "Let's get you clean and something to eat."

She brought him inside the house, and Sebastian wriggled and squealed as Jinn put him beneath the running water before tossing the soiled diaper into the trash. The diaper could have been reused, but it would have taken a lot of bleach, and she didn't want to deal with that mess. The child played happily, as though it were a normal day, and he wasn't naked and neglected and starving. Jinn plundered through her fridge and pulled out some of her manufactured protein, customized to look and taste like chicken nuggets. Though there was always a question of how accurate her replication was to the original, since she had never eaten an actual chicken nugget. Those had long since been replaced with the cheaper and more simply manufactured proteins.

Sebastian had splashed water all over the bathroom before

Jinn returned to towel him off. Nothing like diapers existed in her house, so she wrapped him in an old dish towel and dressed him in one of her old T-shirts, which swallowed his small frame. The toddler giggled at the absurdity, then saw the nuggets on the table. He rushed over and excitedly started shoving them in his mouth.

"Slow down, li'l man," Jinn chided. "They're not going anywhere."

As Sebastian happily devoured his lunch, Jinn showered and put on a set of fresh clothes. She traced around her eyes with a dark pencil before applying some oil to her eyelashes and color to her lips. As she pressed them together, she wondered why she bothered. The time it took just to extract the pigment from the ash and flowers was probably excessive for something so trivial, but when she checked the mirror she was satisfied. The monitors were clear, ensuring that everything was locked up tight again. Finally prepared, she stepped into her boots to make the trip to find out what sort of mess Maddie was in now.

Holding Sebastian's hand, Jinn walked down the street, passing houses beginning to sag under the weight of time. At the front of the small yard, a gate barely held on to the crumbling fence that opened to the front walk of the house where Sebastian lived with his mother. The lawn was overgrown, like most of the houses on the street, and the door was slightly ajar. Nudging little Sebastian slightly behind her, tension settled into her bones. She knocked loudly on the door, pushing it open.

"Maddie?" she called out, "you home?" No response. Even Sebastian had gone quiet. "Maddie? I'm coming in."

Chapter 2

Damn

The putrid stench of death hit Jinn the second she opened the door. She turned to Sebastian, his round eyes looking at her expectantly. She gently guided him backward toward the steps.

"Mommy not wake up," he said for the second time, his eyes glistening.

"Sit here and wait for me, okay?" she said gently, settling him down onto the porch steps. "Don't go anywhere, I'll be right back." He sat down and started picking at the crumbling stone.

Jinn's eyes began to water from the smell as she pushed through the door. The living room was filthy. Dirty clothes were piled on the torn couch, and rotting food, buzzing with flies, moldered and leaked across the floor. Anger and sadness fought for dominion in Jinn's consciousness. Poor little Sebastian, he had no choice in this. She picked her way across the trash and opened the bedroom door, where the stench became even more oppressive. There lay Maddie's stiff corpse, the source vaporizer still clutched in her hand. Retching, Jinn closed the door and leaned against the wall for support.

Jinn stumbled into the room across the small hallway. She assumed it belonged to Sebastian, though it was just as disgusting as the rest of the house. Holding her breath, she picked through some of the soiled clothes to find something he could wear and a stash of reusable diapers. A little stuffed elephant peeked out from underneath a pile of trash. It was also filthy, but it was the only intact toy among the mess. The handful of things she'd grabbed was paltry, but she needed to get out of there. What was she going to tell Sebastian?

She stepped outside and took a few breaths of fresh air before sitting down next to Sebastian and putting on the best kid-friendly smile she could muster. "Hey buddy, we're gonna go back to my house, okay?"

"My name's not buddy," he said, smiling back. "It's Sebastian." He stood and took her hand once again. "Ellie!" he shouted and reached for the stuffed elephant. Jinn started to pull it away since it was covered in dirt and who knows what else, but with a grimace, she allowed him to hold it. She could wash it when she got home.

They made the short walk back to her house while she debated what to do next, the toddler babbling nonsensically the whole way. It amazed her how he was able to just exist in this world of squalor—what had to be a difficult and lonely life—and still have such childlike wonder and happiness in his eyes. This was all just an adventure for him.

Once home, Jinn distracted Sebastian with a tablet loaded with games so she could wash his clothes and stuffed animal. Her heart was heavy, but she knew who she needed to call.

"You get the tiny human sorted?" Pseudo asked when his face appeared on the screen. His glasses were crooked on his face, as usual.

"Not exactly. What are you doing?" Jinn answered, looking at the dark background in Pseudo's screen.

"Roxanne's being a bitch again," Pseudo said, looking off screen. "We might lose connection."

"How bad?" Jinn asked.

"Nothing major, she's just scrambling signals," he answered. "I think the code's corrupted. Won't take long; just gotta find it."

"I need to call Juniper," Jinn said. "Will it work?"

"Doubt it. The longer reaching signals seem worse," he said, pushing up his glasses, which only made them more crooked. "What happened to Maddie?" Jinn had tipped him off mentioning Juniper. Finding an abandoned child in what was left of Atlanta was not exactly rare.

"What about interplanetary?" Jinn asked.

"Don't know. We haven't received signals from Exodus in over six months," he answered and rolled his eyes.

"Is it possible we just aren't picking them up?" she asked, trying to keep her voice steady.

"No. You know this," he answered with annoyance. It was not the first time they had had this conversation.

Jinn checked the date on her screen—July 23, 2176. She made a quick mental calculation. Her parents' ship would still be in flight for another four months, depending on how much time they had spent at the relay stations.

"What happened to Maddie?" Pseudo asked again.

Jinn remained silent, thinking.

"They're not coming back, Jinn." Pseudo's eyes penetrated her screen, trying to will her into understanding.

"I know," she huffed.

"Do you?" Pseudo asked, then snorted. "What's up with the youngling?"

"Bastian's fine," Jinn answered, forcing herself back to the present. "Maddie overdid source."

"She in trouble?" Pseudo asked. There was a hint of worry in his voice. He didn't know Maddie, but Jinn knew he was uncomfortable with her being involved with someone controlled by source. It was difficult to keep away from since most of the city was under its influence in one way or another.

"Not anymore," Jinn said.

"Ah—deadsies?" Pseudo responded, as though he were discussing a houseplant.

"Yeah," Jinn took a deep breath. "I'm gonna take Sebastian to Juniper. He'll be happier there."

"Lucky for him then," Pseudo answered. Jinn flinched and shook her head. He wasn't wrong.

"Watch the lab while I'm gone?" Jinn asked.

"Fine, but I'm not touching that shit," Pseudo responded.

"You know, protein isn't scary. It's basically a plant," Jinn chided, amused by Pseudo's disgust with her work.

"It's gross," he answered with a shudder, "and it smells."

"Everyone around here who gets to eat because of my work would disagree," Jinn declared. "Sebastian likes it."

"Yeah, well, they probably wouldn't eat it if they saw how it's made. Biology's gross."

"You eat it," Jinn grinned. Pseudo just grunted in response. Sebastian, hearing his name, wandered in and started pulling at Jinn's hand.

"I gotta go," Jinn said, looking down at the toddler with a smile. "Don't forget to check on the lab."

"Ugh, fine," Pseudo said before disconnecting.

"Where's Ellie?" Sebastian asked, his curly hair falling into his shining eyes.

"We'll get him in a minute," Jinn answered, kneeling to his level. "Listen, I'm gonna take you to meet some friends, okay? They live in an awesome place with tons of food and toys. What do you think?"

"Mommy come too?" Sebastian asked, with a childish look of apprehension.

"No, sweetie. Mommy's gonna stay. It'll just be you and me." She smiled down at him, trying to make this all seem as normal as possible for the little boy. He smiled back, and Jinn thought she saw relief in his eyes.

"Where's Ellie?" he asked again. Jinn gave him a small squeeze before leading him to the laundry room to get his freshly cleaned, stuffed animal.

As Jinn prepared for the trip ahead, Sebastian became like a shadow. She could tell he was afraid to leave her side. So, despite the difficulty of trying to accomplish some sort of preparation, she allowed his clinging and forgave his constant pestering. Jinn had attempted to contact Juniper, but apparently Roxanne, the radio tower Pseudo had restructured to connect their small network of communication, was indeed being a bitch.

Eventually,it became clear that Sebastian was tired, and it was already getting late in the afternoon. It would be best to wait until morning to leave. Jinn sat down on her couch and pulled out a tablet that she used in her work with food production. She checked the dates. She'd need two days to get Sebastian to Juniper, where NOMAD, or the New Order of the Modern American District, could take care of him. Then, it would take two days to get back. That should give Jinn at least a week before the rolling fall storms. She'd have to deconstruct the greenhouse and reinforce the walls of her lab, but those things didn't take much time. She'd done it for the last three years and had worked out most of the kinks by now.

Sebastian curled up beneath a blanket with his head leaning against her leg. He was sleeping soundly in the way that toddlers do. He almost smiled in his sleep. She looked down at him with empathy and stroked the child's curls.

Jinn wasn't even supposed to be here. Her parents had secured passage on the last Exodus ship, and it was highly unlikely that anyone left on Earth was going to have the resources or expertise to launch any more. Her parents had waited as long as they could for her to get her act together. Biologists in any field, like Jinn and her mother, and physicists like her father were in high demand on the still relatively new

Mars colony. But her own weakness and stupidity had caused Jinn to lose her seat, and her parents had finally left without her. Jinn shook her head and scoffed at herself. She was twenty-eight years old and acting like a child. Sebastian was taking the loss of everything he knew without so much as a second thought. She just needed to do the same.

Chapter 3

Traveling

Jinn woke the next morning as Sebastian stirred. They ate a quick breakfast of cereal and manufactured sausage before going outside to get her bike from the storage shed. The battery was fully charged, so she should make it most of the way before she needed to find a charging station. She put on her leather riding jumpsuit and packed his few clothes and reusable diapers as well as a change of clothes for herself. She also brought along bottles of water and snacks. Her taser, which Pseudo had modified, was strapped to her belt next to a very pretty, but not particularly functional, dagger she liked to carry. The black stainless steel hilt was inset with lab-grown rubies and etched with a phoenix filigree. The smooth, straight blade was also black except for the edges that shone bright silver where it was sharpened. Pseudo had shown her how to keep it sharp, and it was handy as a defensive weapon.

Jinn had tried to pack Ellie in the bag, but Sebastian pulled it out as soon as her back was turned. The disappointment in his watery eyes tugged at her chest when she tried to explain that Ellie would be safer in the bag, so she found a canvas strap and attached one end to the elephant and the other around Sebastian's waist, which he found delightful. Even with the chin straps pulled tight, Pseudo's helmet was too big for the boy, but better than nothing. After one final check, they headed north.

As the interstate opened up, the empty roads and buildings made Jinn feel small. The whine of her electric motor echoed from the walls of the enormous overpasses, and Sebastian would point and shout on the rare occasion they passed another vehicle. She had heard stories from her grandparents about how these roads were once so packed with cars that it took hours to cover even a small distance. Once self-drivers became standard, traffic was less of a burden, but there were still more people than space. It was difficult to imagine. She even remembered when she was just a child herself, that her great-grandmother had come to visit her family and had called Atlanta a wasteland. At the time it was strange, but the Exodus mission had shuttled thousands off the planet since then, and Jinn began to understand what her great-grandmother had meant.

Sebastian sat in front of Jinn and held Ellie close. He was on the adventure of a lifetime. Nothing but smiles and giggles came from him with everything they passed. There was no existential contemplation because he didn't know what had been before, only what was in front of him. After a couple of hours, Sebastian started to fidget, so they stopped for a short break so they could walk around. Hopefully, that would settle his restlessness.

They followed this schedule through most of the trip—ride for an hour or two, then stop for a break. It was, for the most part, uneventful. There was limited traffic on the roadways, and aside from a very precarious-looking overpass, the roads were mostly clear of debris and hazards. As the battery power started to wane, Jinn began to look for a charging station. There were many along the route, but it was a bit of a gamble to find one that still worked. After the third stop they were finally able to recharge. A small building stood close to the station sending delicious smells wafting to them, so she took Sebastian's hand and walked toward it accompanied by his constant chatter. It would take an hour or so to charge the bike, depending on how well the charger worked, so she went to see if they could get something to eat.

They stepped through the door into an open space with a few mismatched tables and chairs. A short, heavy, dark-skinned woman worked behind a stove, and they were greeted by a stout man, younger than the woman but with similar features.

"Hello. Welcome to Delilah's Kitchen. How are you?" the man said in a voluminous baritone.

"Hi, we are good," Jinn forced a smile but held tight to Sebastian's hand. "Do you take credits?" Jinn had a good bit of money saved up, although most everyone bartered if they could. Jinn usually paid for things in manufactured protein.

"Yes, we do. My name is Jonah," he answered with a smile and opened his arm to guide them to a table.

"Thanks," Jinn said and sat Sebastian down in a chair next to her. He immediately started picking up and playing with everything on the table.

"Would you like some tea?"

"Sounds awesome, Jonah, thanks," Jinn answered and attempted to smooth her helmet-styled hair. Sebastian was already turned around backward in his chair, looking at everything in the room.

After a moment, Jonah brought two plastic cups with a lukewarm liquid, but at least it was sweet. He handed one to little Sebastian, who drank from it greedily. Jinn and Jonah both smiled at him softly.

"Delilah grills spectacular chicken," Jonah offered, "with carrots and potatoes. Would you care for some?"

"Sounds amazing," Jinn said while Sebastian stared at Jonah with wide eyes.

"We will get that going for you," Jonah smiled, a sincere smile, as though he truly enjoyed what he was doing. She smiled back, some of the tension easing from her shoulders.

Jinn played with Sebastian, mostly to keep him occupied while they waited for their food. When Jonah brought the two steaming plates to the table, her mouth started to water. The meat had come from actual chickens. This was surprising, but they likely raised the birds themselves. Still, it was a risk to try and run a service like this one. A lot of hungry people roamed the area, and most of them were not in their right minds, thanks to source. Even though the restaurant did not seem like much compared to the standards of, say, the twenty-first century, it was still a lot more than most people had.

Jinn and Sebastian quickly tucked into their meals, Sebastian letting out little squeals of pleasure as he munched the potatoes and carrots, while Jinn cut his chicken into small pieces.

A tingling sensation crawled up her spine, and Jinn glanced toward the door as three men entered. They were quiet, and their eyes were glazed over. Not the usual euphoric expression of people blitzed on source but more like the edgy discomfort of early withdrawal. Jinn had left her dagger on the bike, but her taser was still clipped to her belt. She subtly loosened the strap.

Jonah approached the men with the same smile and greeting, and very quickly had them sitting at a table within Jinn's line of sight. They kept looking around furtively, constantly moving and fidgeting with the items on the table.

Though Jinn was tense, and she sensed that Jonah was as well, the men only seemed interested in sitting and having a meal. Still, Jinn kept them in her periphery while Sebastian finished up. Naturally, he was completely unaffected by the newcomers.

She stood and took Sebastian's hand, walking him to the counter where Delilah was busy cooking and singing to herself. Jinn waited as she finished getting the plates ready and turned to face her.

"Enjoy your meal, hun?" she asked, her voice tinged with a Southern accent that made it smooth as honey.

"It was delicious, thanks so much," Jinn said.

"What about you, little man?" she asked, leaning over to look at Sebastian, who nodded vigorously.

"Jonah said you accept credits?" Jinn asked.

"Yes, ma'am, I'll scan them here." She turned to a small machine with a chip reader. "It'll be forty-eight credits for you both." She smiled again at Sebastian. Jinn let go of his hand to work the RFID card from a closed pocket on her riding jacket. She placed the card close to the reader and waited for the acceptance beep when the air was pierced by a shrill scream and Delilah's frightened gasp. She spun around to see the tallest of the three men holding Sebastian with a blade to his neck. The toddler screamed and squirmed with everything he had.

"Stay calm, bud," Jinn said, putting her hand out toward him.

"Gimme the card and passcode," the man ordered, squeezing Sebastian until he screamed again.

"Here—take it," Jinn threw it down on the ground between them.

"I want your account, too," he shouted at Delilah. Jonah had backed away slowly, coming to stand protectively next to his mother.

"*Don't give it to them*," Jonah hissed.

"The baby," Delilah whimpered. The man squeezed harder, causing Sebastian to choke.

"Okay, okay here." Jonah handed him the card from behind the register. The man took it while one of his companions picked up Jinn's card from the floor. He dropped Sebastian roughly, leaving him a sobbing mess. They turned and fled from the building.

Instinctively, Delilah rushed over to make sure Sebastian was alright, while Jonah just watched in shock, the kind smile stripped from his face. Delilah rocked little Sebastian, wiping at a small strip of blood on his neck.

"Be right back," Jinn growled and stormed out the door. Jinn spotted the men and broke into a run. The modified taser pulled easily from her pocket. She took aim and pulled the trigger. Three bursts of light shot from the gun, landing squarely on the tallest man's back. He immediately hit the ground, his entire body racked with convulsions. The other two took off at a sprint, but Jinn was faster. The taser needed time to recharge, but she wouldn't need it. As she closed the distance, she leaped and caught the second man around the waist. Using her momentum, she rolled forward, slinging his body over hers and flung him into the third. They both began to struggle to get up, but she stood over them with the taser inches from their faces.

"Cards—both of them," she barked, looking back at their counterpart, who was not just convulsing but had lost all control of bodily function. Pseudo hadn't warned her about that particular side effect. "Unless you want to be the next one to piss yourself." She stepped forward, and both men cowered, putting their hands over their faces.

"Cards," Jinn said again, a razor-sharp edge to her voice.

"Here, here," the shorter one said, digging them out of his pocket and handing them over. He had tears streaming down his face. Jinn almost pitied him. Almost. That drug would make you do awful things. She took the cards from him.

"Run," she said, keeping her taser level. They both scrunched their eyebrows in confusion.

"Go!" she roared, and they took off, each of them tripping at least twice before they gained traction. Jinn walked back toward the restaurant, stopping for good measure to kick the man whose convulsions had only slightly abated.

Sebastian and Delilah still huddled on the floor when Jinn pushed back through the doors. Jonah, wide-eyed and shaking, raised an ancient shotgun toward her.

"Whoa." She ducked and put her hands up. "Just me." She looked through her raised hands at Jonah, who still trembled but lowered the weapon. Slowly, she reached into her pocket for the RFID card that belonged to the restaurant and handed it to him. He took it, collapsed into a chair, dropped the gun to the floor, and put his head into his hands. Sebastian escaped from Delilah's grip and ran over to Jinn with his arms wide. She picked him up and hugged him close.

"Your boy is strong," Delilah remarked.

Jinn opened her mouth to speak but closed it again.

"What is it, child?" Delilah asked, putting a hand on her shoulder.

"He's . . . he's not mine," Jinn said. "He was my neighbor in Little Five. I'm taking him to NOMAD."

"Oh, I see," Delilah said. She likely knew that meant something tragic. She patted little Sebastian's back a couple of times, her eyes getting misty.

"Thank you for looking out for him," Jinn's voice cracked.

"Thank *you* for getting our credits back," Delilah said, her voice brimming with appreciation. "That was all we had. We would've been undone. I've been cooking for other people for as long as I can remember, but customers are coming in less, and credits just don't work like they used to." She went over and put a hand on Jonah's shoulder. He pulled in his breath and sat up, wiping his eyes. He patted her hand a few times.

"That was close. We could've lost everything," Jonah said, looking up at his mother. "I know we've been hoping things would get better, but maybe we should head for NOMAD, too, Momma."

"You're right," Delilah said with a wistful look around the restaurant. "I think it is finally time to leave this old place behind."

"Thanks again," Jinn said.

"Safe travels, friend," Jonah said, his kindness pulsing through the trembling baritone.

"Same," Jinn said. Clutching Sebastian's tiny hand, she went back to the bike. Her thoughts were heavy. NOMAD was the largest organization left in North America. They were a society that had broken off from the main infrastructure and lived in what they considered a more earth and environmentally conscious manner. They were not particularly tolerant of people they considered lazy or wasteful, but they were doing much better than most of the people left over in the cities. Many who were unable to secure a seat on the Exodus ships had left the urban environments behind to join them. Jinn had considered it herself, and she was pretty sure Pseudo was just waiting for her.

Chapter 4

Nomad

After the nightmarish events at the restaurant, Sebastian was calm for the ride, and they traveled until well after dark. They found an abandoned motel where they could sleep and were lucky enough that one of the charging stations still had power. Jinn charged the bike while they slept. They had a quick breakfast and rode on, stopping for breaks and snacks occasionally. By late afternoon, they were getting close to their destination. Jinn had tried to contact Juniper a couple more times, but her phone wouldn't make the connection. She talked briefly to Pseudo, who reported that someone had gone into Maddie's house in the middle of the night but left. Jinn hadn't bothered to lock up after leaving the dead woman's home, so it was most likely scavengers, not that there was much in that house to take.

The hills had been rising steadily when the hollowed-out skeleton of a dirigible finally came into view, its latticework of wooden struts sticking into the air like a massive rib cage. She tried to remember the last time she had seen it airborne. She couldn't have been much older than Sebastian. Just before reaching the dirigible, they came upon Juniper's residence. Her home had been dug out of the side of one of the foothills and was very spacious, but all you could see from outside was a door and a couple of small windows. Their electric cart was gone, and Jinn worried whether anyone was home. Sebastian's eyes were filled with wonder as they dismounted the bike, especially when they caught on the flattened area where the enormous machine sat idly. Once upon a time, it had been used as transportation for food and medicine to the urban population. But like everything else, it was discontinued as Exodus transported more and more people off the planet.

Juniper swung the door open before Jinn and Sebastian had covered the distance. Her long silver hair swirled around her, and a kind smile spread across her face.

"Jinn, how great to see you," Juniper said, age giving her voice a soft crackle.

"Hey Jun," Jinn said, coming in for a warm embrace. "How is Mae?"

"She's great," Juniper said, then added, "She is actually off delivering a baby for the Tolentinos."

"That's great," Jinn said and smiled. She didn't know the Tolentinos, but if everything turned out well, Mae would be floating once the job was done. Mae was Juniper's wife, and they had been together since well before Jinn had known them.

"Who is your handsome friend?" Juniper said with the over-enthusiastic cadence reserved for small children as she leaned down to Sebastian's level. The toddler grinned and pushed his face into the side of Jinn's leg.

"Sebastian, meet Juniper," Jinn said to him. He peeked one eye out and squealed before burying his face again.

"His mother?" Juniper asked.

"Source," Jinn answered, shaking her head. Juniper could

guess the rest.

"Sebastian, are you hungry? I have some yummy oranges that I just picked this morning." Juniper spoke with a singsong voice that reminded Jinn of a schoolteacher. Curiosity got the best of him, and he looked hopefully at Juniper. She led them inside and grabbed an orange from the island and started to peel it.

Jinn admired their home. The back wall of the home was buried deep in the hillside, partitioned with wood and plaster. A loft floated near the top where children would play, encircled with a banister and safely gated stairs. There was no shortage of happy parents bringing their young ones around for Mae and Juniper. There were no walls; everything was open except for the bathroom with plumbing that led off the side of the hill and flowed into a natural sewage lagoon.

"Tea?" Juniper offered.

"I would love some, thanks," Jinn answered.

"Why don't you show Sebastian the loft? There are a lot of things up there that the other children have left."

Sebastian finished eating his orange, his face and fingers sticky. Jinn smiled at him and took him to the bathroom to clean up before leading him up the spiral staircase. He was fascinated by the winding stairs, though they made Jinn feel slightly claustrophobic. At the top, Sebastian immediately ran to the railing to look out over the rest of the house, his face bright with amazement. Jinn smiled; this must seem like an enormous height to the small child. Soon he spotted the toys and stuffed animals haphazardly lying around and picked up a toy motorcycle, which he immediately started pushing around and making engine noises. Jinn turned as Juniper came up the stairs holding two teacups with steaming liquid. Jinn took hers graciously.

"How have you been, Jinn?" Juniper asked, directing her toward a couple of chairs in the corner.

"Things are good," Jinn lied. Things were normal, but good

was a stretch. "How are things here?"

"Same as always," Juniper smiled. "How have you been holding up since . . ."

"It's hard, but I'm alright, focusing on my proteins and helping people get enough to eat. Though it seems more people come around daily looking for food. It's hard to keep up."

"And Pseudo?"

"He's Pseudo." Jinn shook her head with a smile. "He barely exists but keeps all our coms and electric running. He's watching the lab while I'm here."

"He is an interesting little creature," Juniper chuckled. "We could use more minds like his around here."

Jinn kept quiet. She knew Pseudo would follow her if she came here, but there was no way she would be able to talk him into leaving without her.

"I would really love for *you* to stay, also." Juniper said, gently touching Jinn's arm.

"I know, I just . . ." Jinn fumbled for a response. "I want to see what my parents' plan is. I mean, they may still send another Exodus ship."

"Jinn . . ." Juniper said, looking into her eyes. They both knew that wasn't going to happen, but Jinn really wanted to believe it might. "You know that they would rather you come here than struggle where you are. You have a place here. Pseudo as well."

"I know, and I doubt they care one way or another. I mean, who leaves their child?" Jinn said with a bit of impetuosity.

"You're not their child, love," Juniper said softly. "You are a grown woman, and they had to make their decision. It was very difficult for them."

"For *them*?" Jinn was incredulous. "What about me? I needed help."

"Yet, you were refusing it," Juniper gently admonished.

"You don't know what it was like. I had no choice. Xandar isolated me from everyone and threatened to hurt them," Jinn said, trying to hold in her emotions.

"I know he did, and you're right. I don't know everything you went through. I just want you to know that your parents did care, and they wanted what was best. But they had no way of providing it, and they did what they thought was right under the circumstances. Whether or not it was the best decision could be questioned, but their intentions were good."

"If intentions meant anything, I'd be on my way to Mars. I didn't *intend* for anything that happened. I was scared, confused, misled . . ." Jinn trailed off, tears welling up in her eyes.

"I know, Jinn, I know," Juniper patted her arm like a loving grandmother. "You make your own decisions, and I am here for you whatever you decide. Just know that I would love for you to be here, and you will always have my support."

"Thanks. Sorry for getting upset," Jinn answered, wiping her eyes.

"No need, love. You have every right to be upset, even angry." Juniper took a breath. "I just want to make sure you know you have people who care for you, and we don't want you to end up in that position again." The insult stung, but she knew Juniper was right. It would be easy to fall into the trap again if she wasn't careful.

The rest of the afternoon was spent in happier conversation. As afternoon turned to evening, they shared a meal of chicken and dumplings, made from real chicken of course, and Sebastian was happier than Jinn had ever seen him. As callous as it felt, Pseudo was right. Sebastian's life would be a lot better here than he ever could have hoped if Maddie was still alive. Juniper had given Sebastian his own cot, where he slept peacefully.

Maybe it was finally time to listen to Juniper, and she should bring Pseudo to live within NOMAD. There was much more stability here, and they weren't struggling to keep old infrastructure alive long past when it should have died.

NOMAD had simply started fresh and rebuilt society using knowledge from the mistakes of past generations. She'd talk to Pseudo and see what he thought. She finally drifted off to sleep, fantasizing about life within NOMAD.

—

Jinn woke to an intense buzzing sound and fought to blink away slumber. Juniper and Sebastian were still sleeping. Mae had not returned home, but that wasn't unusual. She liked to stay for a while with the new mothers and would probably return happy and exhausted in the morning. Outside the windows was still pitch dark. Jinn squinted at her phone, trying to focus. It was a security alert. Her panic room had been activated.

Panic room was a stretch. It was just a cellar that Pseudo had wired up and reinforced with a steel door. Somewhere she would be more protected if her place were ever attacked by roaming bands of people desperate for source. Withdrawal from the drug went from discomfort to desperation quickly, and they would do just about anything to get something of value to barter for more.

Pseudo. Jinn's brain finally caught up with her. Something must have happened, and Pseudo fled to the panic room. She had to get back now. She jumped out of bed as quietly as she could and put on her riding leathers before packing the few things she had brought with her. Juniper stirred in her sleep then sat up in bed blinking in the darkness.

"Are you alright?" Juniper asked in a hushed whisper.

"Yes . . . I mean no . . . I . . . Um . . ." Jinn collected her spiraling thoughts. "My panic room's been activated. I think something's wrong with Pseudo," Jinn whispered.

Juniper crawled out of bed and went into the kitchen, gathering some provisions for Jinn to take with her. As Jinn finished packing her bag, she walked over to Sebastian, who was sleeping peacefully in his cot. She reached down and touched his soft curls. She was going to miss the little bugger.

"Here, take these," Juniper said in a hushed voice, handing Jinn a small bag with some fruits and cheese.

"Thank you so much," Jinn said, taking the bag, "for everything." She could feel emotion choking her up.

"Of course, dear," Juniper said with a smile. "Come back soon, okay?"

"I will. Promise." Jinn meant it and truly hoped she would not have to break it. Taking her things, she slid out the door into the night air. It was chilly but not cold. She disconnected the bike from Juniper's charging station and sped away into the darkness.

Chapter 5

Pseudo's in Trouble

Jinn pushed her bike to breakneck speeds. Forced to stop, she charged the bike at Delilah's Kitchen again. Apparently, they had made their decision quickly and left, because the restaurant was already boarded up. She hoped they would be accepted among NOMAD. They deserved peace as much as anyone.

Once the bike was recharged, she rode through the rest of the day without stopping, and as it reached nightfall, she was close to home. The street was dark as she parked her bike at the end of the block and out of sight of her house. Jinn carefully approached and tried her door; it was unlocked but didn't seem to have been broken. As silently as the creaking door would allow, she slid into the house, holding her taser close to her chest. The living room and kitchen had been rifled through, but nothing significant was missing. She crept into the single bedroom and peered around the door frame. It had been ransacked, but there was nothing particularly valuable in there, so she did not think on it long. The bathroom was empty as well.

Jinn made her way down to the basement, straining her ears for any movement around her, and stopped in front of the door to the panic room, which was tightly sealed. She uncovered the keypad next to the door and attempted to punch in the sixteen-digit security code, silently cursing Pseudo for being so excessive. The second time it went through, and the heavy bolt scraped open. The door swung inward, and she found Pseudo lying on the small cot reading a book he had downloaded on his phone.

"Sup, Jinn?" he said without looking at her.

"What the hell, Pseudo?" Jinn asked, putting her taser back in its holster and leaning forward, hands on her knees.

"What? There were people . . ." he answered, as though it was perfectly normal to spend an entire day hiding in a panic room.

"What people?" Jinn asked as she collapsed to the floor. A twenty-four-hour adrenaline kick was no picnic. She was ready to pass out from exhaustion.

"I dunno," he answered, finally rolling over to look at her. He was wearing his usual round glasses, retro-style cargo shorts, and a loose-fitting T-shirt with his name printed on it. His hair was even more rowdy than normal, and he was barefoot. "Some men came in yelling and cursing, and I didn't hang out to see what they wanted. Pretty sure they had no idea I was here."

"Did they go in the lab?" Jinn asked, struggling to keep her eyes open. Pseudo shrugged. "You're so helpful."

"I know," he chided, throwing his legs over the side of the cot and sitting up. He was so small—he seemed much younger than his nineteen years. "Should we inventory damage?"

"Yeah, I suppose," Jinn said, dragging herself upright. She ran her hands through her unkempt hair and across her eyes.

They headed upstairs and checked the lab first. All the manufactured protein had been taken, but her equipment was still intact. The greenhouse was untouched. They went back into the house and checked the kitchen and living room. Again, the food had been taken but not much else. Finally, they went into the bedroom.

"Anything missing?" Pseudo asked, looking around at the mess.

"Don't think so," Jinn answered, picking through the piles of clothes and knickknacks that were thrown everywhere. All the drawers on the dresser had been dumped and rifled through, but nothing was missing that she could see. "Think they were looking for something?"

"Maybe, but I dunno how they'd find it." Pseudo snickered.

"My room was not this trashed before, asshat," Jinn snapped.

"Sure," Pseudo said with sarcasm. "It was just as clean as the rest of the house."

"Not everyone is as meticulous as you are about *everything*." Jinn raised an eyebrow at him. "You're the weird one, not me."

"You say that like it's negative." Pseudo grinned, completely comfortable with his eccentricities. Jinn envied that about him.

"Well, what else?" Jinn asked.

Pseudo calculated as his eyes swept around. "They said your name."

"My name?"

"When they came in, they called out your name, so they had to've known you."

"Most people know me. I give them food," Jinn said.

"Yeah, but those people just ask."

"Fair point."

"You think this has to do with the youngling?" Pseudo asked.

"I don't know how. I'm not sure many knew he existed," Jinn answered thoughtfully. "Maddie only talked with her suppliers, but she kept him away from that. She told me once that he had a special hideout room for when those people came over."

"Like your panic room."

"Yeah. Still, I don't see how he could be connected. I'm not even sure Maddie knew who the father was." Jinn sat down on the end of the bed, and almost immediately her eyes grew heavy.

"I'll reset you," Pseudo announced, noticing her fatigue. "I've gotta get back to Roxanne, she's almost back up."

"Okay lock up on the way out. I'm gonna pass out here," Jinn answered, falling backward on the bed. "Oh, and put up the bike. It's at the end of the block."

"Seriously?" Pseudo shouted from the living room.

"I was rushing back to save your ass," Jinn shouted.

"Fine," Pseudo shouted and slammed the door.

Chapter 6

Now What?

Jinn woke the next morning feeling groggy but rested. She caught a glimpse of herself in the mirror and grimaced. Dark circles appeared under her eyes, and her skin was pale and stretched across her face. A quick shower and some comfortable leggings and a T-shirt made her feel somewhat more human. She slicked her hair back and checked the mirror, content enough with the person looking back at her. Her eyes tightened when she returned to her wrecked bedroom and started setting things back to right. Most everything was scattered, but nothing appeared to be missing. She racked her brain trying to figure out what the people responsible for the mess could possibly have been looking for in her bedroom. Maybe stashed credits? Too bad for them, she didn't leave any behind.

She got her room reset and headed outside to the lab. Again, things were a mess, but they didn't take any of the equipment, which is about the only thing she owned worth bartering. Even that was difficult because only other people with labs would want it. They took the proteins that were ready to be harvested, but that was it. Resetting the lab was much quicker work than sorting through the mess of her bedroom.

Back inside the house, she cleaned up the common area and then the kitchen. Something was on the wall; it looked like scratches. Her brows furrowed. Someone had taken one of her knives and carved into the wall. It was difficult to read, but it appeared to say *I want you back*. Her blood turned to ice.

She finished cleaning up the remnants left behind by the intruders, then started the task of reinforcing the lab for storm season. Within the first few minutes, she ran into a problem. Strengthening the windows with the steel beams from her storage shed should have been simple, but the windowsill was tilted slightly. Apparently, the walls here were starting to sag, too. The frame of the old structure was becoming soft, but she had hoped for a few more seasons before needing to completely rebuild.

She went inside and flopped down on the couch, hanging her head between her shoulders in defeat. She already had to explain to her neighbors why they would have to wait for their proteins. They would understand, but it was disappointing. The rest of the proteins were still growing, and it would be about a week before they were ready to be harvested. Now she was going to have to open up a wall to brace the sagging frame. Otherwise, the lab would end up collecting too much moisture and potentially lose even more of the proteins. Then there was that ominous message on the wall. She leaned back on the couch and dug her phone from her pocket to call Pseudo.

"Yep?" he answered after a few buzzes. The screen was pointed directly into the light in his ceiling, and he was nowhere to be seen.

"What are you doing?" Jinn asked, not surprised at how often that was the first question of the conversation.

"My com cable's been chewed through, damn rats," came his

muffled voice from somewhere. "So, I'm following the cable to the antenna to see if it is salvageable before I head down to steal another one for Roxanne."

"Who uses com cables?" she asked.

"It's how my computer talks to Roxanne."

"Oh," Jinn responded, feeling slightly annoyed that she had not guessed that already.

"Sup?" Pseudo asked, suddenly appearing on the screen, looking even more disheveled than usual.

"Can you come over?" Jinn asked. She glanced at herself in the bottom corner of the screen, already annoyed with her appearance. Always so critical of herself, she wished she could be more like Pseudo sometimes, not so constantly aware of how she was perceived. This was going to be an intense conversation, and she didn't want to be distracted by her own self-consciousness.

"Like . . . now?" he asked, furrowing his brows in annoyance.

"I can go there."

"Um, I guess," Pseudo responded, clearly uncomfortable with a sudden visitation without a clear purpose.

"Okay, I'll be there in a few," Jinn said.

"Bring food," Pseudo said, then disconnected.

Chapter 7

Should We?

Jinn arrived at Pseudo's apartment with the requested food. Really, Pseudo's place was less an apartment than a room. The building was once known as the Hotel Clermont, which had serviced Atlanta for centuries. Now the abandoned building was home to several of the city's squatters, most of whom were reclusive like Pseudo. They had an unspoken arrangement to leave each other alone. Though truthfully, they were the team that kept the infrastructure running in the city. Unlike Pseudo, most of them lived under the control of source and consequently the cartels that distributed it. The cartels tried to keep them supplied and content in exchange for the luxury of things like electricity, running water, and communication.

Pseudo's room was immaculate as usual. Jinn walked in brandishing a portable bowl of chicken nuggets and steamed potatoes. It was the same thing she'd fed Sebastian.

"Score," Pseudo said in lieu of a greeting and immediately

jumped from his workstation to take the bowl of cold food.

"Gross," Jinn said, watching him stuff potatoes in his mouth.

"Nom-nom-nom-nom," he responded with his mouth full. Jinn rolled her eyes.

"What's your opinion of NOMAD?" Jinn asked, scanning the multiple monitors and keyboard arranged on Pseudo's table.

He chewed thoughtfully for a moment before swallowing. "I don't have opinions."

Jinn cocked an eyebrow at him. "You know what I mean."

"Actually, I don't," Pseudo said and popped another nugget in his mouth.

"You think we'd be better off if we were there instead of . . ." She gestured to everything around them.

"It'd be different," Pseudo said. "We wouldn't have to always be on the lookout for Xandar and his scumbags. I'm sure it would have its own challenges, but starvation and security wouldn't be among them."

"Well, what do you think? Should we go?" Jinn asked.

"Are you ready?" Pseudo asked, looking at her directly. Jinn hesitated, meeting his eyes. He lifted his eyebrows.

"You've always been right, Pseudo. Mom and Dad aren't coming back, even if they wanted to. I've known that since they left. I just wanted to hope, I guess." Jinn's eyes dropped to her feet. This was the first time she chose to believe those words. Emotion settled heavily in her chest, and tears stung her eyes.

More slowly this time, Pseudo said, "Are you ready?"

Jinn remained silent, not trusting herself to speak.

"You know I'm with you wherever you go," Pseudo said, getting up to wash the empty food container. He stepped up to the tiny sink, turned on the water, and said over his shoulder, "You're the only human I like enough to be around."

Jinn smiled despite herself. This was the closest thing to sentimentality that Pseudo ever expressed. He dried the container and walked over, handing it back to her.

"So, are you ready?" he asked once again.

Chapter 8

Interviews

A week later, Jinn and Pseudo found themselves in front of NOMAD's membership council. First, they interviewed together, with the council asking questions about their education and abilities. They also wanted to know about their relationships with each other and with anyone outside of NOMAD. They disclosed their relationships with Juniper and Mae. Though Pseudo had never met them in person, he had been in contact with them on occasion for Jinn's sake, and they'd taken a quick liking to him. The councilors had sent Jinn to wait outside the Chamber while they interviewed Pseudo alone. Jinn was nervous for him. He was not the most socially adept person and tended to miss a lot of social cues. But to her knowledge, NOMAD was not interested in how charismatic you were, just what you could bring to the table and whether you would be willing to contribute to the society. In that respect, Pseudo was invaluable.

Jinn took in the stone walls carved with intricate designs. The Chamber, as they referred to it, was the home for most of the political discourse among their society. Like most of the buildings, it was carved into the side of a mountain. She found herself admiring the workmanship and noticing the layers of rock through which the Chamber had been carved. There was a laser-like precision to the room, and she wondered if that was how they had accomplished the excavation.

The heavy oak door swung outward, and Pseudo walked out, rubbing his temples but wearing the same benign expression he generally had. Jinn raised her brows at him expectantly.

"Your turn," he said and cocked his head toward the door.

Jinn deflated a little. She had hoped for more of a reaction. She nodded at him and reentered the Chamber. The room was rounded, with benches carved out of the rock on each side of a walkway that led up to the council's elevated seats. She was reminded of images she'd seen of twentieth-century courtrooms, but instead of oak and mahogany, everything was made of limestone and shale. As she approached, she paid closer attention to the wooden table and chair that stood out as the only things not carved directly into the stone. A small machine sat on the table with wires running from it. Three women sat as members of the council. All of them were older, probably in their sixties, with short gray hair and serious faces. Now that she was alone, their stark white robes made Jinn feel that her own riding leathers were dingy and informal.

"Hello Jinn," the woman in the middle spoke. She had introduced herself earlier as Councilor Adams. The woman on her right was Councilor Swan, and Councilor Jamison sat to her left. Adams's severe face broke into a surprisingly warm smile.

"Hello, Councilors," Jinn said, nodding respectfully at each one.

"The device on the table is a polygraph," Councilor Adams said, looking at the machine. "I would ask you to attach the white tabs to your temples. It will let us know if you attempt any untruths. Do you understand?"

"I understand," Jinn answered, picking up the tabs. The trailing wires led to a small metal box. The tabs had a strange adhesive quality without residue. She placed them on her temples where they stuck fast and then felt a moment of panic. She did not know how to take them back off. The machine next to her made a strange buzzing tone.

"No need to worry; the tabs will come back off without any pain." The councilors smiled. Apparently, Jinn was not the first interviewee to be worried about this. She took a deep breath, and the machine quieted.

"First, we are going to ask you some basic questions to calibrate the machine, then we are going to ask for a lie. Please state your name," Adams said looking down at the notes in front of her.

"Jinn Marshall."

"Your age," Adams asked looking at the polygraph.

"Twenty-eight," Jinn replied, feeling a little worried.

"Education?" Adams asked.

"I have a doctorate in molecular and cellular biology from Georgia State University." Jinn slowly started to feel more comfortable with the questions.

"Now I am going to ask you what color clothes you are wearing, and I want you to answer incorrectly," Adams instructed. All three of the councilors paid close attention to the polygraph. "What color are your clothes?"

"Um, green?" Jinn answered. The polygraph made the strange buzzing noise again.

"Okay, now truthfully, what color are your clothes?" Adams asked, looking closely again at the notes in front of her.

"Black," Jinn answered, and the buzzing stopped. She smiled despite herself, feeling as though she had passed a sort of test.

"Now that the preliminary questions are done, we are going to discuss some of your history and personal philosophy. We want to make sure that you are a good fit for NOMAD and that we are compatible with you as well. Are you ready to begin?" Adams said gently.

"Yes."

"Why do you want to become part of NOMAD?" Adams asked.

Jinn took a breath before launching into her prepared pitch. "NOMAD is a peaceful society. You have made yourself known for your ability to live alongside nature, respecting the Earth as our home. You have managed to traverse the sometimes-extreme changes to the planet over the last century and have persevered through population decline and Exodus." Jinn had practiced this answer for the last week. She knew it was what the council would want to hear, but the truth was she believed it. She had known Juniper her entire life and was more aware of how NOMAD worked than most people outside of their society. She watched the councilors make a few notes.

"And why now?" Councilor Jamison spoke up.

"As you know, I lost my seat on the last Exodus ship. I tried to maintain my status quo in Atlanta, but it is becoming clear that living in the city is just not sustainable," Jinn replied.

"What caused you to lose your seat?" Jamison asked without looking up.

"I, um, I was caught up in a bad situation," Jinn responded, glancing toward the polygraph.

"Could you elaborate, please?" Councilor Swan asked.

"I was . . . I was addicted to source," Jinn answered. She could feel her hands shaking. She knew that this was something that NOMAD had absolutely no tolerance for, but the councilors had been aware of her history through Juniper.

"How long has it been since you have taken the drug?" Adams asked, looking pointedly at the polygraph.

"Over three years," Jinn answered. "I had been sober for almost six months before the Exodus launched, but they were still too apprehensive to allow passage."

"Do you regret this?" Adams asked.

"Yes," Jinn answered honestly. She was not sure what answer they were looking for, but it was the truth. "My family is now en route to the Mars colony. Aside from Pseudo, Juniper, and Mae, I don't really have anyone left here on Earth. I am hoping that NOMAD can be a fresh start."

The councilors paused their note taking. Jinn focused completely on controlling her breath to try and calm her nerves.

"You say that you have not taken source for over three years. Do you still feel as though you are addicted to the drug?" Swan asked.

"That is a difficult question to answer," Jinn said. "The short answer is no, but it is still prevalent where I am currently living. There are times when I feel pulled toward it, like it would just be easier to give in, but I am strong enough to resist. Especially with the support of Pseudo. He has never tried source and has seen what it does to people up close and personal. I am thankful every day that he is still in my life after all of this." Jinn could see the councilors slightly nodding as though they approved the answer. That sent a wash of relief over her.

"How was it that you were able to break the addiction?" Jamison asked.

"Um, well, that's complicated," Jinn answered. "I had been involved, um, romantically, with Xandar." Everyone knew that name. He was the cartel leader in Atlanta and had consolidated all the lines of manufacturing and distribution of source. The intense addictive qualities made it easy for him to control pretty much anyone that he wanted. "I was convinced I had my life under control, but that was the addiction because I did not. Xandar and source were controlling everything about me—where I went, who I talked to, what I did—everything." Jinn paused for a minute to keep her emotions in check. She wanted to tell them about how Xandar had manipulated her into believing that everyone was against her. How he had eventually become so controlling and abusive that she was too scared to do anything without fear of repercussions. It was when he tried to force her to distance herself from Pseudo that she had finally broken through the fog and realized Xandar was pulling all the strings. When she refused, he began to threaten the people she cared about. He threatened to find Pseudo and kill him. It always bothered Xandar that Pseudo wasn't addicted to source and was therefore never under his control. Xandar also threatened to use Jinn's addiction to ruin the names of her parents and make sure that they lost their place on the Exodus. Eventually these threats caused her to pull away from the only people that mattered.

What she told them was, "Pseudo found me when I was out running supplies for Xandar. Pseudo stopped me and tried to tell me he missed me, but I was blitzed out of my mind. I had this strange feeling that it would be the last time I'd see him, so I gave him a hug. When Xandar found out he flew into a rage, beat me mostly to death, and threw me out on the street.

"Pseudo found me a place to hide so that I could get through the withdrawal," Jinn finally said with tears in her eyes. "He stayed with me, keeping me from leaving to find more source, reminding me that if I left, Xandar would find me and probably kill me. It took almost a month to get my right mind back, and once I did, I was able to see just how far gone I had been. I decided then that I was done. It was difficult, especially once I was able to come out of hiding, but I made it. Thanks to Pseudo." Jinn tucked her trembling hands between her legs. She had to focus on her breathing to slow her heart rate. This was a part of her past that could not be denied, but she hated it with every fiber of her being.

"I despised the person I had become," Jinn continued. "I was like a frightened little kid, completely under the control of something, *someone* else. I never want to be that person again, so I turned to protein manufacturing and working on myself. I try to stay physically active, and I have an intense kickboxing and Tai Chi routine. If I start to feel like I am sliding back, then

I exercise or throw myself into my work. On the occasions it becomes too hard I will lean on Pseudo, but thankfully that hasn't been necessary for a long time now." Jinn hoped more than anything that this would be an acceptable answer for them. She could not imagine trying to make this decision. Addicts were notoriously unstable. She would understand if they did not want to take the risk.

"How is it that Pseudo had been able to find you?" Adams asked.

"After seeing me that day, he tracked my phone," Jinn smiled softly. "Had things turned out differently, I probably would have been upset with him, but it happened to save my life."

"Do you think you would be likely to attempt to take or try to find source again if you were to become part of NOMAD?" Adams asked.

"No." All three of the councilors watched the polygraph closely.

"Anything else?" Adams traded looks with the two others, who shook their heads. "Jinn, is there anything you would like to add, or any questions for us?"

"Um, do you . . ." Jinn trailed, contemplating the question. "Do you have any contact with the Mars colony?"

"No, I'm sorry, we don't," Swan answered, giving Jinn a look of empathy.

"I understand. Thank you," Jinn answered, disappointed. She didn't expect them to have a line of communication, but she couldn't help but hope. "I don't have anything else." She reached up and wiped her eyes.

"Thank you, Jinn," Adams spoke up. "If you would, wait outside with Pseudo while we deliberate."

"Of course, thank you," Jinn answered and stood up to leave. She attempted to pull the tabs from her temples but found them stuck fast.

"Slide them upward, and they will come loose like a

chameleon's toes," Adams said with a slight smile. Jinn slid them upward and found that they came off easily. She considered them for a minute before placing them back on the table. She met the eyes of the councilors and said, "Thank you again."

"Thank you, Jinn," Adams nodded toward the door.

Chapter 9

Decision

An hour later, Pseudo and Jinn stood before the councilors. Jinn was a bundle of nerves, terrified that her history was not only going to destroy her own chance at a decent life, but Pseudo's as well. Her gaze turned in his direction. He was his usual blank canvas. She was genuinely unsure of how he felt about the whole situation. Would he be angry if they were denied? Would he finally see her as the burden she had been to him since university? Thinking about it rationally, she doubted it. Not because she didn't deserve it, but because he had never shown any sign of that type of thinking before. *Was he even capable of getting angry?*

"Pseudo, Jinn," Councilor Adams began. "After listening to your appeals and our discussion with Juniper and Mae, we have made our decision. It is not one that we take lightly."

Jinn swallowed. That didn't sound promising.

"Juniper feels very strongly that you would both be a

welcome addition to NOMAD and is confident that you will find a home here, but we are apprehensive given your history and connections," Adams continued. "We have come to a somewhat unprecedented consensus."

Jinn raised her eyebrows. Pseudo remained inscrutable.

"You both will be given a six-month probationary period to join NOMAD. If within the six months we determine, for any reason, that either of you is unfit for your respective posts, then you will both be dismissed without further question," Adams concluded.

"What does this mean for us?" Jinn asked, relieved but unsettled by the idea of probation.

"We will give you a few days to go and gather your things," Adams said. "Then you will return, and we will work together to determine your posts within NOMAD. You will be asked to carry your own weight within society, as we are only as strong as our weakest member. However, if we feel that you are unable to perform your duties or that your own goals or ambitions are not aligned with ours, then you will be released. Since you came in together, you will be appraised together."

"Pseudo doesn't have the history I do. Would you consider assessing us as individuals?" Jinn asked, eliciting a glance from Pseudo.

"He does not have a history of addiction, but he was willing to enable yours," Jamison stated.

"That's not true," Jinn argued. "He was—"

"Our decision is final," Adams interrupted her. Jinn snapped her mouth closed and looked at the floor, tears stinging the corners of her eyes. Guilt and shame threatened to overwhelm her, but she knew arguing would only create more problems.

"I apologize," Jinn said without looking up. "Thank you for this opportunity."

"Thank you," Pseudo chimed.

"Now go," Adams said with a smile. "Gather your things,

and I would recommend packing light. We do not have much need for material possessions here within NOMAD."

Jinn lifted her eyes and smiled, despite herself. If Pseudo was going to be judged because of her, then she would just make sure that they passed.

Chapter 10

Happily Ever After?

Soon after, Jinn and Pseudo were again at Juniper's house, where Pseudo had left his roadster. It was a strange bubble-shaped car he had managed to fit with a thermodynamic energy converter that Jinn didn't quite understand, but it eliminated the need to stop at a charging station. Though it was not the most comfortable ride, it was surprisingly fast. The car had been the capstone project for his thesis in applied physics and robotic engineering, and he'd only improved its performance since. The top of the car was fitted with micro-solar panels for some extra charge, but that also made it more desirable to drive during the daylight. It was already approaching evening, so they decided to stay with Mae and Juniper for the night and leave early in the morning.

Jinn grinned broadly as they approached the home when she spotted Sebastian playing happily in front. He saw them approaching, and his little face lit up in recognition. He ran to her, and she swooped him up in a big hug while he squealed.

"This the youngling?" Pseudo asked, smiling at the boy.

"Yes, this is Sebastian," Jinn said, her voice taking on a childlike cadence. "Sebastian, meet Pseudo."

"Hi," he said, waving a chubby hand. He immediately started squirming to get down and go back to playing. Jinn released him, noticing that he had already gained weight in the week since she had last seen him. His eyes were brighter, and he was smiling. Her heart swelled.

"He's cute," Pseudo said.

They both looked up as the door opened and a tall man with dark hair and deep-set eyes stepped out. His face was kind, though serious; he was wearing dark denim pants and a shirt that Jinn noticed fit him quite nicely.

"Hello." The man spoke with a smooth voice and a broad smile.

"Um, hi," Jinn said awkwardly, causing Pseudo to snort.

"I'm Lucas," he said, putting out a hand.

"Jinn," she said, recovering slightly. "This is Pseudo." She shook his hand, and he put his hand out for Pseudo also, but Pseudo just shook his head. He was finicky about human contact. Lucas nodded back, not taking any offense.

"I've been caring for Sebastian. Mae wanted to give him a checkup," Lucas informed them.

"Great," Jinn said. "How's he been?"

"Good, considering," Lucas said, smiling slightly in Sebastian's direction. "He's had some tough moments, but he's adapting. It's amazing how much happier someone can be when there's food."

Jinn chuckled slightly. "I'm glad to hear it. Poor kid's had it rough."

"So I've been told." Lucas reached up and brushed his curly dark hair from his eyes. Jinn caught the slight definition of muscle in his arms. "You brought him here?" he asked, noticing her gaze.

"Yeah." Jinn's cheeks flushed.

"Before this gets weird, can we go in?" Pseudo asked, causing Jinn's blush to deepen.

"Yeah, sorry," Lucas said, stepping from in front of the doorway.

"Sorry," Jinn said. "Pseudo is . . . well . . . He's kind of a jerk." Pseudo just snickered as he walked past them.

"Takes a lot more than a bit of social awkwardness to offend me," Lucas laughed. "We're headed home anyway. I'll see you around?"

"Yes, we were accepted into NOMAD today," Jinn said, her smile brightened as she searched for a reaction from Lucas.

"Cool. See ya." He walked over and gathered Sebastian up in his arms, the child giggling.

"Yeah, uh, see ya," Jinn said, feeling repulsed by her own awkwardness. Her excitement about becoming a member of NOMAD was considerably out of proportion to Lucas's. She figured she would at least have gotten a congratulations or something. Maybe it was that he didn't know her history. Or maybe he just didn't really care. Jinn was surprised at her disappointment at this thought.

Jinn shook her head and walked inside to find Pseudo eating an orange and sitting with Mae and Juniper, everyone wearing huge smiles. Juniper walked over and gave Jinn a hug.

"I am so happy for you both," Juniper said.

"Me too. I think this'll be great for both of us," Jinn said with a smile. "When we get back tomorrow, what should we pack? I'm tempted just to leave it all and start fresh."

"I can understand that," Juniper said. "You may want some of your comforts though—clothes, blankets, maybe some of your research. I am sure that NOMAD would be happy to build on the manufactured proteins, and they would be a boost to our usual diet."

"True," Jinn said thoughtfully. "I also left my bike. I do want that."

"I would, too," Mae interjected with a chuckle. "I'm not sure you would know how to exist without that bike. Or how to dress for that matter."

Jinn scrunched up her face, looking down at her leather jumpsuit. "You're probably right." She laughed.

Juniper opened a cabinet and produced a small bottle of wine. Jinn was amazed. She had not seen actual wine in ages. Ever since source became prevalent, alcohol was almost non-existent within the city. There was no demand for it. Juniper poured four glasses of the deep red liquid and handed them out. "To our newest members," Juniper said, raising her glass. They all raised their glasses as well.

"I truly hope you find a home here," Mae responded.

Jinn took a sip of the wine. It was sweet, slightly bitter, and had a pleasant warming effect. Pseudo regarded his glass curiously before sipping it but quickly put it down. Jinn wasn't surprised. He had the palate of an eight-year-old.

"Thanks," Jinn said. "Really, thank you both for everything you've done for us."

"Of course, dear," Juniper said, reaching over and squeezing her hand. "You are both very welcome." Juniper took a breath. "This feels right."

Chapter 11

Implosion

Jinn and Pseudo woke early the next morning. They wanted to gather their things and get back to NOMAD as quickly as possible—the novelty of a new and better life crystallizing in front of their eyes. The trip back was quick and uneventful, but when they arrived at Jinn's house, something was wrong. Jinn wasn't sure what it was, but her skin tingled with anticipation. Pseudo parked the roadster on the street where they hesitated.

"What's happening?" Pseudo asked, his eyes narrowed on the house. The porch light was on, but otherwise everything appeared normal.

"Something's not right," Jinn said softly before noticing the soft red lights in the lab blinking slowly. Someone had been in there. She quickly pulled out her phone, but the battery had died on the way, and Pseudo's roadster did not have a charging port. "Is your phone working?" she asked him.

"No, died last night, why?" Pseudo squinted at the blinking

lights. If they'd had their phones, they both would have gotten alarm notifications. Hopefully, someone had gotten hungry, broken in, and was long gone. Jinn doubted she had that kind of luck.

"Should we circle around?" Pseudo asked. Jinn shook her head.

"If anyone's there, they've seen us," Jinn said. "Might as well go say hi."

They exited the car, trying to be as quiet as possible. Jinn pulled her taser from her belt when she saw that her front door was ajar. She kept Pseudo behind her and stepped into the living room. It was empty. She went and checked the bathroom, with Pseudo close behind, but nothing was amiss in there, either.

Finally, she approached her bedroom. She pushed open the door, and her blood turned to ice. Xandar lay across her bed, flipping through one of her books. Jinn recognized *At the Mountains of Madness* by H. P. Lovecraft. That was one of her more prized titles. The novella itself was close to 200 years old. The impulse to snatch the book from his hands almost overwhelmed her, but she remained locked in place.

"Hello, Jinn," Xandar said, without looking up. He was dressed as always in a blazer, slacks, and shiny leather shoes. His blond hair was perfectly trimmed and gelled. His appearance contrasted with his lazy posture draped across her bed. Jinn put a protective hand back toward Pseudo, but he wasn't there. "You've still got this ridiculous piece of shit," he said, tossing the book onto the floor.

"What do you want?" Jinn asked, mind racing.

"I was surprised when we ran the surveillance on Maddie's house and discovered you were still here. I've missed you." Xandar asked, cold blue eyes piercing through her, almost as though he believed his words.

"Stay away from me," Jinn snapped.

"I guess I shouldn't be surprised." He looked hurt, an

expression that made Jinn's skin crawl. "You've always had a hard time seeing what was right in front of you. You're so negative." He shook his head in disapproval.

"I'm leaving," Jinn said. "I only came to get a few things."

He looked shocked, but Jinn ignored it as she moved to start gathering clothes. "What do you mean you're leaving?"

"I mean, I'm leaving Atlanta," she answered.

"Where are you going?"

"I'm not telling you that," she said, stuffing clothes into her bag.

"Yes, you will. You owe me that," he growled.

"What are you talking about?" Her hands were trembling.

"You think you can just take my son and disappear?" he asked as he came closer. Then he glanced over Jinn's shoulder. Her mind was going a thousand places. *Was Sebastian Xandar's son? Would he find out that she had taken him to NOMAD? Where was Pseudo?* Jinn really hoped Pseudo had managed to disappear; he was surprisingly good at that. She stepped backward as Xandar got up from the bed and started walking toward her.

Suddenly, Jinn's arms were gripped from behind, held in place by a strong person, most likely one of Xandar's goons. Panic stabbed through her until it was silenced by a small voice.

"Jinn?" She turned and saw Pseudo being held in a similar position, his face contorted in terror. He was minuscule next to the monster holding him. The brute had a bald head and no neck, muscles bulging from everywhere. His bulbous nose had been broken, most likely on several occasions. Her vision went red.

She released her feet from under her, her full weight dropping suddenly, which caused her arms to twist painfully, but knocked the goon off balance. She tucked her feet back underneath her and launched herself straight up. The crown of her head connected with the goon's chin and produced a satisfying crunch. Stars exploded in her field of vision, but the man involuntarily released her, his eyes rolling back. She spun around and connected her knee with the monster's groin, and as he leaned forward grasping at himself, she brought her weight down behind her elbow to the back of his head, rendering him unconscious.

The man holding Pseudo started trying to back away, but she was too quick. In a practiced maneuver she pulled the taser from her belt and swept up behind him, placing the barrel directly on his back and pulling the trigger. He immediately went into convulsions, dropping Pseudo in the process.

"*Run!*" she hissed.

Pseudo stumbled to his feet and took off toward the door. She spotted Xandar across the room watching everything unfold as though it were all going according to plan. Jinn's head was throbbing, and she was pretty sure she'd fractured her elbow, but the goon wasn't about to get away with hurting Pseudo. She pulled her dagger and rushed at the monster. The man caught her arm before she could sink the knife into his chest. She saw his bulbous eyes move over her shoulder and turned just enough to see Xandar close the distance between them and pull something from the pocket inside his blazer. The pinch of a needle pierced her neck, and a familiar wave of euphoria washed over her. The first man was still sagging against the wall, his face bloody and his jaw set at an unsettling angle. It looked like he was attempting to smile. At least he would have to take his meals through a straw for the foreseeable future. A comforting, though not helpful, thought as she struggled against the grip of Xandar's second man.

The euphoria deepened, and she realized what was happening. Source. Xandar was trying to bring her back under his control. She spun and broke free from the goon's grip, knocking him backward with a kick to the stomach, then turned to face Xandar, her taser just inches from his face. He froze.

Jinn's equilibrium faltered under the influence of the drug, but she was able to focus on her hatred and rage. As she started to squeeze the trigger, she heard a pop, and pain blossomed in her abdomen. Warm sticky blood poured from her stomach. Her own shot went wide as she fell to her knees.

"This isn't how I hoped it would end." Xandar stood over her with a look of mild disappointment. "That's too bad." He shook his head and knelt to examine her wound. His goon stepped into view holding an antique revolver, smoke still seeping from the barrel. "We could've been together. You've broken my heart . . . again," Xandar said as Jinn's vision started closing in on her.

No, Jinn thought. *This can't be it. This can't be happening now.*

"I guess I'll just have to pay a visit to your friend Juniper," Xandar said, his voice laced with disappointment. "You had so much potential, Jinn." He tossed the empty syringe at her as she fell to the floor.

Her mind's processing turned into bursts and whispers. She could see Pseudo worried, scared, alone. Juniper was disappointed. Guilt. Fear would explode and then disappear in moments of lucidity. Death was so close. The world around her was incoherent; she was struggling to breathe. Her heart pounded, and she could feel the hole in her abdomen throbbing with each beat. She tried to move, but her muscles would not obey. Reality swirled around her, bending and contracting as though she was underwater. Darkness started to envelope her; it was warm, comfortable. Maybe death wouldn't be so bad. Maybe, maybe this is how it should be. No more worries, no more struggling, no more guilt. Maybe it was time to just let go. She closed her eyes.

"Jinn, wake up," she could hear Pseudo's voice whispering. "Jinn, you dead?" She heard him again, barely. *Yes*, she thought. *Xandar finally killed me.* Suddenly she could see a kaleidoscope of colors. Greens and blues and reds she had never seen before. "Well, you're breathing, and you have a pulse, so don't die on the way, you hear me?" His voice sounded far away, like he was yelling through a tunnel. The world around her started moving violently. Then she was cold. She shivered uncontrollably. The shadows of death reached for her again, and she welcomed the warm darkness.

Chapter 12

Wake Up

Pseudo pushed his roadster to its breaking speed. He glanced over at the compress he had made from towels, praying to whatever gods would listen that Jinn would make it back to NOMAD.

After he'd run from the room, he watched the events unfold from her window. Pseudo knew he was not strong or particularly fast, as these were physical features he rarely needed. His weapon was his mind. His mind was boiling over with questions. *Why did they drug her? What were they after? Where did they find an actual gun?*

Xandar had threatened to go after Juniper, but that would be a terrible idea. NOMAD had a strong defensive system. Pseudo also knew that Xandar was arrogant, stupid, and could potentially hurt Juniper or Mae before anyone could help. So he had to get there first—not to mention that was likely Jinn's only chance at surviving this encounter.

Xandar and his men had left in an old-school truck that sounded like it ran on an internal combustion engine. Pseudo had not seen one of those used as a personal vehicle in, well, ever. Where did he get the fuel for it?

He glanced at Jinn. The towels were soaked through with blood. Starting to get light-headed, he then made the mistake of looking down at himself. His skin crawled with the compulsion to get the blood and dirt off and as far away as possible. He took some deep breaths and focused all his attention on the road ahead. He had to keep his mind occupied. *It's not there.* He told himself. *It's not there.*

His mind turned to Xandar instead. Rarely did someone bother him so much. But he knew, *he knew*, Jinn was smarter than that. Xandar had duped her, and Pseudo still couldn't puzzle out how. Pseudo had only met him once before Xandar started to isolate Jinn. The stupid drug helped speed that process along, especially since Jinn had known that Pseudo wouldn't approve. But even that first meeting, Pseudo had known something was not as it seemed with Xandar, and he didn't understand how Jinn had missed it.

Jinn held a microbiology fellowship with Tomorrow's Sunrise Pharmaceuticals, where she met Xandar. Pseudo didn't know what Xandar's position was, but he appeared important and very well off. He was always traveling. He took Jinn with him overseas on a couple of occasions, and Jinn told Pseudo that she and Xandar would eventually be traveling with Exodus. Jinn had promised at the time to find a way to get Pseudo on board with them, although he was still technically a minor.

Even Pseudo had to admit that Xandar was very charismatic. But if Jinn had just paid attention, she would have seen the reality. Past the tailored clothes and charming smile, Xandar's eyes were cold, calculating, like he was appraising everyone and everything in relevance to how much he could gain from them.

The first time Jinn admitted to blitzing with Xandar, she

told Pseudo that she felt good, felt alive, felt more connected to Xandar than she had with anyone. Pseudo tried to explain that drugs will do that and that it was a bad choice, but she swore she had it under control. It was just a one-time thing. He shook his head at the memory, pretty sure even Jinn knew that was bullshit. For a short while though, everything was picture-perfect from the outside. Romantic getaways, hopeful future. Pseudo could see cracks in the veneer, but Jinn blinded herself to them, and she thought she was happy.

Pseudo swerved to avoid a piece of crumbling overpass that had fallen onto the road. His roadster's battery was waning. His lights were going dim. It was not so obvious at first, since he rarely drove the roadster at night. He reached for a switch below the steering wheel, turning off some of the auxiliary power. It would kill the climate control—that was the least of his worries. But once the air stopped moving, Pseudo gagged. He could smell the blood and bodily fluids coming from Jinn bleeding to death next to him. He pushed the roadster just a bit harder.

After Xandar was culled from Exodus, things turned bad. Jinn never told Pseudo the reasoning behind Xandar's elimination, but she was determined to do something about it. Her plans and ideas became more unhinged as she sank further into addiction. She started fighting with her parents, avoiding Pseudo, believing that everyone was set against her. She said they didn't understand her, that they just needed to get to know Xandar and they would understand.

Xandar had always kept Pseudo at arm's length. He was friendly enough while Jinn was around, but when she wasn't, Pseudo didn't even exist to him. Jinn had changed her hair, her style, even the way she spoke was manipulated by Xandar. Pseudo tried to bring it to her attention, but that was the thorn that made her pull away from him.

Pseudo had stepped back. Partly because he was hurt that Jinn was pushing him away at Xandar's request, but mostly because he knew that there was no way to help her until she figured it out for herself. Paranoia was a symptom of both the drug and Xandar's manipulation, and he knew that she wouldn't have been capable of listening to Pseudo, regardless of how obvious it was. Of course, Xandar and Jinn's relationship had come to a violent end. Luckily for Jinn, Pseudo had been able to anticipate it. Otherwise, she probably would have died three years ago.

Daylight broke well before the derelict dirigible finally came into view. Pseudo's panic had subsided into a numb, almost mechanical single-mindedness. He had to get her to Juniper; she would know what to do. He reached over and touched Jinn's forehead. It was cold and damp, but it crinkled slightly at his touch. The sheet he had used to drag her out to the roadster was bunched up at her back and spilling over onto the floorboard, causing her to sit at an odd angle.

Why? Why? *Why*? This is the reason Pseudo didn't tolerate humans. They were stupid and selfish and unpredictable. Generally, he accepted this. It's just how people are programmed. But now Jinn is dying, bleeding all over his roadster, and there was nothing else he could do about it. The bullet had gone through her, and he could see the compress was completely soaked. He didn't want to think about the compress on her back.

Chapter 13

Jinn is Dying

Pseudo skidded into the yard at Mae and Juniper's home. He leaped out of the roadster and ran to the door. Over the last hour, Jinn's breathing had become shallow, and she'd turned a sickly green color. It was close to noon. He didn't know what he would do if they weren't home. He pounded on the door. Juniper opened it—fear etched across her face.

"Jinn's dying," he said between breaths.

"Mae!" Juniper shouted and ran to the roadster. Pseudo followed. "What happened?" she asked as she opened the pod where Jinn was strapped into the seat, unconscious.

"We were ambushed," Pseudo said. "Sebastian is Xandar's kid."

Juniper's eyes flew wide and locked onto his.

"They drugged her," he continued, "then shot her."

"Shot her? With a gun?" Juniper asked as Mae came hurrying toward them.

"Sure looked like one and sounded like they do in movies," Pseudo said.

"She's been shot?" Mae asked in disbelief. "Here, help me." Mae positioned Juniper and Pseudo so that they could help carry Jinn into the kitchen. They moved her inside and laid her out on the table. Mae ran to get her medical supplies, and Pseudo wondered if she ever treated injuries this traumatic. Jinn's breathing was still shallow, and she was not responding to anything at all. Pseudo took a step back, knowing that he'd only be in the way.

"We have to call Lucas," Juniper said as Mae cut Jinn's clothes and Pseudo's makeshift compress off her.

"Why? What is happening?" Mae asked, dousing the wound with grain alcohol.

"Apparently Sebastian is Xandar's son," Juniper said.

"I don't understand," Mae said. "Why would no one know this?"

"I don't know, but I doubt it had anything to do with sentimental feelings for the boy, just something else that Xandar is supposed to own and control," Juniper said.

Mae finished cleaning the wound and pulled out a curved needle and thread. "Good thing she's not conscious, this is going to hurt." She began stitching the wound where the bullet had left Jinn's body.

Pseudo turned away. He couldn't watch Mae stitching up his friend. *The human body is so gross*, he thought. He flinched. Juniper was speaking to him.

"You said he drugged her. What did he give her?" Juniper asked again as she dug through Mae's bag looking for a poultice that would help to prevent any infection.

"Source," he answered. "He wanted her hooked again so that he'd have control."

"Is he coming here?" Mae asked. She gave Pseudo an accusatory look.

"Probably," Pseudo answered. "He doesn't know where *here*

is though."

"Are you sure?" Juniper asked.

"No."

"Do you know how much source he gave her?" Mae asked, finally done dressing the gunshot wounds.

"No, it was in a syringe. They shot it in her neck."

"What about you? Are you hurt?" Juniper indicated down to his clothing covered in blood.

He gasped audibly when he looked down at himself. "Oh, oh no," his eyes shot toward the ceiling trying to calm his disgust. "It's not my blood," he said quickly.

"Go clean yourself up, Pseudo," Mae said, pointing toward the bathroom. "There are some robes in there you can put on for now."

"Thanks," he said, his eyes never leaving the ceiling. He could hear them speaking in hushed voices as he walked into the bathroom.

Chapter 14

Recovery

The next several days were tense. Jinn stayed mostly unconscious. Juniper attempted to wake her from time to time to drink some medicinal broth, and Mae checked on her every couple of hours. Pseudo disappeared when it came time for them to change the dressings on her wounds. He could tell that Mae was uncomfortable with their situation, but she continued to treat Jinn as best she could—probably for Juniper's sake. Pseudo stayed mostly to himself. He wasn't socially adept at the best of times, and right now he could barely function. He had no idea what to do. Mae had gone out once or twice for NOMAD, and brought him back a couple of changes of clothes. They were ill-fitting but functional. He was never fussy about his appearance anyway.

He finally worked up the nerve to ask Juniper about their collection of books, and after that he spent most of his time by Jinn's bedside reading. There were a lot of old books about societal issues that he found interesting. His parents were from Venezuela, though that country was overrun soon after he was born. They had given him up as a baby, and he spent his childhood in American foster homes. As if his skin and hair color had not been problematic enough, his social and intellectual peculiarity surfaced at an early age.

The home he had left when he was fourteen was the worst. The parents claimed to be traditionalists. They kept about twelve foster children, treating them as second-class humans. They tried to force Pseudo to be normal according to their views. Any time he showed his intelligence or acted strange by their definition, he was punished—usually locked away somewhere. He preferred this, at least until they stopped allowing him to read. When they were approached by Georgia State University admissions, his foster parents naturally led the recruiter to believe that the reason Pseudo was such a prodigy was because of their strict child rearing. At first, his foster parents refused because the programs at the university didn't align with their religious beliefs, but they soon realized that they could claim the child prodigy while simultaneously getting him out of their hair. Of course, Pseudo was eager to go.

At GSU Pseudo became close to one of the physics professors who recognized his genius. She had encouraged him to see a therapist at the university, but he'd been through so many within the foster system that he was not interested. She finally relented, allowing him to just be his awkward, eccentric self. She did, however, help him find a way to legally emancipate himself from his foster family. They tried to fight at first but were quickly discouraged. He wasn't worth the fight for them anymore. Sadly, the professor passed away soon after Pseudo had been emancipated.

The professor had also tried to get him a seat on Exodus, but the governing body was uncomfortable allowing someone that young, especially with no legal guardian. Her advanced age prevented her from claiming that role. He was not bothered by this, though. The idea of leaving the planet was of no particular interest to him. He liked puzzles. He liked trying to figure out the crumbling infrastructure of Atlanta and how to salvage it, and to be honest, he had done a great job. Jinn was his only real contact. He supposed she was his only friend. He forced himself to look over at her. She was sweating. *Gross.* He took a damp cloth and wiped her forehead, but quickly gave up and went to wash his hands. *Humans are so disgusting.*

"Would you like something to drink?" Juniper asked.

Pseudo flinched. He hadn't noticed her come into the kitchen area.

"Pseudo, are you alright?" Juniper asked, placing a hand on his arm.

"Um, yeah, sorry," he said, looking down. "You startled me."

"I can see that," Juniper chuckled. "When was the last time you had something to eat?"

"Um, I, uh . . . "

"Come on, I'll make you a sandwich," Juniper said, pulling some things out of the cupboard.

"Thanks," he said and sat on one of the stools next to the island.

"You have a hard time with other people, don't you?" Juniper asked. She was kind, not judgmental. Pseudo shifted a little on the stool. "It's okay, you can't bother me," she continued. "I always felt like I was different from everyone when I was young," she said as she prepared his food. "Not like you, but different in my own way. It turns out that is exactly what made me who I am, and it turned out to be exactly what NOMAD needed. It really didn't feel like it at the time, though."

"What do you mean?" Pseudo asked. This intrigued him.

"Well, I just, I guess I had a hard time with a lot of what was happening," she said. "This was during the early stages of Exodus. Only a few people had made it off Earth at the time, and there was a very hard distinction between NOMAD and, well, everyone else. This was hard for me to understand, because in my mind we were all human; we should all have the same ideas and goals, but we clearly didn't." She paused, lost in reminiscence. "I began here as a healer, like what Mae does now, and there was an infection."

"Spastic meningitis," Pseudo said. "I read about that. It messed up Exodus for a while. Allegedly when they were researching cures is when they accidentally created source."

"Yes," Juniper said, lost in the memory. "We, NOMAD, found a treatment. It didn't work all the time, but even when it didn't cure the disease, it helped ease the pain. NOMAD didn't want to share this with the outside, but I was not able to keep it. That's actually how I met Mae."

"Wow," Pseudo said.

"Mm-hm," Juniper said, handing him a sandwich. She smiled as he took a huge bite. "Well, it got me into a lot of trouble at the time, but eventually we ended up opening trade to the urbanites and went on to prosper, none of which was likely to happen otherwise."

Pseudo chewed thoughtfully. He wondered if that was why Juniper and Mae lived just outside of NOMAD. They didn't quite fit. It made sense.

"Anyway, the point is, different doesn't bother me as much as it does some members of NOMAD. So, you have nothing to fear from us," Juniper finished.

"I wasn't afraid," Pseudo said, a little more defiantly than he intended. He picked at his sandwich before asking in a softer voice. "What do we do now?"

"We wait, love," Juniper said softly, looking at Jinn. "That is all we can do."

Pseudo nodded as he polished off his sandwich. Others had said similar things to him before. That he was special, that he was unique and accepted. It usually wasn't true, but he really wanted to believe Juniper. He took his book back over to wait next to Jinn.

Chapter 15

Pushed Out

It was late at night when Pseudo awoke to the sound of hushed voices. He opened his eyes to see Mae and Juniper standing close to each other near the door. Mae was still wearing her scrubs, and her medical bag sat on the floor next to her. Her face was creased with concern, and Juniper had a hand on the curve of Mae's neck.

"What are they supposed to do?" Juniper asked, her hushed voice full of concern. "Sending them back to Atlanta would be a death sentence."

"I don't know," Mae answered. "They are very adamant, especially after learning of the boy's patronage."

They glanced over as Pseudo stirred on his cot. He closed his eyes and pretended he was asleep.

"Jinn hasn't even regained consciousness," Juniper whispered, clearly upset. "And Sebastian is a baby. What is he supposed to do?"

Why are they talking about Sebastian? Pseudo strained to hear the conversation.

"The council says their decision is final. They are going to inform Lucas in the morning," Mae said.

"You're okay with this?" Juniper asked.

"Of course I'm not okay with this," Mae shot back. "This is bigger than us, Juniper. Letting them stay here could possibly even put *us* in jeopardy."

"Who gives a shit?" Juniper asked. Pseudo's eyes flew open, and he stifled a gasp. He had never heard Juniper speak like that.

"Language Jun. You sound like an urbanite," Mae hissed. "And I do, and my patients do. And the judiciary needs you. We can't just abandon them."

"We don't have to cave to them either," Juniper said, probably more loudly than she had intended. She pulled in a deep breath then whispered, "We can't just toss them out."

"Do you have a better idea?" Mae whispered.

"Yes, fuck the council. If they don't like it, they can deal with it. I'm not going to send them to their deaths."

Mae gasped. "Jun, you can't talk like that." Mae paused. "Maybe . . . maybe we could hide them out for a while, but that won't last long, especially if Xandar manages to find his way here."

"Even if he did, Xandar wouldn't make it past the garrison," Juniper said.

"Jun, he has guns," Mae whispered. "Are you willing to put our people in danger for them?"

"We don't know that he has guns," Juniper dismissed her.

"Jinn was shot," Mae responded.

"We know he has *a* gun," she countered. "Guns were purged decades ago. I doubt he has many."

"Still," Mae said, "we don't know what he is capable of. And I am not sure it is worth it to keep them here."

"Did you really not expect this to happen at some point?"

Juniper countered. "You and the council know that things have been getting worse each season. It was only a matter of time before people started knocking at our gates."

"Doesn't mean we need to provoke it," Mae answered, then lowering her voice, she continued. "Besides, Jinn was so blitzed on source when she showed up, how do we really know what happened?"

Juniper was quiet for a moment, so Pseudo spoke up.

"That was forced on her," he said, startling them both. "It wasn't a choice. She was trying to protect me. I told you that."

"We know," Juniper said softly.

"And you know what the withdrawal is like for that drug," Mae said, her eyes steely. "She is likely to wake up with a craving that she is unable to resist."

"That's why she needs our help," Juniper said. "We can't just ask them to leave."

"What about Sebastian?" Pseudo asked.

Mae and Juniper locked eyes. Finally, Mae spoke. "The council thinks it is too dangerous to keep him here if he is really Xandar's child."

"They're just gonna throw out a three-year-old?" Pseudo asked. "I mean, forcing Jinn and me to leave would suck, but what's a toddler supposed to do?" Pseudo's mind started spinning. He could feel old emotions creeping up on him and had to tamp them down quickly.

"I . . . I don't know," Mae said, looking defeated.

"Well, we are not going to figure it out right now," Juniper said, looking weary. "Let's sleep on it before we decide anything."

"Yes," Mae said. "It has been a long, emotional day. Believe me when I say that I fought this tooth and nail. I just . . . I wasn't heard." She ran a hand through her short silver hair.

"We can talk tomorrow," Juniper said. "We can't just expect them to walk out with nowhere to go."

"Tomorrow," Mae agreed. She walked into the bathroom to

shower for bed. Juniper quickly washed the teacups and left to change into her bed clothes. For what may have been the first time, Pseudo acknowledged their age. Though they didn't seem like it, they were both likely in their eighties, if he had calculated from the spastic meningitis era correctly. He lay down on the cot and looked over at Jinn. She was still asleep, but her brow was creased. He wondered if she had heard any of that. *Jinn, please wake up.*

Chapter 16

She Awoke

Jinn was cold. The world around her was dark and loud, but she couldn't make sense of it. She reached for the warm shadows over and over again, but they stayed just beyond her fingertips. Images and nightmares plagued her. Pseudo, scared and covered in blood. Her vision going red before darkness fell again. Xandar standing over her, holding an elongated syringe with a green bubble of poison seeping from the end of it.

A gunshot.

Her eyes snapped open. There were voices around her. They sounded angry. Where was she? She turned her head, and her vision swam. Nausea forced her to lean over the edge of the cot and start heaving. There was nothing in her stomach to retch but bitter-tasting bile. A stab of pain shot through her abdomen. *What the fuck is happening to me?* She sensed a sudden flurry of activity.

"Jinn?" She heard a voice. *Pseudo?*

"Jinn, can you hear me?" Another voice.

"Give her some space," a third voice entered, putting something underneath her face, which was hanging clumsily over the side of the cot. A child giggled.

When she finally finished heaving, hands helped her turn back onto the bed. A cool cloth was pushed against her face. She was sweating. Her hair was wet, and her clothes soaked. Someone pulled the blanket off her, causing her to shiver violently. She desperately wanted to leave consciousness again. She heard more giggling. Giggling? Jinn was being forced to sit up, and a glass was pressed against her lips. The liquid was warm and slightly salty. She took a few sips before giving up. Her stomach rebelled, but she swallowed it. They helped her back down, making sure she was on her side.

"Jinn, please, *te necesito.*" She was certain that it was Pseudo this time. Her mind started slipping again. She tried to open her eyes, but sleep was stealing her away—peaceful, silent sleep.

Except it wasn't peaceful or silent. It was filled with violence and overdosed, bloated bodies. Fear was always on the horizon. Pseudo, hurt and terrified. Sebastian screaming. Pain, the never-ending searing pain that gripped her completely. Her shadows would slink close to her from time to time. She would reach for them desperately. Jinn was so cold, shivering, her teeth chattering. The voices would come and go, and she was unable to distinguish which were real and which were figments of her imagination. Juniper and Mae arguing. Pseudo whispering in Spanish. The ever-present shadows offering peace and comfort but staying just out of reach. Sebastian crying.

Slowly this time, she opened her eyes. Pseudo was sitting next to her reading something. Not that it was surprising; he was always reading something. Sharp pain stabbed her abdomen as she pushed herself up onto her elbows. Pseudo glanced up from his book. *Violeta*, it said on the cover. It was familiar. She'd read it in one of her college courses. She shifted on the cot with the pain in her abdomen. Memories started resurfacing, but she struggled with differentiating what was real from what had been hallucinations.

Pseudo's eyes lifted from his book as she stirred. She knew him well enough to see the concern in his face, though he was good at hiding it. She closed her eyes again, still nauseated. Chills caused her to tremble. With sudden clarity, she recognized the symptoms of withdrawal. She remembered being stabbed with a needle before everything became hazy and disconnected. Xandar had dosed her.

"Jinn, you back?" Pseudo asked, putting his book down.

"Do I have a choice?" she muttered, keeping her eyes closed. Her body was racked with a violent shiver, pain coursing through her again.

"Nah," he responded, picking the book back up.

"How long have I been here?" Jinn questioned, as much to herself as Pseudo. Her eyes moved around the room, finally realizing that she was at Juniper's.

"Almost a week," Pseudo answered without looking at her.

"Wha . . . what happened?"

"You were dosed. But you fought anyway, and they shot you," he answered.

Jinn vaguely remembered seeing the strange revolver that Xandar's goon had been holding.

"Where are Juniper and Mae?" Jinn asked, attempting to sit up.

"They're with the council," Pseudo responded, finally setting his book on the table.

"The council?" Jinn repeated. "Why?"

"Short version—they don't want us to join anymore. And since they found out Sebastian's lineage, they don't want him either." Jinn flinched as though he had slapped her. Pseudo just stared at her for a moment, considering her response. "Juniper, Mae, and Lucas are trying to convince the council otherwise, but I dunno if they even agree with each other," Pseudo continued.

Guilt hit Jinn in the chest, knocking the breath out of her. Pseudo was going to be hurt again by things that he was not involved in. Sebastian had finally found a stable home and was about to be taken away from it. And Juniper and Mae were fighting, all because of her. She lay back on the cot, trying to regain control of her emotions. *Why? Why was this always the case? Why did people continue to try and help her. Could they not see that she was toxic?*

"Stop," Pseudo said, looking miffed.

"Stop what?" Jinn was shocked out of her spiral.

"Stop the self-pity, self-loathing bullshit."

"What?" she repeated. She hadn't said any of that out loud.

"Whatever guilt or insecurities you feel are yours to handle, but we need you here. So, take this ridiculous, self-fulfilling prophecy, and tell it to fuck right off." Pseudo was looking directly at her. This was not like him. She smiled, despite herself.

"You're such an asshole," she said.

"Yep, eventually you'll learn I don't care," he said, picking his book up again.

"Yes you do," she teased.

"Keep telling yourself that," he responded, sticking his nose back into his book and pointedly ignoring her.

Chapter 17

Exile

Mae and Juniper burst through the door with Lucas and Sebastian close behind. Jinn could immediately tell that Sebastian was not his usual happy self—he was clinging close to a protectively hovering Lucas. Everyone was agitated. Jinn tried to remember if she had ever seen Juniper angry before.

"I need some tea." Juniper started noisily moving around the kitchen. Lucas and Sebastian made their way up to the loft so that the child could take some comfort in the toys. Jinn could feel the tension emanating from Lucas, but he was quiet.

"Jun, what are they supposed to do? They have to think about the well-being of NOMAD as a whole. We can't save everyone—" Mae was close to shouting.

"We could," Juniper snapped, turning to face Mae after setting the kettle on the stove. "We have the resources to help anyone who actually wants it. You're right, we can't just give away everything we have built, but we can help anyone willing to come in. And we have the ability to defend ourselves from the ones who are just trying to take it from us."

"That is exactly why we need to protect it," Mae answered. "We can't go provoking people like Xandar. We need to keep the peace."

"That is what you and the council don't seem to get," Juniper said, her voice going quiet. "Keeping total peace is an impossible task. The urbanites are getting more desperate by the day, and it is only a matter of time before they come trying to break down the gates. But if we keep turning people away because of some perceived threat, we are only going to destroy ourselves." Juniper paused and took a deep breath. "How can you justify banishing a toddler?"

"Yes, it seems cruel," Mae said with resignation, "but he's not *just* a toddler. He's a flash point, and people will fight for their children."

"Only if they care about them," Jinn spoke up, causing everyone to turn toward her in surprise.

"Jinn's awake," Pseudo added unnecessarily.

"You think he won't come after his child?" Mae asked.

"I don't know," Jinn answered honestly as Mae came toward her. "I know he couldn't have cared too much, given how I found the kid. The entire time I was living in Little Five Points, he didn't come around. The only reason it's an issue now is because he's gotten it in his head that someone told him no. He has to prove he's in control." Mae began checking Jinn's vitals and probing her abdomen, causing her to grunt in pain.

"This is what I am talking about, Jun," Mae said, looking at Jinn apologetically. "By taking in the kid, and Jinn, we are provoking him. We don't know how he is going to react."

"Doesn't matter though," Jinn answered growing frustrated.

"Provoked or not, he'll eventually come after NOMAD," Pseudo added to the conversation.

"What do you mean?" Mae asked him.

"He's delusional." Pseudo shrugged as though this answered everything. Mae started to remove the dressing on Jinn's wound. He shuddered and walked into the kitchen with Juniper, keeping his back to Jinn.

"How do you see this playing out?" Jinn said. Then she hissed in pain as Mae removed the gauze.

"That is the point. There is nothing to play out if there is no provocation," Mae answered, pouring a sour smelling antibacterial liquid across Jinn's skin.

"There is though," Jinn responded through clenched teeth as the liquid burned and bubbled over her sutures.

"She's right," Lucas answered from the loft, drawing everyone's eyes upward. His face was cold. "Xandar has most of Atlanta under his control, but the city is dying, which you know."

Mae picked up her medical supplies. Lucas made his way back down the spiral staircase with little Sebastian following close behind, trying to balance with a toy in each hand. Sebastian found a corner to play in while Juniper poured several cups of tea. Mae helped Jinn from her cot and then onto one of the stools around the kitchen island. Pseudo took the seat next to her, and Lucas stood to the side. Juniper continued to bustle pointlessly around the kitchen as Mae put her supplies back in order.

"Xandar's been talking about a hostile takcover of NOMAD, but he doesn't have the resources or intel," Lucas continued. "Yet."

"What are you talking about?" Mae asked, clearly flustered.

"I said I was in logistics before coming here six months ago?" Lucas glanced at Juniper and Mae who both nodded in encouragement. "That was true, but . . . I worked for the cartel." Lucas watched their faces, gauging their reactions. Juniper raised her eyebrows.

"That can't be true. The councilors would not have let you past the interview if they knew you worked for Xandar," Mae said as she leaned on the island with her face in her hands.

"They didn't ask," Lucas said. Mae narrowed her eyes at him. "They asked what I did, and I told them. They asked who I worked for, and I answered that, but I didn't mention that the man I worked for was part of the cartel's logistics. They probably could have figured it out if they looked hard enough, but I told them that I no longer have ties to any of those people. And that was the truth of it."

"The councilors' arrogance is going to be the downfall of this district," Mae muttered under her breath.

"I thought I recognized Sebastian," Lucas continued. "I wasn't sure 'cause Xandar didn't have much to do with him, but I had a feeling. That's why I stepped up. I tried to get Maddie to let me help when he was an infant. I knew she wouldn't be able to handle a baby, but Xandar wasn't having it."

"How do you know all this?" Jinn asked.

"He had me keep tabs on Maddie for a while since he ran a lot of distribution through her, but he didn't like how critical I was of Sebastian's situation," Lucas answered. "I guess he was insulted that I tried to help, so he put me out, to use his phrasing. Had I been addicted, it would've been a problem, but I wasn't. So, I fell off his radar for a while before coming to NOMAD. He's arrogant. He never saw me as a threat."

"He said that?" Pseudo asked.

"No, but he said I wasn't cut out for my position if I was worried about the comfort of babies," Lucas rolled his eyes. "It's all stupid, but I wanted out. I acted like I was desperate for source and pretended to beg for his forgiveness long enough for his ego to swell. Then, I took the opportunity to disappear."

"How long did you work for him?" Mae asked.

"Took a delivery job when I was fifteen," Lucas answered. "My parents were addicts, so I never had the inclination to use, but I caught on quickly that I needed to fake it to get by. When everyone else is blitzed, it isn't hard."

"Why work for him?" Jinn asked, trying to make sense of

things.

"Didn't know there were options," Lucas shrugged, "and truthfully, there weren't. If you weren't part of the cartel, you were begging. I worked my way up within the network, but I wasn't ambitious. I just wanted to survive, so I stayed under the radar. Xandar assumed I was weak. I didn't care."

"So, what is this about him planning to come after NOMAD?" Juniper asked, resting on a stool on the opposite side.

"The city is dying. Food's running low, infrastructure's crumbling. Everyone who isn't addicted has left, and he don't have the resources to keep up. He had a standing order for anyone to bring him information about NOMAD if they found it."

"Why NOMAD?" Juniper asked.

"You have food," Pseudo supplied. Lucas nodded.

"Did he have some sort of strategy?" Mae asked.

"Dunno," Lucas said. "Xandar's arrogant. He thinks everyone is just going to cave to him, and, thanks to source, he's usually right."

Jinn shivered; the chills of withdrawal still hammering at her even after a week. "Withdrawal is horrendous," she added. "Most people would do anything to escape it."

"Exactly," Lucas said. "That's given Xandar a false sense of control."

"So what? We are just doomed, no matter what?" Mae asked, exasperated.

"No, but placating him will only give him the impression that NOMAD is weak and scared," Lucas said.

Everyone fell silent, fidgeting with their teacups and weighing the situation. Sebastian was making childlike noises from his little corner, but even those were subdued. The air hovered as though a weighted blanket had been thrown over the household.

"Well, it doesn't matter anyway," Mae said, straightening

her back. "The council has already made their decision, and telling them that Lucas worked for Xandar would only reinforce it."

"So, what now?" Pseudo asked in an uncharacteristically small voice.

"You have another week for Jinn's recovery, then you have to leave," Juniper said, her voice choked with emotion. "All of you."

Chapter 18

Lucas

Jinn sat up on her cot when a door slammed—Juniper and Mae leaving yet again. Guilt plagued her that Juniper was fighting so hard for her, for them. Jinn had spent most of the night tossing and turning, but couldn't come up with any workable solution. Xandar would learn that she was still alive, and he would find her. The thought was paralyzing.

Sebastian squirmed precariously on a stool at the kitchen island, enjoying some cereal and making a mess of things. He was eating and chattering away while Lucas made coffee and offered noncommittal responses to Sebastian's ramblings. Jinn smiled despite their circumstances. Lucas was smiling as well. The perpetual happiness of Sebastian was contagious. As Jinn watched, she realized that though Lucas was tall, he was also graceful. His dark hair fell in curls around his forehead, and his hazel eyes were glittering. She noticed his muscular arms and chest as he reached into the cabinet to put away the coffee beans. His skin was smooth and tanned, emanating a golden glow.

"Want some coffee?" he asked, catching her gaze. A slight smile played at his mouth.

"Please," Jinn said quickly, averting her eyes, her cheeks flushing. She winced and stood up, slowly making her way across the room to sit next to Sebastian.

"I eat cereal," Sebastian said, waving his spoon at her.

"I see that," Jinn said, smiling. She winced again as she settled onto the stool.

"You still hurt?" Sebastian asked, his big brown eyes watery with concern.

"Yes, I am. I'll be okay though."

"Yeah, you'll be okay." He grinned and shoved another spoonful of cereal into his mouth, dripping milk down the front of his shirt.

Lucas turned to face her with a mug in hand, then he passed the sweet cream. Jinn took it and poured a healthy dollop into her mug. She kept her eyes averted while she swirled her coffee, but she could feel him watching. It seemed he was enjoying her embarrassment. She shifted in her seat and finally met his eyes. He was grinning.

"What?" Jinn asked.

"Nothing," Lucas said, throwing his hands into the air. "You're easy to read."

"What does that mean?" Jinn asked. She wanted to wipe the smirk off Lucas's dumb, pretty face.

"Admit it, you like me," Lucas said cocking an eyebrow.

"I don't even know you," Jinn said and lifted her nose into the air.

"I like you Lucas," Sebastian said around a mouthful of cereal. Jinn smiled. Her wall was being cracked by a toddler.

"I like you too, Sebastian," Lucas said, smiling at the milk covered child. "Let's go get you cleaned up."

Sebastian hopped down from the stool and headed toward

the bathroom while Lucas gathered the bowl and spoon and wiped the milk from the counter. Jinn sipped her coffee, purposefully ignoring Lucas's glances. He was enjoying this. It made her itch.

Lucas helped Sebastian, then the toddler found some toys and went about entertaining himself, checking every so often to make sure they were still there. Lucas sat on the stool next to Jinn and grabbed his coffee cup that was still mostly full. Jinn tried to win the battle of wills, but the silence became too much for her.

"No more diapers?" Jinn asked innocuously.

"Nah, he figured the toilet out pretty quick. I think he's happy not to have to wear them anymore."

"So, what's your story, Lucas?" Jinn asked. "You said you worked for Xandar, but what else? Why'd you offer to take care of Sebastian?"

"Dunno," he said shrugging his shoulders. "Seemed like the right thing to do."

"That's it?" Jinn said, deadpan look on her face.

"Yeah, I mean . . . Never really thought I wanted kids, y'know? My parents weren't exactly the best models. It just seemed too damn hard."

"Makes sense," Jinn answered. "My parents were pretty awesome, but I never wanted kids either."

"Were? What happened to them?" Lucas asked.

"Left on Exodus," Jinn said, looking into her coffee. Awkward silence settled over them.

"Ah," Lucas said. "Feels like we're getting a bit heavy for our first date," Lucas said, and quirked an eyebrow.

"This is a date?" Jinn's cheeks started tingling again. His hazel eyes shined with mischief.

"A first date's usually coffee . . . No?" Lucas said, his lips curled in a smirk. He leaned over and nudged her with his shoulder. She bit her lip, working to keep her nerves under control.

"I doubt she'd know," Pseudo suddenly piped in as he strolled up to the coffee pot and poured himself a cup. Jinn shot him a death glare. Lucas laughed out loud.

"He's not wrong," Jinn said, resigned. "I haven't exactly been on the dating circuit, but to be fair, most of the available people in Little Five aren't the type to plan a future with."

"Yeah, I know the type," Lucas said with a sigh. "Hell, I used to be one."

"Me too," Jinn said before realizing it. Suddenly they both appraised each other with this new set of data.

"Why'd you stop?" Lucas said, his tone turning serious.

"Almost died. Pseudo saved me, kinda forced me to dry out," Jinn said. He didn't need the details. "What about you?"

"Tried it . . . twice actually, but it always reminded me of the bullshit I had to deal with as a kid, so I guess it never became a habit. I kept up the appearance that I was hooked. It wasn't hard since everyone around me actually was." Lucas shook his head as though the memory disgusted him. "I became the addict without the addiction—self-absorbed, arrogant, and after a while it was even hard for me to tell what was real and what was an act."

"How did you get around the polygraph?" Jinn was incredulous. Between the application and the interview, she couldn't come up with a possible way to fool the council.

"I didn't." Lucas pressed his lips together.

"What?" Jinn's mouth dropped open.

"I stuck with the truth as far as it needed to be told, but I was able to deflect anything incriminating. As long as I kept my composure, the machine didn't register. Their machine is not as sophisticated as they want to believe. I'm not sure NOMAD is as put together as they let on."

"Because of their polygraph machine?"

"Because of their council," Lucas said. He swept his eyes around the room as though to make sure no one else was listening. "The organization keeps growing, and they're having a harder time keeping people under control. Some members of the council want to close the doors completely."

"And they told you this . . ." Jinn asked, staring in disbelief.

Lucas shook his head with a slight smile. "They let me in because I'm good with building and logistics, so I saw where resources are allocated. If I back up I can see the big picture."

Jinn tried to wrap her mind around all of it. She didn't know Lucas. It was possible he was just an arrogant ass, but she was inclined to believe him.

"What about you?" he changed the subject. "You don't exactly strike me as an addict, but you knew Xandar?"

"Yeah," Jinn answered staring at the counter. "It'd been over three years for me, but then Xandar dosed me. We have a uh . . . history."

"You *dated* Xandar?" Lucas's eyebrows shot up. "You must be something special to catch his attention."

Jinn's skin crawled. She knew he meant it to be a compliment, but the very thought of Xandar thinking about her at all made her feel sick. She rolled her shoulders, and Lucas seemed to catch how uncomfortable she had become.

"How are you now? He finally asked softly.

"I think I have gotten through the worst of it, but I can feel the craving like I never quit." Jinn dropped her gaze, disgusted with herself.

"It's okay," Lucas said. He put his hand over hers. A shiver ran through her at the soft touch. "We have your back." He gestured toward Pseudo.

"Thanks," Jinn said and leaned slightly into him. "But you don't know me."

"I'd like to," Lucas said.

Pseudo snorted.

"What?" Lucas asked him. His lips curled into a smile.

"Could you be more pedestrian?" Pseudo asked, then mimicked Lucas in a high-pitched voice, "*I'd like to*." Pseudo rolled his eyes.

"Hey, I can be whatever cliché I want," Lucas responded with a huff.

"Good luck using that on *this* bitch," Pseudo said nodding toward Jinn. Lucas's mouth opened in surprise. Jinn threw her spoon at Pseudo, then grimaced when the flex hurt her abdomen. Lucas put a hand on her back in a comforting gesture. Jinn enjoyed the touch more than she wanted to admit. When she swallowed the last of her coffee and slid slowly from the stool, Lucas moved his hand to her waist to assist her. Once her feet were on the ground, she looked up at him, his bright hazel eyes close to hers. He smiled and brushed her hair away from her face before taking a step back to allow her space. She clumsily made her way to the couch and sat down. Sebastian came and hopped up on the couch beside her.

"You'll be okay," he said, and laid his head over on her lap.

"You're right, little buddy," Jinn answered, tousling his curls. She glanced at Lucas and then at Pseudo. They had found an interesting book on Juniper's shelf about the future takeover of robots in the year 2050. It would seem that prediction had missed the mark. They smiled as they talked, and Sebastian started snoring lightly. Jinn couldn't place this feeling in her chest. It should be fear or anxiety. There was so much to fear in her future. But she was almost hopeful.

Chapter 19

Mae

The next four days were hectic, but not difficult. Juniper and Mae's place had taken on the appearance of a refugee camp. There were cots set up for Jinn, Pseudo, and Lucas, and a bedroll laid out for Sebastian, though he usually slept next to Lucas. Being a toddler, he had the innate ability to destroy the place with toys and whatever else he could get his little hands on. Meanwhile, Juniper and Mae were trying to make sure that everyone was able to eat, and that Jinn's wounds were kept clean. Pseudo looked almost as frazzled as the house, despite his constant efforts to keep it cleaned up. Jinn was getting stronger daily and tried to help but was only able to stay on her feet for short periods of time. Lucas spent most of his time chasing Sebastian. Between toys, food, clothes, and medical supplies, the place was fairly wrecked.

Pseudo and Lucas had connected on an intellectual level. They were both fascinated with technology, and Pseudo enjoyed trying to impress Lucas with his knowledge and ability to work with entire mainframes and infrastructure. Lucas impressed Pseudo with his ability to see complex big-picture puzzles and come up with plans and schedules for routing everything from food to power. Jinn and Lucas had shared a few more moments after the coffee, but they were usually interrupted. Alone time was a scarce thing, and everyone was starting to notice.

Mae had softened to them all being there in her space, though she never admitted it. Juniper, on the other hand, was furious with NOMAD for causing this rift. She went daily to speak to the council, hoping that she could change their minds—even threatening to leave—but they were firm. They probably knew it was a bluff anyway.

They had two days left until the council's deadline, and Jinn was washing dishes while Pseudo was buried in a book, as usual. Suddenly, Lucas burst through the door carrying a frightened Sebastian who had been outside playing.

"Motorcycles, coming in fast," Lucas hissed. He moved around the island and placed Sebastian in the cabinet. "We're gonna play hide-and-seek, ok buddy?" Lucas glanced back and forth between Jinn and Pseudo. Mae and Juniper were thankfully within NOMAD. "Stay here, and be very quiet so no one can find you, okay? We're gonna trick the bad guys."

"Okay," little Sebastian whimpered and curled into a ball while Lucas closed the cabinet door.

As quickly as she could, Jinn went over to her pack, pulled out her taser, and directed Pseudo to hide behind the island against the cabinet where Sebastian was hidden. She was considering whether he would fit in the cabinet as well, when someone started pounding on the door.

"Little pig, little pig, let me iiinnn ..." the voice said, dragging out the last word. Jinn rolled her eyes at Lucas. She could tell by the way the voice was slurring that he was blitzed. Lucas was positioned behind the couch with a taser as well, though his was not going to be nearly as severe as hers. He almost appeared to be praying.

Jinn waved to get Lucas's attention. *How many?* she mouthed. Lucas shrugged and held up three fingers. The pounding began on the door again.

Suddenly there was a muffled voice further away, and Jinn could sense their attention being pulled from the door.

"Who are you? What do you want?" a familiar voice echoed.

Shit, that's Juniper. There was an exchange of words that Jinn couldn't make out as the voices crept closer to the door. She ducked into the living room, taking a spot behind the couch next to Lucas.

"I told you, there's no one here," Mae's muffled voice carried through the door.

"Then you won't mind us lookin' around," the man said. His voice was guttural and graveled, someone who had been a longtime user.

"Actually, we do mind," Juniper answered. Then there was a soft thump, almost causing Jinn to leave her concealed spot. Lucas put a firm hand on her shoulder. The door opened.

Jinn could see three men. The one leading the way was tall and skinny, with a scraggly beard and huge sunken eyes. Behind him was a short, stocky man who appeared to be in his fifties, but was likely much younger. Standing in the doorway was the third, a young blond with papery skin and wide-set eyes that were pulled downward by a long droopy nose. His pale oily skin reminded Jinn of a sea creature that lived at the bottom of the ocean. He held Juniper by her arms. Mae was standing in front of him, holding her hands out in a placating gesture. All three had the telltale dilation of their pupils. Scraggly beard took three steps in before Jinn hit him with her taser. He fell to the floor convulsing. The ruckus caused fish face to let go of Juniper and push past the others into the house.

Jinn launched herself out from behind the couch with her dagger, but she was too slow. Fish face managed to turn around and land a punch straight to her gut. He was wearing something metal across his knuckles, and her sutures tore with blinding pain. She landed on the floor, bleeding and fighting to maintain consciousness. Lucas leaped out and tased fish face, causing momentary spasms. He turned and grappled with Lucas as the taser finally gave out. Jinn tried to get up to help, but the pain was causing her vision to swim.

The stocky man headed toward the island where Pseudo and Sebastian were hidden. She forced herself onto her feet as he reached the other side. Pseudo grunted as the man grabbed him by the shirt and threw him to the side like a rag doll. Pseudo kicked and scrambled with all that he had, but he was no match for Xandar's hired muscle. Jinn stood up and immediately fell again as the man bent down to peer into the cabinet. Sebastian screamed when he was dragged out. Pseudo jumped up and flew at the man but was knocked aside easily. Jinn checked her taser; it wasn't quite charged yet. The man struggled to drag the kicking, screaming, fighting toddler by the arm.

"I got 'im," the man yelled. "Let's get outta here."

"Make sure he don't get hurt," fish face, still brawling with Lucas, shouted back. "We need the reward." Jinn clenched her teeth, forcing her feet underneath her. She couldn't let them leave with Sebastian.

Then there was Mae. The octogenarian launched herself with a fire and fury that Jinn had never seen. A life of working with NOMAD had kept her strong. She grabbed Sebastian and attempted to wrench him free from the kidnapper's grip. Using everything she had, Jinn pushed herself off the floor and stumbled toward them. She lifted her taser and pulled the trigger.

Time slowed. In the instant between when the charges left the taser and landed in the man's chest, he landed a blow to Mae's temple that snapped her head backward. Mae grabbed Sebastian as she fell, pulling him loose from the man's grip before cracking her head on the granite countertop. Juniper ran the few steps across the room to catch Mae. Pseudo swept

Sebastian up and turned to hide him from the violence. The man hit the floor convulsing.

Jinn watched Pseudo as he cradled the child who was bruised but otherwise healthy. Lucas, having finally knocked fish face unconscious, immediately set to work immobilizing the intruders. Jinn dragged herself over to Juniper. She was looking down into Mae's slack face. A knot formed in Jinn's chest. *No*, she thought, *please, no.*

Juniper was rocking back and forth, humming slightly. Then she leaned over and planted a kiss on Mae's lips. Jinn saw Juniper's shoulders hitch as she waited for Mae to respond.

"Please, Mae," Juniper whispered. "Please don't go." Tears started streaming down Juniper's face. Jinn came up behind her and touched her shoulder, but Juniper did not feel it. "I love you," Juniper whispered. She started to repeat the phrase over and over, and after a moment she leaned over, holding Mae close to her breast. Juniper lifted her eyes and released a piercing scream that shook the very mountain to its core.

Chapter 20

Fallout

The air was frozen. The sound of Juniper's keening wails made the world shiver. Lucas moved to further secure the three intruders with cord and duct tape. Jinn pulled herself up against the island, the shock of everything falling all around her. Her mind was slipping when Pseudo came over and dumped Sebastian unceremoniously into her arms. Pain jolted through her, but it was the wake-up she needed. Jinn straightened, clutching the child and ignoring the torn stitches. She did not have time to feel sorry for herself right now, but her own tears started to fall as she hugged Sebastian close.

Lucas and Pseudo finished tying up the intruders and Lucas came over to take Sebastian from Jinn. She squeezed the boy again as Lucas took him, then she put her arm around Juniper's shoulder. Jinn couldn't speak. She hugged Juniper as Juniper held on to Mae. Slowly, Juniper quieted, her cries diminishing into soft sobs. She pulled Mae close and kissed her softly.

"I'm so sorry," Juniper said. She kissed Mae again, tears falling onto Mae's face. Pain tore at Jinn's abdomen as she stood up, allowing Juniper her space with Mae. Pseudo had faded back into a corner. He had pulled his knees up to his chin, reminding Jinn just how young he was.

Jinn jumped when Lucas touched her shoulder, his eyes wet with tears. He gestured toward the door. She nodded and waved Pseudo over as well, though she wasn't sure if he noticed. She followed Lucas outside then sat down heavily on the ground with her back to the wall. She put her head between her knees and started counting breaths to calm her whirling mind. Lucas lowered Sebastian on the ground, and the child started poking at things but would not wander out of arm's length. Lucas sat down next to Jinn and leaned his head back on the wall before pulling in a deep breath and blowing it out through his mouth.

"We need to talk to the council," Lucas said, keeping his eyes closed. "I can go. Stay with Sebastian 'til I get back?"

"Yeah," Jinn answered. "What about them?" She nodded toward the house, referring to the captive intruders.

"They probably won't wake up, but if they do just tase the fuckers," he answered. "Or kill 'em—I don't care. Doubt anyone else will either."

Jinn snorted. She would probably enjoy killing the bastards. They both looked up as Pseudo came out the door, his eyes wet and puffy and his hands shaking. He sat down with them. Silence fell heavily around them. Even Sebastian came over and leaned against Lucas's legs.

"What about us?" Pseudo finally asked.

"I honestly don't know what's gonna happen," Lucas said. "This's exactly what they were afraid of. We've just proven that it is not safe for us to be here." Lucas leaned over and put a protective hand on Sebastian. "Especially him." Lucas's voice caught on those last words.

"Well, what are we supposed to do?" Pseudo said, suddenly angry. "It's not our fault these psychos have taken over everything." He crossed his arms over his knees and started rocking back and forth. It was hard for Pseudo when he didn't have an answer.

Jinn reached over and put a hand on the back of his neck, massaging gently. She started taking deep breaths and subtly compelled Pseudo to mirror her. She could feel her own anger simmering. "We'll figure it out," she said.

The door opened again and Juniper stood there, her eyes glazed and far away. Blood was smeared on her face and down the front of her shirt. Jinn stood up quickly and embraced her. Juniper responded, but only slightly. She put her arms around Jinn, her movements slow and lethargic.

"I'm so sorry, Juniper," Jinn said through tears.

"It's not your fault," Juniper said, though the words were empty. All the emotion had drained from her body. "I need to speak to the council."

"I'm coming with you," Lucas said, standing up. Juniper's eyes turned toward him, but her gaze went right through.

"What do you want us to do?" Jinn asked her.

"Wait for me," she said simply and started walking.

Lucas quickly leaned down to Sebastian, "I'm going with Juniper. I need you to stay with Jinn and Pseudo, okay?" Jinn reached over and took his tiny hand.

"Okay," Sebastian said and sniffled, then he hugged onto Jinn's leg. Pseudo stood up, taking a step closer. He had all the appearance of a protective older brother. Lucas hurried to catch up to Juniper, leaving the three of them standing and staring after them.

—

NOMAD was efficient. In a short span of time, a few people dressed in white scrubs had come in and taken the three intruders out, ensuring they were constrained. The intruders were treated like objects, without emotion, only duty. The crew wasn't overly harsh, but they also weren't gentle. Two of the intruders had woken up but were still too dazed to be coherent. The other was still unconscious as they were taken away. Jinn wondered what was going to happen to them, but NOMAD refused to share any of that information, especially where Jinn and Pseudo were concerned.

The council also sent people to assist with the preparations for Mae. Two more women in white scrubs took Mae's body away to be prepared for the final rites. Juniper seemed to be floating, as though none of this was real but was just a list of tasks that needed to be checked. Still, she kept up with everything. Juniper joined in the throng of people who came in to clean the house and prepare for the death ceremony. Jinn and Pseudo helped remove all the cots and prepare a space for Mae to rest while loved ones came to say their farewell.

When they returned with Mae's body, she was wrapped in multicolored linen. Her hair was styled in her usual way, and her face had been made up so that she appeared to be sleeping peacefully. She rested in a plain wooden box ornamented with ivy, roses, calla lilies, and hyacinths.

For the next forty-eight hours, Juniper sat up next to Mae's body. She wore a red veil covering her face and a heavy red dress symbolic of mourning in NOMAD society. She would welcome and offer refreshments to the guests coming to say their final farewells. At first, Jinn tried to help, offering refreshments and comforts. But she quickly learned that she only made most of them uncomfortable. Everyone remained cool and polite. They spoke softly and worked to make sure that Juniper knew she was not alone. Condolences were offered and gratefully accepted. Jinn, Pseudo, Lucas, and Sebastian just did their best to stay out of sight.

After the forty-eight-hour wake, the council arrived at Juniper's house for the final procession. They took Mae in her pall, and six men that Jinn had not seen before carried her down into the valley toward the river. Jinn and Lucas each took a side of Juniper, who was beyond exhausted at this point, and supported her for the mile-long hike behind Mae. It was at this point that Juniper began to shed tears, quietly at first, but by the time they made it to the river she was openly sobbing.

Several members of the community took up their places behind large tribal drums decorated with Celtic knots and triads. They started drumming as the procession slowed. A woman began to sing, her clear voice like a bright strand weaving through the rhythm of the drums. Her haunting melody pierced through Jinn's stoic facade. They placed Mae on a raft that held a bed of dried sweetgrass and oak timber. Juniper walked toward the pyre and took a handful of hyacinths, those had been Mae's favorite, and laid them across Mae's chest. Juniper then removed the veil from herself and placed it over Mae, covering her face completely. The six pallbearers covered Mae in oil and handed Juniper a torch. They pushed the pyre toward the river. Once the pallbearers were about waist-deep in the water, they settled the raft to float on top of the water and held it steady for the final send-off. The drums and the singing stopped, even the wildlife held their breath for Mae. Thick silence fell while Juniper hesitated.

With a feral yell befitting a wild animal, Juniper launched the torch into the pyre. Within seconds, the entire raft was rolling with bright blue and orange flames. The drums started pounding again, harder than before, and working their way into a frenzy. Several people were holding burning sage sticks and dancing in circles. Someone handed sage to Juniper as she emerged from the water. Juniper held it for a moment before she fell to her knees. Jinn rushed over, but Juniper just shooed her away, handing her the burning sage. Juniper wailed in that space until her voice gave out. Then she lay down on the ground and sobbed.

Someone brought a blanket and placed it over her, allowing her the space to grieve while the ceremony continued. Jinn and Lucas tried to fade into the background as best they could while everyone around them celebrated Mae's transition from life.

Some cried, some laughed. Honey-infused wine was flowing freely, and there was abundant food brought in by the revelers.

Eventually, Juniper was able to rise from the ground and join the ceremony, which now resembled more of a festival. She circulated and talked with others. They were sharing memories of Mae with each other and the rest of the community. It was all very kind and cathartic, but there was an underlying current of unease. Pseudo had stayed behind with Sebastian, and people avoided Jinn and Lucas as much as possible.

Jinn found herself leaning into Lucas at one point during the evening as they shared their own memories of Mae. Juniper had been childhood friends with Jinn's mother and was married to Mae long before Jinn was born. Jinn was having a hard time reconciling that Mae was gone.

Lucas had not known Mae nearly as long, but she'd been a very big part of the last six months of his life, making sure that he was assimilated with NOMAD and then helping Sebastian transition. Mae had been smart, strong, determined, and most of all, her world revolved around Juniper. Jinn and Lucas both agreed that they'd never encountered a more perfect companionship than Juniper and Mae's.

"What have I done, Lucas?" Jinn asked, openly crying now.

"This wasn't you," Lucas said, pulling her into a hug. "*They* did this. No one else."

Jinn leaned into Lucas's chest, feeling his arms envelope her. She sighed, then began to sob. Lucas held her close, allowing her grief to be spent. When she finally looked up at him, his eyes were also streaming with tears.

"I'm so sorry, Jinn," he whispered.

"Yeah . . . me too," she answered. They stayed there, leaning on each other as the ceremony began to wind down.

Juniper finally walked over to them. She was clearly exhausted and had taken more than a few drinks of the honeyed wine, but she seemed alright.

"How are you, Jun?" Lucas asked, putting a hand on her

shoulder.

"I'm going to be okay," Juniper said, leaning onto his shoulder. "I was not ready to lose her, but I never would be." Juniper took a shaky breath, and her gaze lengthened. "We had a wonderful life together." The tears started streaming down her face again. She eyed Jinn with resolve. "It hurts like hell, and there are moments that I want to scream in pain and anger. I *never* expected to outlive her." Juniper chuckled slightly at this bit of morbid humor. "But I have so much to be happy for." She squared her shoulders and took a breath.

"We all loved her so much," Jinn said, her own tears falling.

"I know," Juniper said, "and she deserved every bit of it." She squeezed Jinn's hand and then Lucas's. "Let's go home."

Chapter 21

Please Go

Juniper slept for the next three days. She would wake up in a daze and find something to eat and drink, then listlessly wander back to her room. Just as Jinn was starting to fear that she would soon succumb to her broken heart, Jun woke up. She was able to move about the house on her own again, and though she would break down from time to time, she was beginning to accept her new reality.

Then the council showed up wearing their formal white robes.

"Juniper, how are you handling things?" Adams asked after they were seated in the common area. Jinn prepared some tea, while Lucas, Pseudo, and Sebastian stayed up in the loft.

"I am coping," Juniper said. She eyed the three of them skeptically.

"We wanted to come and check on you. We had not heard anything for a while," Swan said, graciously accepting the tea.

"I am managing well, thanks to my companions," Juniper said. There was an edge to her words.

"And you've been eating?" Jamison asked.

"Why are you here?" Juniper said quickly, her patience spent. "I know you have more of an agenda than checking in on an old woman, and you most certainly never show up in dress."

"Well, yes," Adams said, looking back and forth between Swan and Jamison. "We wanted to ask about your plans moving forward?"

"Plans?" Juniper asked.

"Yes, are you going to go back to your duties with NOMAD?"

"Of course, why wouldn't I?" Juniper said, narrowing her eyes at the councilors.

"Juniper, you have to understand, we ruled that your companions are not going to be able to remain under the protection of NOMAD," Swan said, looking at the floor.

"My house is outside of NOMAD's garrison. You aren't expected to protect them," Juniper said, growing quickly hostile.

"Yes, but we cannot support them, or you, if you are supporting them," Swan finished.

Jinn felt as though all the air had been sucked out of the room. The silence was palpable.

"Mae died *for them*," Juniper's voice was cold as steel. She slowly rose to her feet.

"Jun, Mae died *because* of them," Adams said softly, trying to placate her.

"No," Juniper said. "She died because of you."

All three members of the council pinched their expressions.

"Juniper—" Swan began, but Juniper cut her off with a glare.

"I have spent my life in service of this community," Juniper hissed. "Mae gave up *everything*, including her place on Exodus, to stay here with us. And your fear of confrontation cost her life. You know that it is only a matter of time before more people start flooding the gates, and eventually they will break them down. But you believe whatever lies you have told yourself."

"Juniper, you have to understand. We have our community to think about as a whole," Jamison said.

"Who do you think you are talking to?" Juniper snapped. "NOMAD still exists because of the efforts of Mae and myself."

"Juniper—" Adams said.

"Leave now," Juniper said, her shoulders shaking with rage.

"Juniper, please," Swan said, almost begging.

"Leave."

"We will be back in a week," Adams said. "We obviously all need some time to settle."

The members of the council marched out the door while Juniper sat down heavily on the couch. Her shoulders hitched a couple of times before she took a deep breath and leaned back and closed her eyes. Jinn moved to stand in front of her.

"Jun, you okay?" she asked tentatively.

"No, Jinn," Juniper said without opening her eyes.

"What can we do?" Jinn asked.

"I don't know," Juniper answered. "I'm too old for all this nonsense."

Sebastian took this opportunity to trip over his own feet and land heavily on the floor. He started wailing, looking for someone to pick him up. Juniper leaned forward and watched as Lucas picked up the child and coddled him. Her eyes went misty.

"Jinn," Juniper said softly, her eyes never leaving Sebastian. Jinn turned toward her. "I know we were hoping to change the councilors' minds, but is there somewhere else you can stay for a while?"

"Well . . . yes," Jinn answered. "I mean . . . we've been preparing for that eventuality. What did you have in mind? Do you want to come with us?"

"I just can't take all this on," Juniper said. Her shoulders sagged.

"I don't understand," Jinn spoke, though she knew. Her world was crashing. She had finally allowed herself to hope the future could be brighter and better with NOMAD, and now it was clear she was going to lose that, too. All thanks to some stupid decisions she had made a lifetime ago.

"I might be able to eventually clear the way for you all to come back, but NOMAD is not going to budge on this. Especially without Mae," Juniper said, her voice taut with resignation.

"What're you gonna do?" Lucas asked.

"I'm done," Juniper said simply.

"Juniper," Jinn whispered, tears forming in her eyes.

"Jinn, I love you and I always have, even through your hard times," Juniper said, looking directly at her. She turned to Pseudo. "Pseudo, I've only just met you in person, but I feel like I have known you for a lifetime." She turned again to Lucas, who was still holding Sebastian. "Lucas, you have made a huge impact on my life in the short time I have known you. I know that you are strong, and you will make a great guardian for little Sebastian."

"Jun, I . . ." Jinn started, then hesitated.

"I'm sorry, Jinn," Juniper said. "I have done all that I can. Your history, Lucas's history, and Sebastian's lineage is just too much." Juniper's voice hitched with a subdued sob. "I've spent my entire life with NOMAD. But without Mae, I don't even know how I am going to get up tomorrow, or even worse, try to sleep tonight. I just . . . I just can't."

"I understand," Jinn said. Her voice had lost all its inflection. "You want us to leave now?"

"Yes," Juniper whispered. "Please, I just can't take any more."

"Pseudo can hide us in the Clermont." Jinn lifted her eyes to Pseudo. She refused to allow her mind to wander. Solve this problem first, then worry about the next. Pseudo nodded briskly.

"I'm so sorry," Juniper said as she stood up.

"Don't be," Jinn said with conviction. "You've always been a wonderful friend to my family. You're a strong, amazing person, and you have nothing to apologize for. I love you."

"We all do," Lucas added. He was still holding Sebastian, who was no longer crying but could sense the weight in the room.

"Call me if you need anything at all, and we'll come running," Jinn said. She glanced at Lucas and Sebastian, and then Pseudo, who were all nodding with her.

"I truly hope so," Juniper said. "I am going to go back and talk to the council. I will call you if anything changes." With that, Juniper left. Jinn, Lucas, and Pseudo stared at each other, not really believing what was happening.

Thoughts began to swirl around in Jinn's mind. At first, she was confused, unsure what to do next. She moved to gather her few belongings. Lucas and Pseudo followed suit. As she packed, her mind moved from confusion to anger. Initially, the anger was directed inward. If she hadn't gotten involved with Xandar all those years ago, none of this would have happened. If she wasn't so easily manipulated and controlled by source and her own self-doubt, she could have come out the other side of this without a problem. Hell, she wouldn't even be on this planet. She'd be most of the way to Mars by now alongside her parents.

Tears stung her eyes. She had been so afraid of the past that she had done everything possible to hide, to make sure that it could not bleed into her current life. She hid her identity, kept herself small and unnoticeable, even fled to NOMAD. Jinn's self-pity suddenly curdled inside of her. Disgust with herself and everything that she had become welled up within her. What had happened to the headstrong woman who had entered the university? The woman who would argue relentlessly with classmates and professors about the best practices for terraforming another planet. Who the hell was this scared little girl? The tears started flowing at this point.

"You okay?" Lucas asked, putting an arm around her shoulders.

"No." Jinn laughed without mirth. "No, I'm not okay, but I'm going to fix it."

Chapter 22

Time to Face the Demons

Gray light spilled across Jinn's face as she held open the curtain, her eyes glazed and trained on the horizon. The storms were coming in. It seemed they came earlier and stronger every year. The weather's instability was worse with each season. When Jinn was young, there had only been a couple of weeks during the fall where travel was limited due to the random storms that would spring up out of nowhere, then disappear as fast as they had come. Now, they lasted months. The rain waxed and waned but never really stopped, and sudden meteorological violence swooped in and retreated with more destruction than she remembered. Most of the buildings in Atlanta had been reinforced to withstand the storms, including the Clermont, but the threat still lingered just over the horizon.

She paced in front of the window. Once upon a time this room would have been a place of luxury. The enviable penthouse floor of the famous Clermont Hotel. It had been close to a decade since someone paid for the services of this place. The other squatters relegated themselves to the lower floors. Jinn and Lucas with Sebastian shared adjoining rooms, each containing two beds and a kitchen space. They would share a bathroom with a shower and double sinks, the mirror having taken on a slight sepia tint with age. The furniture and decor were generic and old, but still comfortable.

Sebastian giggled and ran up and down the hallway. Yet again, this was all just an adventure for him. Lucas was sitting on the threadbare couch near the door so he could keep an eye on Sebastian as he frolicked. Lucas's face was drawn, eyes empty. Silence weighed heavily for a minute before he finally leaned back and placed the back of his hand over his eyes.

"Is this . . ." Lucas gestured around the room. "Is this it?" He sighed. "Is this what we are now—just surviving in an abandoned hotel?"

"No," Jinn said with conviction.

Lucas cut his eyes over to her without lifting his head. "No?" He snorted a humorless chuckle. "Do we have a choice?"

"We always have a choice, Lucas," Jinn said, grinning slightly.

"What's that supposed to mean?"

"It means we can make a choice," Jinn said, then took a deep breath. "Options: We can stay here and survive, probably the safest choice." She paused in thought. "We can leave and try to see if we can make it outside the city on our own, though that's kind of doubtful. Maybe if we had more people, and I'm pretty sure Pseudo is allergic to being outdoors. He'd go if I asked him to, but he wouldn't be happy about it."

"Where'd he go anyway?"

"He lives here," Jinn answered. "He went back to his room on the ground floor."

"He's not worried about Xandar?"

"Nah," Jinn smiled. "Never doubt his ability to hide in plain sight." Her eyes drifted back to the window.

"For some reason that don't surprise me," Lucas said with a genuine chuckle. Then he sighed and leaned back again. "So, what then?"

"Hmm?" Jinn slowly turned her head to look at him.

"I don't want Sebastian in danger, but this is no life." Lucas leaned forward, looking down the hall where the toddler had squatted to examine something on the floor.

"I dunno," Jinn answered with a shrug. "I'm tired of hiding. I've spent the last three years scared and watching over my shoulder for Xandar." She blew out her breath. "It helped that he thought I was dead."

"He runs the city; his influence increases each season," Lucas said. "I dunno what we can do about it." He stood up and started pacing. "Maybe we should leave."

"And go where?"

"I don't know, Nashville? Birmingham?" He gestured around him.

"Or . . . we can get rid of Xandar," Jinn said.

"Okay," Lucas scoffed.

"If we could cut off source, he would lose his whole economy," Jinn said.

"Sure, totally plausible. Let's do that," Lucas rolled his eyes, coming back to focus on Jinn.

"Listen, I know you grew up with source and the cartel, but there are still a lot of people who'd rather exist without it."

"You realize what you're saying?" Lucas asked. "Xandar has a veritable army. There's no way to just stop source."

"Sure there is," Jinn said, laughing.

"You have a plan?"

"Nope," Jinn said and then laughed again. Lucas cocked an eyebrow at her as if he questioned her grip on reality.

"Three people trying to take down Xandar is suicide," Lucas said, turning his head to look at Sebastian again.

"Give me some time," Jinn said. "And don't underestimate

Pseudo."

"What about Sebastian?" Lucas asked, then put his arms around Jinn's shoulders, pulling her close to him.

"We'll keep him safe," Jinn said, leaning into him. He smelled of sage and lavender. Juniper must have given him some soaps before they left. She rested her head on his shoulder. After a moment, he pulled back and looked down at her. His hazel eyes ignited.

Jinn could see the brown flecks in his irises. Her heartbeat quickened and stuttered as he pulled her closer. The contact was exhilarating and confusing. *Afraid.* She was afraid. Of what? Her heart started racing, and her chest and throat tightened. Suddenly, she couldn't breathe. She tried desperately to keep her composure but had to fight for each breath. Lucas pulled back at her change in demeanor, concern written on his face.

"I'm sorry." Jinn's voice was a hoarse whisper as she backed away from him.

"I . . . Um . . ." Lucas stuttered, unsure what to say.

Jinn could feel tears stinging her eyes. "I'm sorry," she whispered and rushed through the bathroom into the adjoining room. She pushed the door shut and locked it, then sat down heavily behind it. Tears began to flow freely. Jinn was confused, desperately trying to figure out what was happening, where all this was coming from. Collapsing onto the floor, she cried. Lucas's touch felt so good, so safe. But the last time she had been close to someone had been . . . *Oh. Xandar.* Her whole body shook with emotion. Embarrassed, confused, but mostly she was pissed—furious that Xandar could still have this much control over her. First, her friends and the university, then her parents, Juniper, and NOMAD. They had all left her behind because she had allowed Xandar to take control of her life. Now, she found herself afraid to get close to Lucas. There was no other direction left to go. She was not going to run from her past anymore. It was time to face it.

Chapter 23

My Stuff

"Slow down," Pseudo griped into Jinn's earpiece. "I can't see what you're looking at."

She was going back to her house in Little Five Points. Mostly she wanted her bike, but there were some other personal belongings she hoped to reacquire. Pseudo had checked out all her security systems. Luckily, they were still online. She raised her hand to eye level and gave a thumbs-up.

Pseudo had fashioned a communication system using an earpiece and augmented reality glasses. With these, Pseudo could see everything that Jinn was seeing or he could switch to an infrared display, but on a screen safely housed in the Clermont. He had also set it to overlay her vision with the infrared, but the contrast was turned down to almost nothing so that it wouldn't interfere with her true vision.

It was dark outside. The streets were empty as she crept up to the house. "Sweep the area," Pseudo said into the earpiece.

Jinn made sure her line of sight covered the entire property. "There's something in the greenhouse," he said. She turned her head in that direction. Her true line of sight was obstructed, but she could see a faint orange smudge in her AR when she went across it.

"One of the lights?" Jinn whispered.

"Doubt it," he answered. "The main house is empty though."

With another sweep of the street, orange smudges lit up in one of the houses, but there had been residents in that house for as long as she'd been living there. They would come and trade for protein occasionally. The doorknob turned easily in her grip. Thankfully, Pseudo had not bothered to lock it when he'd had to drag her out of there. But it was stuck. With her shoulder, she forced it open, but not quietly. She quickly pushed inside and found a place to hide momentarily and look around. The infrared smudge in the greenhouse was still stationary. That was good. The bedroom was empty, so she slipped inside and took the empty pack from her back to gather some essentials: a couple of changes of clothes, some toiletries, and makeup. Wistfully looking at her book collection, she decided she would have to come back for it, eventually.

Her back door was lighter and much quieter than the front, and she managed to make it out soundlessly. Some shrubbery that had overgrown next to the house made for a good hiding place as she glanced over at the greenhouse. Fat raindrops splattered against her head. *Shit*, she thought, *I really needed this to wait*. A blinding bolt of lightning flashed across the sky, followed by an earth-shattering clap of thunder. Whatever was in the greenhouse started moving.

"Definitely not a light," Pseudo said. Jinn wanted to curse at him but needed to stay silent. They watched as a person slunk out of the door holding a bag loaded with her harvest. Jinn didn't mind; there was enough of a cache stored at the Clermont to last for a while yet. She tapped the temple of her glasses to turn off the infrared momentarily. Jinn recognized the person coming out of the greenhouse. Her name was Stacy. She lived a couple of blocks down and usually bartered with Jinn for food. It made sense that she noticed Jinn had been gone for a while. It was a wonder anything was left. Most everyone around knew that she had security systems set up on pretty much everything, but scarcity creates need. Most likely, when Stacy was convinced that Jinn wouldn't return, she went for the food that would otherwise go to waste.

Jinn stayed in her hiding spot while Stacy glanced around and left with her spoils. Once Stacy was out of sight, Jinn headed into her shed. This was going to be the tricky part, because there was no way to bring the bike out quietly. She slipped inside just as the rain started pouring. *Great.* Her helmet sat on the seat of the bike. She put it on and readied herself for an expedient escape, though she wasn't sure what she was running from yet. It would be beneficial to wait for the rain to calm down, but there was never a guarantee it would stop soon. She needed to get out of there.

"Look back toward the door," Pseudo hissed into her ear, startling her so that she almost knocked the bike over. She took a deep breath, then tapped her glasses. Now there were two orange splotches—the one that was Stacy froze as the second heat signature approached.

"They look like they're talking," Pseudo narrated. He had a much clearer picture of the interaction. Eventually, the smudge that had been Stacy was able to walk away. "I guess Xandar doesn't want his people to make a lot of noise," Pseudo speculated. The other figure walked back into the house across the street. Maybe she would be lucky, and they were just sharing the stolen food. Stacy started walking briskly up the block, heading back toward her place. Jinn could see her head pivoting back and forth with each step.

"Should I break for it?" Jinn whispered.

"The rain would cover the noise," Pseudo said, and another blinding flash and clap of thunder answered him. "It's dangerous. The storm's hooking not far from you. Couple of miles maybe."

"All the more reason to get the hell outta here," Jinn said. She put on her helmet and zipped up her leathers, then disconnected the charging port. She swung her leg over the seat and hit the button for the garage door. Her trepidation built as the door slowly rolled upward. Jinn started the bike and kicked it into gear. Within seconds she was down the driveway and barreling through the streets. The rain had slowed slightly, but on the speeding bike it was like needles against her skin.

"You got someone's attention," Pseudo said in her ear. "There's a green military jeep following you." Pseudo had patched himself into the street cameras, or at least the ones that still worked. He was able to follow her route without much issue.

"Military jeep?" Jinn asked, almost inaudible above the wind and rain.

"Xandar raided Fort McPherson, according to the online rooms," Pseudo said by way of explanation.

"'Course he did," Jinn growled, speeding through streets as much as the bike would allow. Admittedly, the bike was not particularly fast, but it was highly maneuverable. Pseudo had Jinn turning through tight alleys and moving across catwalks to lose the tail. The storm helped, but the jeep was difficult to shake.

Speeding through the towering buildings of downtown, her connection with Pseudo was spotty at best. Once the jeep was no longer directly behind her, she darted down an alleyway and pulled the bike behind a stack of pallet wood that had likely been sitting there for decades. She cut off the bike and ducked behind it. The jeep sped by as she peered through the slats and expelled a breath she didn't realize she had been holding.

"They're coming back around," Pseudo hissed in her ear, causing her to jump out of her skin.

"Goddamn it, Pseudo," Jinn growled, crouching low to the

ground. The jeep came by again, more slowly this time. "Any idea who it is?"

"No," Pseudo answered.

Jinn waited. Silence and fear stretched out and became weighted by the incessant rain. Crouched behind her bike until her legs were ready to give out, she checked her immediate surroundings, then silently slid into a sitting position. The rain came down in torrents, but she was resting slightly underneath an awning that prevented the worst of the deluge. The water still puddled up around her and ran in rivulets down the alleyway. She shivered. The cold was not severe, but the combination of being wet and exposed made it quite uncomfortable.

Suddenly, movement stirred behind her. A wooden privacy fence served as a barrier for the alleyways between the two blocks. Her AR picked up two figures huddled under a large umbrella-like structure on the other side. One of the people started coughing. It was wet and full of phlegm. Jinn assumed that he was a habitual source user. She slid closer to the wall to try and hear them. Thankfully, due to the storm, they were practically shouting at each other.

"Jeez, Shenk, y'alright?" One of the voices asked as the other continued his coughing fit.

"Yeah," the voice that belonged to Shenk replied between breaths. "Gimme that water," he gasped. There was a pause, and Jinn watched as the two men interacted with each other. He tipped back what Jinn assumed was a water bottle then went to hand it back, but the other person was not paying attention. Jinn focused on a tiny bright spot on the infrared, then the acrid sent of vaporized source. They were blitzing.

"Jesse—" Shenk spat, knocking him on the arm with the water.

"Damn—the fuck's wrong w'your hand?" Jesse asked when he went to take the water back.

"Busted a fuckin' pod," Shenk answered.

"I've busted pods before. They ain't never done that," Jesse said, clearly disgusted.

"They do it to me," Shenk answered. "Ain't the first time. Sometimes it'll get on my mouth too."

"The fuck man, you should prolly quit," Jesse said. They both laughed at this, and Jinn could feel her skin prickle.

"It goes away. It's some dumb allergy or somethin'," Shenk said.

Jinn considered this. Could someone be allergic to source? There was a stimulant in it similar to what used to be known as nicotine; that was not what created the high feeling, though it probably increased the withdrawal symptoms. The men continued to speak, but not about anything useful. Mae had said something about a rash on Jinn's neck when Pseudo had brought her to them. She touched her neck where the needle had pierced her skin. Determined to see Shenk's rash, she strained her eyes through the slats in the fence. There was pretty much no field of vision, so she moved between the boards until she found a decent perspective. It looked as though Shenk had broken out with smallish pustules down his arm and all over his hand.

No way.

Pseudo's voice broke into her thoughts. "Jeep's gone. Not sure where it went, but it detoured from Little Five and headed across I-20." Jinn turned her glasses in the direction of the two men so that Pseudo would see why she was staying silent. "Ah," he responded when he saw the bright figures on his screen. "Anyone we know?"

Jinn shook her head back and forth to signal no.

"Well, we can wait for 'em to clear out. Looks like the storm is gonna let up soon, though there's some nasty ones coming in behind it."

Jinn gave a thumbs up. After a few more minutes Shenk and Jesse finally went on their way, and Jinn was able to move her bike back out into the rain.

Chapter 24

What is This?

Jinn arrived safely back at the Clermont, though she was soaking wet and cold. She stashed her bike in the neighboring parking garage and connected it to a charger. She could hear the rumbling of the storm outside, pelting the building with rain and what sounded like small hailstones. The lightning and rolling thunder had become almost constant, but she felt safe inside. Safer here than at her old house, anyway.

Jinn climbed the stairs, dripping all the way to the top floor. Pseudo had told her that the elevators worked fine and were perfectly safe. She usually trusted his judgment but couldn't bring herself to get in the metal death traps. Sebastian was playing in the hallway as usual when she finally opened the door to her floor. He was running back and forth on his own personal racetrack with Lucas looking on. Lucas stood up as soon as he saw her. She was sure she looked like a drowned rat.

"You okay?" he asked with concern.

"I'm fine," Jinn huffed. "I'm cold, and I think my house is being watched, but I'm safe and I'm here. So now I am gonna get in the shower and try to get some feeling back in my extremities."

Lucas smiled at her and stepped aside. Neither of them had addressed her previous panic attack. Jinn wanted desperately to explain herself to Lucas, but every time she tried, the feeling of being suffocated rose in her chest again. Lucas had given her plenty of space, which was comforting but terrifying at the same time. She smiled back and went into the bathroom and locked the door.

Frustrated with her inability to just say what was on her mind, she dropped her hands heavily on each side of the sink and raised her eyes to the mirror. Sharp green eyes stared back at her. Strength resided in there somewhere. She just needed to find it again. Her wet riding gear was stiff and stuck to her skin, but she finally removed it, leaving it in a wet heap on the floor. She crinkled her nose as water ran from the clothes. She would pick them up later. Turning the handles in the shower, she waited until the water began to steam before stepping inside. The warmth was almost painful where the cold had settled deep into her bones. She leaned back into the water, luxuriating in Juniper's soap made from honey and lavender. Finally feeling warm, she stepped out of the shower and put on a robe that was a remnant of when the hotel was still operational. It was old, but warm and soft. Lucas and Pseudo were deep in conversation on the faded couch when she emerged from the bathroom.

"Feel better?" Lucas asked. His voice sounded like he was attempting to be facetious, but his eyes belied his worry.

"You have no idea," Jinn said and sat down on the chair facing them. Lucas had managed to wrangle Sebastian back into the rooms, and he was munching on some food while they talked. "My house is being watched," Jinn continued, "which is annoying because I could really use my lab equipment."

"I wouldn't worry about lab equipment," Pseudo said. "This

place houses the biggest gaggle of nerds left on the planet. We can find whatever you need."

"Anyone working on proteins?" Jinn asked.

"Ew, no," Pseudo said, a look of disgust crossing his face.

"You eat it just fine," Jinn chided.

"We do have a lab for it, but as far as I know, none of us use it," Pseudo said.

"Can I see it?" Jinn asked.

"Like . . . now?"

"As soon as I get some clothes on," Jinn said with slight annoyance.

"Fine," Pseudo said rolling his eyes. "It's in the basement."

"I think we'll hang back," Lucas said, referring to himself and Sebastian.

"Shouldn't take long," Jinn said and smiled softly at him.

A few minutes later Jinn was gripping the railing in the elevator, since Pseudo refused to take the stairs. Her knuckles were white, and she was glaring at him the whole time. They rode down in silence, Pseudo's smirk saying all that needed to be said. When they finally reached the basement floor and the doors opened, Jinn was genuinely afraid that she was going to vomit. She exited the elevator and leaned over, placing her hands on her knees before looking up and around. Several corridors led in different directions to spaces housing the working engines of the hotel. A boiler room generated heat, a room full of vats that smelled like a brewery, and a room that contained enormous washers and dryers. They passed several locked storerooms, most likely containing the food caches, before finally reaching a fully stocked and functional organic lab.

Jinn inspected the lattices, growth mediums, and solutions. Everything was there that they needed to begin manufacturing protein, but apparently the people living here lacked the time, or stomach, for it. She checked the availability of bacterial culture growth mediums. She eyed Pseudo. "You think you could get me an empty pod?"

"Why?" Pseudo asked, his voice edged.

"I have a suspicion that I'd like to test," Jinn said.

"I don't wanna have anything to do with any of that if I can help it," Pseudo said, fear creeping into his words.

"I think I can create a cure," Jinn said, fully meeting his eyes.

"You can't cure addiction," Pseudo said. He looked at her like she had grown a second head. She knew this.

"No," Jinn said, "not the addiction, but I may be able to create something to hold off the withdrawal and maybe even eliminate the euphoria."

"What're you talking about?" Pseudo asked with incredulity. "You're no chemist, and even if you were, that'd probably hurt people more than the actual drug."

"I don't think so," Jinn said then smiled at him. "Can you get me a pod?"

"Probably," Pseudo grumbled.

"It's only a theory," Jinn said. "I could be wrong, but I've got to see."

"Fine," Pseudo said. "Don't say I didn't warn you; empty or not we shouldn't fuck with it." As if to punctuate his point, there was a heavy rumble of thunder, and the lights flickered causing both of their eyes to turn toward the ceiling.

"Trust me," Jinn said and smiled.

Pseudo didn't.

Chapter 25

Maybe

It made sense. Jinn had spent a week in the lab testing her theory. Pseudo had posited before that source was accidentally developed when everyone was looking for a treatment for Spastic Meningitis. Even back then, NOMAD rarely used anything like the chemical pharmaceuticals preferred by the Exodus scientists. Mae would have been able to confirm her hypothesis. Tears sprang to Jinn's eyes at the memory. Mae had spent a long time trying to recreate the bacteria that caused spastic meningitis, and it wasn't until she met Juniper that she was able to finally find something that could treat it.

Jinn busted an empty pod Pseudo had pilfered, and then set up some cultures. It had taken a couple of recipes to get them to grow, but finally Jinn had proof that source was not a synthetic compound. It was a form of bacteria. More than anything, she wanted to call Juniper and let her know what she found. But the call wouldn't connect, and Jinn figured it was for the best.

Juniper was dealing with enough right now. Jinn still had a lot of research to do to figure out how exactly it created the euphoria and why it went after the brain. But what she did know for sure was this—if the drug is a bacterium, then she could create an antibiotic.

She learned that temperature was a problem. Source could survive for a while in warm temperatures, but not very long. Jinn theorized that was why it went after the brain. Its temperature usually stayed just below ambient body temperature, so it would last the longest there. Jinn also theorized that it was somehow causing the release of high amounts of dopamine, which creates euphoria without the side effects of most chemically induced highs. The bacteria also became very aggressive when its survival was in jeopardy. This was probably the reason why the withdrawal was so intense, but if she could create an antibiotic, she could at least shorten the withdrawal time. Maybe even reduce the effects of the dopamine, so it would be easier for people to kick the habit. She knew addiction would always be addiction, but just maybe this would help.

Excited that she had been able to cultivate the bacteria, she rushed upstairs to tell Lucas. Her energy abated when she found him still in the room lying on the bed in a similar position to when she had left that morning.

"I made a breakthrough," Jinn announced, trying to force her excitement onto him.

"Yeah?" Lucas said, looking up at her with a limited expression.

"Yes, I've finally figured out the cultivation. It's tricky, but I found it," Jinn said, coming over to sit on the edge of the bed.

"What's that mean?" Lucas asked, sitting up on his elbows.

"This means I can develop an antibiotic," Jinn grinned, proud of her accomplishment.

"So . . . you're growing source right now?" Lucas asked, a slight edge to his voice.

"I, uh . . ." Jinn hesitated. "Well, yeah, I guess."

"You're ok with that?" Lucas asked. He eyed her with skepticism.

"What do you mean?" Jinn asked. She knew what he was getting at, but she didn't want to admit it.

"You were addicted," Lucas said slowly. "You gonna be able to surround yourself with this stuff and not use it?"

Jinn blinked. The statement coming from Lucas stung her pride. "Yes?" she said hesitantly.

"You don't sound very sure," Lucas said. His voice and posture were heavy. He was clearly struggling with their situation. She had not helped matters. Ever since she had run from him, she'd done her best to keep him at arm's length and keep any communication superficial. With her being so involved in research, she hadn't considered how much time he spent alone. She scooted closer to him.

"Lucas," she said, looking directly at him. "I'll be fine."

"Until you're not," he rebuffed.

"Then I'll ask for help." She put a hand on his thigh. He finally lifted his eyes to meet hers.

"Lucas, I'm sorry," Jinn said, trying to reign in the emotions that were swirling around in her mind. She was excited about the progress she had made, but worried about the future. She was offended and chastised by Lucas pointing out the obvious. She was scared. What if all this just turned her into a target?

"For what?" Tentatively, Lucas covered her hand with his own. She could feel his loneliness. The creeping voice in her head started prodding her. *You're the only person around, of course he's attracted to you.* She shook her head, then met Lucas's eyes again.

Then she kissed him. He reacted with surprise and pulled back, searching Jinn's face. She remained where she was, her eyes locked on his. He leaned forward and kissed her back, more slowly this time. Their lips met gently, and Jinn moved her hand up to his cheek. He pulled her closer, the kiss becoming more insistent, searching. He moved his hands to her waist, pulling her against him. She responded by throwing her arms around his neck and sidling closer. Her tongue probing his, her face warm and flushed.

They both pulled back as Sebastian came bounding into the room, though Lucas's hand remained on her waist. Her mind started spiraling. *Damn it, stop*, she chastised herself. Lucas gently massaged her back in response to her change in posture. Thankfully, he didn't say anything. Maybe he understood more than she'd realized.

"I'm hungry," Sebastian said, oblivious to the tension in the room.

"Okay, buddy," Lucas said and stood up. He went to the kitchenette to make Sebastian some lunch.

Jinn saw her opportunity and ducked out of the room. She had to reel in her thoughts. She headed down to Pseudo's room to share her research findings with him.

"Pseudo," Jinn said as she entered his room.

Pseudo lifted his eyes from his computer, annoyance on his face.

"Source is bacteria," she said, smiling.

"That's what you suspected, right?" he asked, looking back at his screen.

"Yes, but now I can cultivate it. I can create an antibiotic," Jinn responded, waiting for Pseudo to be impressed.

"Which is what you were going to do," he said, his voice monotonous.

"Yes, and I have made huge progress. Be happy for me," Jinn said, throwing a wad of paper at him.

"Pass . . . what d'ya need now?" Pseudo asked, finally turning his focus to Jinn. She was picking at something on his bed.

"I need to make a slurry. I'll need the centrifuge to work," she responded before getting up and pacing the room. "And I'll need a carrier fluid if I want injection." She sat for a minute then started again.

"Biology's gross," Pseudo said.

"You've mentioned that."

"What else is on your mind?" Pseudo asked.

"What do you mean?"

"You're being weird usually means you're thinking about something," he said, not bothering to look over at her.

"I've been telling you . . ."

"Anything to do with Lucas?" Pseudo asked, ignoring her.

Jinn froze, her eyebrows lifted almost to her hairline. The time it took her to recover from the shock was enough to confirm Pseudo's theory.

"I kissed him," Jinn said, her cheeks flushing.

"So?"

"What do you mean *so*?"

"I mean, so what? Why does that have you all worked up? Don't you like him?"

"Well, yeah, I just . . . Um . . ." Jinn stammered. "What if he doesn't feel the same way?"

"Are you in fucking middle school?" Pseudo admonished.

"Wow," Jinn responded, becoming defensive.

"I know you, Jinn. You're considering and over thinking every possible thought that could be in his head. Here's the rub though: You. Can't. Think. For. Him." Pseudo finally met her eyes.

"What the hell are you talking about?" Jinn retorted, growing annoyed at her own insecurity and even more annoyed that everyone kept pointing it out.

"What if he doesn't like me, why would he like me, how does he perceive me, blah blah blah fucking blah," Pseudo said. The intensity of his annoyance was surprising. "Look if you want to know what he's thinking, ask him."

"Why are you so angry?" Jinn said, suddenly finding herself amused by Pseudo's reaction.

"Cause it's stupid—"

"It's not—"

"It is. Don't make me prove it." Pseudo turned his eyes back to his screen.

"Fine, whatever." Jinn was on the verge of laughter, which only annoyed Pseudo more.

"*Fine, whatever, me me me,*" Pseudo mimicked, demonstrating his youth.

"You're an asshole," Jinn said.

"Still don't care," Pseudo quipped.

"When you meet someone, I am going to make you pay for all this," Jinn said, a smirk on her face.

"Yeah, okay," Pseudo said. "At nineteen years old I'm pretty sure I could have a more mature relationship than you ever could."

"Damn," Jinn lifted her eyebrows, unable to contain her grin. "Out for blood."

"I don't have time for nonsense," Pseudo said. He pushed his glasses up on his nose and turned back to his screen.

"You asked . . ." Jinn muttered.

"I've got eyes on Junkman's Daughter, and I am trying to follow the distribution channels."

"Oh." Jinn quickly absorbed the information, despite the sudden shift in topic. The Junkman's Daughter had been a fixture in Atlanta for centuries. It was a retail store that carried all sorts of products through the years and made its name in Little Five Points for being a sort of haven for counter-culture. About fifty years prior, it had been sold along with the restaurant next door. The owners at the time managed to get seats on one of the earlier Exodus flights. The more recent owners had tried to keep up the eclectic image and products, but as more people left, they eventually abandoned it for NOMAD. Even Jinn had been through there to pick over the bones. It's where she had found her dagger. Less than five years ago, the store and the restaurant had been taken over by the cartel. They pretend that they are running a legitimate business, but everyone knew better.

"I keep losing 'em on the interstate," Pseudo said.

"Losing who?"

"About once a week, two box trucks drop something at the store," Pseudo said. "Between surveillance and Lucas's intel, I think they're source shipments. Xandar does a pretty good job of keeping things random and secret. I'd imagine it would get fucked if he didn't."

"Right."

"I'm getting close, though," he said, cutting his eyes over to Jinn. Pseudo grinned—something that was rare on his face, but Jinn loved it, nonetheless.

"Cool, me too," Jinn answered. "Let's take this fucker down."

Chapter 26

Lucas Matters

It was late as Jinn slowly trudged up the stairs to the suite. The last couple of weeks had been strained as she continued working on the antibiotic, but she was slowly getting more comfortable with Lucas. A smile crept across her lips at the realization that she was looking forward to seeing him.

"How's it coming?" Lucas asked as she walked into their shared suite. He was lying on the bed reading, with his arm stretched lazily behind his head. The muscles in his arms were slightly smaller, and his skin was drawn. A hint of worry prickled at her over the weight he was losing. Sebastian was sleeping soundly in the opposite bed, clutching his stuffed elephant.

"I think I'm ready to test; it all seems rushed though," Jinn answered. Kicking off her shoes, she climbed onto the bed next to him. Lucas's heartbeat drummed against her ear as he lowered his arm down and wrapped it around her. She could sense his hesitance. It put her on edge.

"What're you worried about?" Lucas asked. He was good at keeping the conversation superficial.

"The only way to create the antibiotic is rough. I know it'll kill the bacteria, but with the way that source goes into overdrive when it's dying, I'm worried the cure may be worse than the disease," Jinn answered.

"How so?"

"Consider the withdrawal symptoms," Jinn leaned up on her elbow. "Fever, tremors, nausea, all that."

"Yeah?" Lucas said.

"Well, I can't be sure that the bacteria won't dump all their toxins at once."

"I'm not sure I follow," Lucas said, putting his arm back behind his head.

"The only antibiotic I've been able to create busts through the cell walls of the bacteria," Jinn explained. "It *may* shut everything down and it's all fine, or it may send it into an even harder overdrive and create a huge toxin dump, poisoning the subject." Jinn took a deep breath.

"Any evidence of that?" Lucas asked.

"Yes," Jinn answered, laying her head back down. "But until I can test on an actual person, I can't really determine how bad the effects would be. They could be drastically reduced, shortened but rougher, or it could kill them."

"Wow, okay," Lucas said. He slid down slightly so that they were both lying comfortably.

"You can't test it on mice or something?" Lucas asked.

"Tried," Jinn answered. "I can't exactly pick up lab rats, but I've tried it on some of the vermin that run around. The results are weird and inconsistent, almost like they are immune to source."

"Huh," Lucas answered. He started stroking her hair. "So, we have to possibly kill a person to see if it works?"

"Yeah, pretty much," Jinn responded, her voice resigned. "If

I had another five years, I might be able to find a gentler solution, but for now I'm stuck."

"Seems ethics are a bit sketchy," Lucas said with a slight smile.

"Yeah," Jinn gave a half-hearted chuckle.

"Pseudo made any progress?" Lucas asked.

"I haven't talked to him in a while," Jinn snuggled closer. "He's running through the underground, getting street cameras onto his network. I think it's too big for him, though. He's trying to come up with something more direct."

"More direct?"

"Yeah, he's been working on some sort of tracker; he's good at those. I'm guessing he's going to ask me to fix one on a truck."

"Huh," Lucas said again. His shoulders tensed.

"You all right?" Jinn asked, leaning up so that she could look at him.

"Yeah," Lucas avoided her eyes.

"You know if you don't tell me what's on your mind I'm gonna think it for you, and I'm sure it'll be a lot worse." Jinn smiled at him.

Lucas chuckled slightly. Jinn had told him about her conversation with Pseudo and how much it had annoyed her that he was right.

"I feel kinda useless," Lucas said, the smile falling from his features. "I'm stuck in these rooms. I dunno what's gonna happen. There's literally nothing I can do except babysit Sebastian."

Jinn furrowed her brow.

"I don't mind the kid," Lucas said quickly. "I'm just in some sort of weird limbo," he paused. "Or purgatory. You're in the lab all the time, Pseudo's doing whatever Pseudo does, and I'm here watching a toddler. I'm bored and frazzled at the same time."

"From what I understand, that's how toddlers work," Jinn said, giving his chest a teasing shove. He smiled down at her.

"I know," he pushed back, smiling. "I just wish I was

contributing." He covered his eyes with the back of his free hand. "With the plan, or research," he turned to Jinn, "with you."

Jinn's heart skipped a beat, and her cheeks warmed. She had to admit that Lucas had been extremely patient with her. The first attempt at intimacy had her running away in tears, and then the kiss that came out of nowhere, and she immediately bolted after. Since then, he had almost treated her like a scared animal, allowing her to get closer to him at her own pace. She sat up and kissed him on the cheek.

"You're amazing, Lucas. You've been here 'round the clock for Sebastian, you've tolerated my fleeting bouts of crazy, and you aren't particularly annoyed by Pseudo—which is a feat all to itself." Jinn smiled at him. "You've been holding everything together, and I'm sorry if we haven't shown you that. You're important, crucial even, to us." She took a breath. "To me." Jinn's hands were shaking. This sort of vulnerability was difficult for her, and Lucas knew it.

He sat up on his elbows and took her hands, leaning closer. Jinn could smell the soap he had been using; his hair was still slightly damp. Jinn closed her eyes and closed the distance, meeting his lips softly. Her mind was swirling yet again, but she concentrated on the feel of his lips on hers and the warmth of his hands. He pushed against her slightly, and she put her head back on the pillows. He broke away from the kiss and looked down at her, his hazel eyes glistening. She reached up and touched his cheeks, slightly roughened by stubble, but the shadow that it created was alluring. He stroked her hair away from her forehead.

"Jinn, I..." Lucas started to speak, but then just leaned down to kiss her again. She pulled him in, her hands reaching around his neck and running her fingers through his hair.

Sebastian stirred on the other bed. Lucas sat up and glanced over at him. Sebastian sat up also, rubbing a tiny fist in his eyes. Lucas shook his head.

"I'm gonna take a shower," Jinn said, moving away from him. He gave her a beseeching expression, so she leaned up and kissed him again quickly, trying to quell the disappointment in his eyes. She said, "Maybe we can finish this conversation in my room once Sebastian's asleep?" Lucas smiled—the first genuine smile Jinn had seen from him in a while. She rolled out of the bed and headed to the bathroom.

Chapter 27

Jasmine

Lucas sat on the bed with Sebastian for a while trying to get him to go back to sleep. Poor little guy had severe attachment anxiety, not that Lucas could blame him. The kid had had a rough time in the few short years he had been around. Sebastian leaned over on him, and Lucas put his arms around the boy and gently rocked. Sebastian finally went back to sleep, but Lucas had also dozed off in the process. He didn't know how much time had passed since Jinn got out of the shower. She was probably already asleep.

He quietly went through the door to the adjoining bathroom, pausing for a minute in front of the mirror. His face was gaunt—he was definitely losing weight. He took a breath and tried the door to the adjoining room. It was unlocked, which surprised him. Jinn sat on her bed wrapped in one of the robes with the Clermont logo stitched in the front.

"It's about time," Jinn whispered smiling at him.

"Don't I know it," Lucas gave her a hungry smile. His eyes trailed across her lips and then followed the curve of her body to the toned legs that she had draped over the side of the bed. Her hair fell in damp curls around her face accentuating her liquid emerald eyes. The mattress dipped as he settled next to her. He pushed a lock of hair away from her eyes and inched closer. Jinn tensed beneath his touch. He waited.

Jinn closed her eyes and took a breath. When she opened them again, Lucas could see the depth of her emotion. It was hard to imagine all she had been through. She smiled up at him and pulled him into a deep, slow kiss. He responded, gently pressing against her. He moved his lips down to her neck and her breath caught.

Gentle and deliberate, his hands moved to the opening of her robe, slowly caressing her soft skin that was warm beneath his touch. The robe slid from her shoulders, and she tensed, either from the chill in the air, or the exposure. Lucas drew back and looked at her. Focused on her eyes, he waited until she was ready before allowing his eyes to roam. At her invitation, he resumed his exploration with his fingers as she warmed to him. Finally, she reached for his T-shirt, and he helped to pull it over his head. Then it was her turn to pull back and look. He smiled and flexed, eliciting a small giggle from Jinn. She pulled him against her.

They moved into each other with hunger. The storms outside the window raged and shook, but only intensified the moment. Lost in the physical, exploring with their hands and lips, and soon pulsing out a rhythm that brought them closer and closer before they were spent, exhausted. Jinn laid her head over on Lucas's shoulder, and he kissed her forehead.

"You okay?" he asked her.

"Never better," her languid whisper drifted through the darkness. He watched her as she dozed, admiring her glossy black hair and smooth skin. He smiled despite himself, unable to be anything but elated that she had finally opened to him. He knew that it had been difficult for her, and his patience paid off. He had found something in Jinn, her conviction and intelligence, her strength. He longed to show her what he could see. As he began to doze, she pulled closer to him. The scent of lavender and the warmth of her skin lulled him to sleep.

Warmth stirred next to Lucas. The gray light of day seeped through cracks in the curtains. The storms were still raging outside, rain pelting the windows. The muted light made it difficult for him to tell what time it was. Jinn was stirring next to him. He smiled.

"Good morning," Jinn said, smiling.

"Is it?" Lucas mumbled, burying his face in the robe that Jinn was attempting to use to cover herself.

"Yep," she laughed quietly and stood up cinching the robe around her. "Y'know, there's a gym here."

"Yeah," Lucas said, catching a glimpse of himself in a mirror.

"You use it?"

"I haven't," Lucas said. "It's difficult when your being tailed by a toddler."

"Makes sense," Jinn said with a smile.

Lucas extricated himself from the tangled sheets and began to dress. Thunder shook the windows, and it vibrated through the floor.

"You want me to stay with him so you can go?" Jinn asked. She looked at him expectantly, and when he didn't respond, she dropped her gaze. "Sorry, should've thought about it a long time ago."

"You don't mind?" Lucas asked.

"Course not," Jinn said with an exuberant smile. "Go. I'll take care of breakfast."

"Thanks," Lucas said with genuine appreciation.

"No worries," Jinn said, moving to get some leggings and a shirt.

Lucas went back to his side of the suite and pulled on some

shorts and athletic shoes. He smiled. For the first time since all this mess started, he was hopeful for the future.

Lucas made his way to the gym, reveling in the solitude and looking forward to pushing himself physically. The equipment was old, and most of the more technologically complex machines weren't functional, but there was still a good number of free weights and a couple of rowing machines that were operational. He did a quick stretch and warmed up before hitting the weights. The old rhythms and solace he'd gained through pushing his body returned quickly.

Very early on he learned that he was going to have to rely on himself for survival. Once he was old enough to walk and talk, his parents left him to his own devices. It was a difficult lesson for a child, but he learned that he needed to be stronger and faster than the other kids if he wanted to eat. Once he figured out how to provide for himself, he started helping the other feral children. They developed something like their own rogue society, though the majority that survived to adulthood just ended up like their parents. As his mind wandered, taking him back to when he was young, he worked up a sweat. Not everyone had fallen into the addiction. He had run into one of his fellow street urchins during his short stay with NOMAD.

He tried to get one of the treadmills to work, but they were too far gone, so instead he finished out his routine on a rowing machine. Once the storms blew through, he would start running outside again; he looked forward to that. The machine pumped, and the burning feeling in his back and arms became pleasurable. Suddenly, something moved in his periphery, and he froze.

"Hello?" Lucas called out, bothered by the fact that he had spent his whole workout in here without noticing anything. He listened, his muscles tense. "Hello?" he called again. In the corner behind some defunct machines, there was definitely something.

Stepping around them, he found the source of the

movement. A smallish woman, maybe early twenties, crouched behind the machines. Translucent blond hair, unkempt and messy, fell around a pale cream-colored face. Her striking blue eyes were wide and watery, though tinged with red. She was clearly terrified.

"You okay?" Lucas put his hands up so as not to appear threatening. He took a step toward her. She wrapped arms around herself and closed her eyes to his approach. Lucas could see that she was sweating, and her face had a sickly green pallor. It was probably withdrawal. He cautiously approached and extended a hand to touch her shoulder. She attempted to draw away from him, but there was nowhere left to go. "I promise I won't hurt you," Lucas said softly, kneeling next to her.

She slowly lifted her eyes to meet his. He smiled at her. "You need help?" Lucas asked gently. She shook her head and pushed him away. He gave her space but remained kneeling. "I'm Lucas," he said, extending his hand.

She eyed his hand for a minute before looking back at his face. Slowly, she extended a shaky hand toward him. "Jasmine," she said, her voice barely a whisper.

"You stay here?" Lucas asked, settling himself on the floor.

"No," she answered, turning her back to the wall and relaxing, barely.

"Do you need something?" he asked.

Suddenly she broke into sobs. Lucas put a hand on her shoulder while she cried and scanned the gym for anything else he may have missed. After a couple of minutes, her sobbing subsided, and she hung her head between her knees.

"Sorry," she said, her voice unsteady.

"Dunno why you're apologizing," Lucas said, giving her a smile.

"I'm trying to get through this," she said, "but I really need some source. You have some? Or anything that I could trade for it. I can pay."

"Sorry, I don't," Lucas said.

"I'm so tired of being this person," she said, putting her face in her arms again.

Lucas's heart broke for her. He knew that sentiment—when someone gets tired of dependence and just wants to escape. Jinn's antibiotic popped into his mind.

"I don't think I can survive this," she said, her voice muffled. "I don't know if I want to."

"Sorry," Lucas said. "Listen, come upstairs with me. I have someone for you to talk to."

"I don't . . . I dunno." Jasmine cut her eyes suspiciously over to Lucas. "Sorry, I'm babbling and full of shit. I should . . . I should go." She picked herself up from the floor and started edging toward the doors.

"Wait," Lucas raised his hands. "We are on the top floor. You don't have to come right now, but we might be able to help. Just think about it." He gently touched her shoulder and stood up. "I'm easy to find. There's a feral toddler with a permanent case of the zoomies who will lead you right to me."

Jasmine furrowed her brow in confusion.

"His name's Sebastian," Lucas smiled. Her look of uncertainty giving him pause, but he turned to walk away. He glanced over his shoulder and gave her a final smile as he left the gym.

Chapter 28

Testing

"How was the workout?" Jinn asked, looking up at Lucas as he entered the suite. She was sitting with Sebastian, playing with some tablets that belonged to Pseudo. He had retired them a while ago, so he programmed a few games for Sebastian's entertainment.

"Good, thank you," Lucas answered. He briefly considered mentioning Jasmine, but decided it could wait. "I really need a shower now." He gestured to his sweat-soaked clothes.

"Don't thank me. I literally did nothing," Jinn answered with a smile. She turned her attention back to Sebastian. Lucas shrugged and headed to the shared bathroom.

While he showered, Jinn found herself lulled to sleep by the repetitive upbeat cadence of the games. Sebastian snored next to her. She registered Lucas moving quietly around the kitchen, but was only roused back to consciousness when he began to wash the leftover dishes from breakfast. With a languid smile, she stretched and rolled her head toward him. Trying not to jostle Sebastian, Jinn slowly climbed out of bed. The child stirred a little but settled back into his nap.

Jinn stepped up to Lucas as he dried his hands. She turned him to face her, pulling him closer. He leaned down and kissed her softly. She kissed him back briefly, then buried her face in his chest and tucked her arms into her sides. He wrapped his arms around her, and she nestled safely into a cocoon of warmth.

"Hey," she said when she finally pulled back.

"Hey," Lucas said and smiled down at her.

"Hey," Pseudo said from the doorway, startling them both.

"Damn it, Pseudo," Jinn cursed, trying to reign in her racing heartbeat. Lucas laughed out loud. "What do you want?" Jinn asked as she spun around to face Pseudo.

"I need a favor," Pseudo said as though he hadn't just scared her out of her wits.

"You finished the tracker?" Jinn asked.

"Yup, now we need to put it on a truck. I should be able to get location and audio. It has a micro camera, but I doubt I'll see much." Pseudo looked smug. He was obviously proud of his invention.

With all the activity around, Sebastian woke up. He sat up in the bed and started babbling, then greeted everyone in turn. Lucas took him into the bathroom for a quick clean up.

"You have a plan?" Jinn asked Pseudo.

"Nope, that's your job," he said, taking a seat on the couch.

"Of course," Jinn rolled her eyes. "You at least have a guess for when the trucks will be back at Junkman's?"

"Couple of days?" Pseudo said, "But I see them when they approach, and they're usually there for at least half an hour, so . . ."

"So . . .?" Jinn was exasperated.

"That's it," Pseudo said. "The rest is on you."

"Okay," Jinn said. "I'll talk to Lucas."

"You know Lucas?" Jinn and Pseudo turned to see a young woman standing in the doorway. Her hair and skin were almost translucent. She was petite enough that a good gust of wind would knock her over. Her expression held a combination of fear and hope.

"Uhhh . . ." Jinn said eloquently, unsure about the stranger with the angelic features. Pseudo just froze.

"Jasmine," Lucas called as he and Sebastian came from the bathroom. Sebastian pushed his way out the door, paying no mind to the new adult in the room, and resumed cruising along his personal racetrack.

"Hi," Jasmine said, looking very relieved.

"Jasmine, this is Jinn," Lucas said by way of introduction. Jinn nodded at the stranger then turned back to Lucas with her eyebrows furrowed. "This is Pseudo." Pseudo gave her a quick nod then left the room.

"Hello," Jasmine said, her eyes trailing after Pseudo.

"He's a little antisocial," Jinn said in defense of Pseudo's behavior.

"That's fair," Jasmine said and smiled. It was genuine enough, but her hands were trembling.

Jasmine suddenly lurched forward, and Lucas barely caught her as her balance shifted. He lowered her down onto the couch. Jinn's adrenaline spiked instantly, recognizing that this woman was in withdrawal.

"This who you wanted me to meet?" Jasmine said after regaining her composure.

"Yeah," Lucas said. "Jinn might be able to help if you really want to drop source."

"Please," Jasmine said, then turned her watery eyes on Jinn. "I can't take this anymore."

"Wait, what?" Jinn asked, glancing back and forth between Jasmine and Lucas. "You told her about . . .?

"No," Lucas responded quickly. "I just told her you might be able to help. She was in the gym and looked like she was struggling."

Jinn was torn. She had not perfected the antibiotic. There was a very real possibility that the antibiotic could kill her faster than the drug. There was also a chance that it wouldn't help at all. With the pharmaceutical companies, she spent years working with a new drug, manipulating the compounds, and running simulations over and over again before she could so much as test it on mice, let alone humans. She really needed a human to test it, but at what cost? All of this rolled around in her mind. Jinn didn't want to reveal too much to the addicted girl, but she also didn't want Jasmine to think she was some sort of savior that could fix all her ailments. However, Jasmine might change her mind if she knew what was at risk.

"Did you explain what the *help* actually is?" Jinn asked Lucas.

"No," he said, shaking his head. "Just that you might help."

"Okay, listen," Jinn said, looking at Jasmine, whose face had taken on a green pallor and was covered in a sheen of sweat. "I dunno if I can help or if it will work at all. I haven't . . . I haven't tried it on a person yet." Jinn glanced up at Lucas. "It's medicine, and if it works, you'll get through the withdrawal faster with less lingering effects."

"How much faster?" Jasmine asked, starting to shiver.

"The symptoms will probably last about twenty-four hours," Jinn guessed. She looked up at Lucas again, taking a breath.

"But?" Jasmine asked, aware that there was more to it.

"But that day is going to be rough."

"How rough?" Jasmine grunted through clenched teeth, hope starting to fade from her eyes.

"I can't say for sure, but the symptoms will likely be intensified," Jinn said, directing her eyes to the floor.

"Are there any side effects?" Jasmine asked.

"Um, no, at least not that I know of, unless you have an allergy?" She raised the last part like a question.

"No allergies," Jasmine said. "But you don't seem

confident."

"Well," Jinn said, "there's a lot of variables, so it could be dangerous. The worst case could even be death, though it's unlikely."

"So, this will either cure me or kill me?" Jasmine asked.

"Um . . . well . . . Yeah, that's the theory. But it only cures the symptoms and craving. You'll have to stay off source on your own," Jinn said, looking pointedly at her.

"I understand," Jasmine said, nodding thoughtfully, then doubled over as a stomach cramp racked her body. "Let's do it."

"You sure?" Jinn asked. She must be in an intense amount of pain to trust a stranger to give her a random medicine that may or may not kill her.

"Positive," Jasmine said. "Death can't be worse than this."

Chapter 29

Side Effects

Jinn was afraid of disclosing too much information to Jasmine. The whole situation was unsettling. Lucas hadn't mentioned having a conversation with an addict during the hour he was gone, but she also understood that running into someone in intense withdrawal was not exactly rare. But had he seriously just invited this stranger up to their room? What if she was dangerous? Did he even consider Sebastian? Lucas knew it would be very dangerous to let *anyone* know that she was cultivating the drug so many people craved. One look at Jasmine, and Jinn knew she would have to worry about that later.

While Lucas and Jasmine waited in the suite, Jinn went down to the lab and grabbed one of the syringes. She pulled in a deep breath as she checked the dosage. So much guesswork, so many variables. A single dose should be enough to destroy the source bacteria because it was surprisingly easy to eliminate. It was the toxin dump that worried her. As far as Jinn could tell, the antibiotic that she had created would not cause too much harm, but if the bacteria were abundant and given enough time, the resulting toxin dump could send Jasmine into seizures and possibly even kill her. The problem was that Jinn only had an educated guess as to how much it would actually take.

She walked back up the stairs with the syringe tucked into her jacket, listening to the storms raging outside. The constant white noise was forever causing her nerves to tingle. A loud thunderclap reverberated the foundation of the hotel, and she froze mid-step. Gripping the railing for a couple of breaths to slow her heart rate, Jinn watched the lights flicker momentarily, shook her head, and continued the climb.

When Jinn entered the suite, Jasmine was lying across the bed where Lucas usually slept. She looked like a small, sick cherub while Lucas leaned over her, dabbing her forehead with a damp cloth. They both had slight smiles on their faces, and discomfort tugged at her chest. *You're an adult, Jinn,* she chided herself.

Lucas lifted his gaze to her, and his eyes brightened. Jinn felt a slight flutter at his smile. She came in and closed the door.

"Should we set you up in your own room?" Jinn asked, "at least until we know how the anti—medicine is gonna work?"

"You don't want me to stay in here?" Jasmine asked, attempting to sit up on her elbows but quickly giving up, drawing Lucas's attention back toward her. Jinn swallowed the annoyance that crept up on her.

"You're fine," Lucas said softly before turning to Jinn. "Sebastian's all set up to hang in your room until it's over."

"Oh—okay," Jinn said, a little surprised.

"You don't mind, do you?"

"No. No, of course not," Jinn's response was a little too animated.

"Good," Lucas said, stepping over to the bathroom to leave

the washcloth in the sink. "I was hoping to spend some more time in there myself." He reached over and pulled Jinn close, brushing his lips against her forehead. Jinn tried to ignore the giddy feeling in her gut.

"He's in there now?" Jinn asked, realizing she had not seen Sebastian running his usual hall races.

"Yeah, napping," Lucas said, releasing her.

Jinn turned toward the bathroom, and from the mirror she spotted Jasmine eyeing her cautiously. Jinn leaned over and washed her hands. She really needed to get hold of this. Jealousy was not a good color for her. Jasmine was beautiful, even in her current state. Lucas was kind and knew that they may be able to help her. And even if none of that was true, Lucas didn't belong to Jinn any more than Jinn belonged to Lucas. They had shared some intimate moments, but they were still two very different people. *Lucas probably doesn't even want to bother with a relationship with me, anyway.* The thought invaded Jinn's brain before she could stop it. She remembered Pseudo's words and chided herself for again trying to guess what Lucas might be feeling instead of just asking him. If she were being honest with herself, she wasn't sure how she would feel about it, anyway. Her mind was still a tangled mess from Xandar's abuse, and she was working on deciphering the difference between her own feelings and the feelings she was *supposed* to feel to avoid repercussions. As her relationship with Xandar had deteriorated, she learned to school her feelings and reactions to avoid Xandar's ire. Over time, she had hidden herself to the point where she could no longer tell which emotions were real and which were the facade she used to protect herself.

Jinn shook her head to clear the tangled mess of her thoughts. She went over to Jasmine, who was still lying on her back, with her arm thrown up over her eyes. "You ready?" Jinn asked.

"Yeah . . . I guess. I don't care," she said from underneath her arm.

"Well, here goes," Jinn said and took out an alcohol swab from the first-aid kit. She disinfected the area on the inside of Jasmine's elbow and pulled out the needle. It was unnecessarily large, but it was all she could get for now. If this worked, she would find a hospital and try to barter for some better syringes. She pricked the needle into a vein and slowly pushed down the plunger. Jasmine hissed in pain but remained still. Once the solution was pushed through, Jinn removed the needle and covered the injection site with some gauze and tape, instructing Jasmine to fold her elbow and keep pressure on it.

She and Lucas watched with anxious breaths. Jasmine didn't change. Then Jinn huffed her breath. "I dunno what I'm waiting for," Jinn said. "It's medicine, not magic. I don't even know how long it'll take to see any effects." As soon as the words left Jinn's lips, Jasmine leaned over the side of the bed and vomited, then began to violently dry heave.

"Oh shit," Jinn said and blinked stupidly.

Lucas jumped into action. He grabbed some towels and soaked the washrag in cool water again. He placed the rag on Jasmine's forehead before quickly cleaning up the vomit. It was mostly bile, but Jinn still struggled against the sympathetic reflex. After a second, Jinn regained her composure and helped Lucas.

"How are you feeling?" Jinn asked, coming close to the bed.

"Hurts," Jasmine hissed through clenched teeth. "Oh, God—" She turned and started dry heaving again as Lucas came over with a spare trash bucket. Jinn put a hand on Jasmine's back. She was fevered, but not dangerously so. Still, this was a very quick reaction. Jinn couldn't help but worry.

Suddenly, Jinn's phone started buzzing. She quickly swiped the screen, and Pseudo's face popped up.

"Jinn, you gotta go. The trucks are almost to Junkman's," Pseudo said without looking at the screen.

"Now?" Jinn asked incredulously. "You said a couple days."

"Not this time," Pseudo said, his glasses glaring as he turned toward his camera.

"Shit," Jinn said, then repeated. "Shit, shit, shit." She lifted her eyebrows at Lucas, who was holding back Jasmine's hair while she shivered and continued to dry heave.

"What's up?" Pseudo asked.

"I just gave this girl the antibiotic," Jinn said and then bit her tongue. She was trying to keep that to herself until she knew how it was going to work.

"And?"

"She's reacting, but doesn't seem life-threatening," Jinn said. "I wanted to be able to observe the process."

"Well, I don't know how long before the trucks will come back again," Pseudo said. "It might not be for a while after two drops back-to-back." If they wanted to be able to leave this hotel anytime soon, she had to catch those trucks.

"Okay," Jinn said. "Okay, I've got it. I'll head over." She swiped her screen, disconnecting the call. She went to the dresser and took out her AR glasses and earpiece. She connected them to Pseudo. "You there?" she asked.

"Loud and clear," he answered through the earpiece.

"Stay on call for Lucas," Jinn said, then turned to Lucas. "I gotta go."

"Right," Lucas said with a nod.

"Try to pay attention to how this plays out," Jinn said, indicating Jasmine.

"Got it," he said. "Go."

Chapter 30

Tracking

J inn crouched behind the large building that was once home to the famous retail store Junkman's Daughter. The eccentric sign was still visible out front, though the paint had faded. The alley behind the store was mostly empty. Areas of the pavement fell away into deep holes the trucks had to maneuver around if they wanted to keep their tires intact.

Thankfully, it wasn't raining. More storms were headed in, but this was a rare calm moment. Several men meticulously unloaded wooden crates padded with dingy paper. They all wore identical black shirts and cargo-style khaki pants, and had close-cropped hair with clean-shaven faces. Fifty years ago, the scene would have been commonplace around Atlanta retailers, but they were oddly out of place in the post-Exodus cityscape. Jinn recognized the clinking sounds of glass pods filled with source. Users were expected to return the pods, though it didn't always happen, thanks to the effects of the drug. They got broken or lost regularly, and Xandar would send out his clean-up crews to collect them.

Jinn assessed her surroundings as the men unloaded the last of the crates. There were cameras directly over the warehouse doors, but they were easy enough to avoid. Jinn raised her hand in front of the glasses, silently asking Pseudo if the area was clear from his perspective.

"You're clear," he said quietly into her earpiece. "They're just on the other side of the door, so keep quiet." Jinn cocked an eyebrow in irritation, not that Pseudo could see her. She glanced around once again before ducking out of her hiding place, careful to avoid the cameras.

Straining her ears for any disturbances, she approached the nearest truck. The engineering of the tiny tracking device was immaculate, a nod to Pseudo's genius. It was small, circular, and reflective in a way that caused it to blend into its surroundings rather than stand out. On the bottom was a powerful magnet. If Jinn could attach it to the frame of the truck, then they would be able to track its location and possibly even pick up and transmit sound.

She crouched in front of the truck and moved to attach the magnet to the bumper. It didn't stick. She stared at the contraption, confused. She tried attaching it to the fender with the same result.

"Do you have to activate the magnet?" she hissed at Pseudo.

"What are you talking about?" he responded.

"It won't stick to the damn truck," she whispered, waving the tracker in front of her.

"Why not?" Pseudo asked.

"How the hell should I know?" Jinn growled.

"Try the rim," Pseudo responded. She could hear him typing on his computer keyboard. Probably trying to figure out why the tracker was not working. "The magnet is a magnet, not electric. It's supposed to magnet."

Jinn crept around to the side of the truck, coming

dangerously close to the camera's view. The magnet still did not react. She shook her head to signal Pseudo.

"Fuck," he whispered. Jinn could hear him typing furiously at his keyboard. "That model truck is mostly fiberglass. You'll have to get it *in* the truck."

"How the hell am I supposed to do that?" Jinn hissed as she crept back to the front, safely out of the camera's line of sight. Pseudo remained annoyingly silent. She slid back around to the side of the truck and slowly reached up for the door handle. She held her breath and hoped that it was unlocked. She lifted the release and, for one exhilarating moment, she grinned as the door caught and pulled open.

"Hey!" a man shouted from the warehouse door.

"Fuck," Pseudo hissed in her ear.

Jinn jumped into the truck quickly, dumping the tracker behind the seat. She pushed the button to start the engine.

"Bitch is stealin' our truck," the man yelled back into the door. Seconds later, three more men came running out.

Jinn slammed the shift trying to put the truck in gear, but she didn't get it before rough hands were dragging her out. She fell painfully onto the concrete, searching for an opportunity to run. They picked her up and forced her back against the truck.

"Well, ain't you pretty." A man slithered into view wearing a similar uniform, but his shirt was red. She could feel the cold door through her jumpsuit. At the sound of the man's voice, her skin began to crawl.

She didn't speak—just regarded the new person with as strong a stare of vehemence as she could muster. Rain started to fall again, creating a cold mist around them.

"And she thinks she's tough," the man said, nudging the man next to him with his shoulder, eliciting grins and laughter from the others. Jinn attempted to shake her arms loose of her captors, unsuccessfully.

"Don't let them get you inside," Pseudo whispered.

"I think we can have some fun before we turn her over," the

man said, the men around him snickering. He smiled, which made Jinn's stomach turn.

"You don't wanna do that," she said, pulling in all her strength to make her voice even.

"You don't know what we want," the man answered. He pushed his face in close to hers. His teeth were deteriorating, and his breath smelled sour. Jinn had to fight a wave of nausea.

Jinn lifted her eyes and smiled, a wholesome, happy expression that thoroughly confused the men holding her arms. A slight tilt of her head and coquettish lift of her eyebrows had the men loosening their grip. Eyes traveling to each of them in turn, she waited until they were confident she was going to comply with whatever they wanted. Her gaze settled on the man who was leading the group.

"You *really* want me?" she asked in a lust-filled whisper. She batted her eyes dramatically.

"What are you playing at?" the man said. "You blitzed?"

She blinked a few times, trying to appear as vacant as possible. Their grips loosened on her arms. Her shoulders drifted forward as though she had spent all her energy.

"Answer me," the man shouted. His lackeys both flinched, and she saw her opportunity.

She jumped and planted her feet against the side of the truck, then propelled her body forward, driving her shoulder into the man's face. Landing heavily on top of him, the pavement scraped at her knees as he floundered to stand back up. The other two lost their grip on her arms, and in a fluid motion she pulled her taser from its holster. The group leader had only managed to get up onto his knees before she stuck the taser to his chest and pulled the trigger, leaving him in a convulsing mess. She raised it again and pointed it at the others, who froze with their hands in the air. She silently prayed no one would call her bluff. Keeping the taser level and switching back and forth, daring them to move, she backed away. Once she had enough space between herself and the group, she turned and sprinted, darting down the alleyway toward her bike.

"Fuck yeah," Pseudo yelled in her ear.

"I'm not out yet, Pseudo," she called back, between breaths. She didn't take the chance to turn around, not allowing herself to slow until she got to her bike and tore out. She headed in the opposite direction of the Clermont, making sure no one was tailing her before she returned to the hotel.

The wind whipped around her as she analyzed the encounter. Obviously, the guys had a boss or manager that they answered to. They were quick about saying that they would have to turn her over, but she didn't know who they would be talking about. They didn't seem too worried about being told on by the others, which was not surprising considering they were probably all addicts. She hoped they didn't get a good enough look at her on the camera, or even better, that the lead jackass would be too embarrassed to report that someone had been there. She did, however, make it appear that she was only trying to steal the truck, not plant something in it. Hopefully, they would be too humiliated to admit being bested by a woman. Even if she did have a tricked-out taser. They probably wouldn't even consider the possibility of a tracker. She tried her best to ignore the tingling fear that Xandar would soon learn she was still alive. Again.

Chapter 31

Withdrawal

Lucas glanced up from his notebook as Jasmine writhed in the bed. She was sleeping, however fitfully. He'd seen many people going through withdrawal from source, but it had appeared as though all of Jasmine's withdrawal symptoms were unleashed simultaneously. After about two hours of vomiting and fever, she had finally fallen asleep, or more accurately, passed out. She was still fevered, though it was subsiding. Making notes of everything for when Jinn returned, he wished there was something more he could do to ease Jasmine's discomfort.

He glared at his phone. Jinn had been gone for almost four hours, though it hadn't seemed that long. He was blindly acting as nurse and caretaker for Jasmine, and trying to take care of Sebastian, who of course needed almost constant attention.

He finished writing his notes and set the notebook to the side before walking over to look at Jasmine. Her color was starting to return. She was naturally pale, but her skin was delicately translucent, as opposed to the sickly green that she had been before. He couldn't help but notice that she was quite beautiful. Her hair was soft and almost white; her lips were still pale, but regaining a pink hue. Dark lashes stood in contrast to her light complexion. She appeared so small and fragile that he was compelled to shelter and protect her.

Sebastian came running into the room with his stuffed elephant. He was squealing happily for no apparent reason.

"Hey buddy, shh," Lucas said softly. "We gotta let Jasmine sleep so she can get better."

"Sorry," he whispered dramatically. "Can I have a snack?"

Lucas got up and found some bagged popcorn. He opened the bag and handed it to Sebastian. "Here you go." He smiled at the boy.

"Thank you," Sebastian said a little too loudly, and when Lucas flinched, he whispered, "Thank you."

"You're welcome," Lucas responded with a smile. He turned back toward Jasmine as Sebastian settled onto the couch with his snack. Her eyelids fluttered before she opened them fully.

"Good morning," Lucas said to her, despite that it was late in the afternoon. He smiled at her while she tried to focus.

"Hey," she said finally. "How long've I been asleep?"

"About two hours, maybe," he answered. "Not as long as I expected. How do you feel?"

"Really?" she asked, looking confused. "Um . . . I'm not sure . . . everything's kinda fuzzy. I wasn't in my right mind this morning. I only remember bits and fragments. I remember you and that woman, and . . . she gave me some medicine?" When she shook her head, her translucent hair fell around her face.

"Yeah," Lucas responded. "That was Jinn. She's been working on something to help source withdrawal." He checked her over, trying to assess her health.

"It seems to have worked," she said with a hint of a surprised smile. "I feel better than I have in a long time, I think."

"How long were you in withdrawal?" Lucas asked her and pulled the notebook off the counter.

"I'm not sure," she answered before growing quiet. "I just couldn't . . . I just couldn't handle it anymore." Her eyes grew misty as she studied her hands.

"It's okay," Lucas answered softly, brushing her hair out of her eyes. They were pale and watery when they met his. He smiled at her. "We understand, probably a little too well."

"What'd you give me?" she asked him, taking a shaky breath.

"I . . . Uh . . . don't really know the details," he lied. He wasn't sure how much information Jinn was comfortable revealing. "Jinn is a microbiologist. She's been working on it for weeks now."

"Oh," Jasmine responded.

"Hi Jasmine, are you better?" Sebastian was suddenly standing at the foot of the bed still munching on his popcorn. "Can I be loud now?"

"Hi there," Jasmine smiled at the toddler. "What is your name?"

"Sebastian," he said and giggled.

"Sebastian," Lucas translated.

"Hi, Sebastian," Jasmine said, then glanced up at Lucas. "Is he . . ."

"My son," Lucas lied again. "His mother passed away."

"I'm so sorry," Jasmine said, looking back at Sebastian. "It's nice to meet you."

"Nice to meet you," Sebastian echoed. "Are you better?"

"Yes, I am," she smiled at him.

"Lucas! She's better!" He grinned up at Lucas.

"That's awesome," Lucas answered with a smile. Sebastian took his popcorn and went back to the couch.

"Your son calls you Lucas?" Jasmine eyed him skeptically.

"I know, it's weird," Lucas answered, feigning self-consciousness. "Something his mother taught him. I just didn't

EXODUS MISSED | 157

let it go."

"Okay," Jasmine answered, though the skepticism didn't leave her voice. "He's adorable."

"Yes, and a handful," Lucas answered with a smile. Jasmine's eyes glazed over.

"I had a son," she whispered.

"What happened?" he asked softly, taking her hand. She took a couple of ragged breaths. "You don't have to tell me if you don't want to," he amended.

"He died a few days after he was born," she answered without looking at him.

"I'm sorry," Lucas said. He didn't press for details.

"I didn't even name him." Tears welled up in her eyes, and Lucas put a comforting arm around her shoulders. "Sorry," she said, taking a deep breath and wiping her eyes.

"Nothing to apologize for," Lucas answered.

"Could I . . ." she blinked, getting her emotions under control. "Could I use your shower? I feel gross."

"Of course," Lucas answered and pulled away from her. "There's towels and robes or you could probably borrow some clothes from Jinn."

"I'll get clean, then figure out clothes," she said with a soft smile.

Lucas stood up from the bed and took a step back. She stood next to him, her head barely up to his shoulders. She pulled him into a quick hug that caught him off guard.

"Thanks," she whispered. "I was trapped for so long."

"Um . . ." He responded, putting his arms around her. "You're welcome, but it's really Jinn you should thank. She let you be the guinea pig."

"Yeah." Jasmine chuckled. "That might bother me later, but for now I feel like I exist again." She released the hug and then turned and went into the bathroom, throwing a look over her shoulder that Lucas was not sure how to interpret. She closed the door behind her, and he sat down on the bed.

He checked the time again. Jinn had been gone for a long time. He knew that Pseudo had eyes and ears on her, so he tried not to worry. Pseudo would've come to him for help if she was in trouble. Still, the apprehension lingered. He just couldn't figure her out. She was all fire and fight when it was necessary. And she was clearly brilliant, since she was able to deduce and then create an antibiotic that worked against source. She was strong, beautiful, and independent. Yet every time he got close to her, she pulled away. He wished that he could just get a good look over those walls. He really enjoyed her company, both socially and intimately, but he could not quite get a clear read on how she felt about him.

Chapter 32

Source

Pseudo's eyes darted back and forth between his monitors. Jinn's feed from the AR glasses was still pulled up, though he was no longer concerned. She was on her way back, just making sure to detour around half of Atlanta so that there was no chance of a tail. He figured she was probably getting some stress out as well. *If she would let me work on her damn bike, I could make it so much faster and more efficient.*

The tracker Jinn had placed was working beautifully. Though it landed close to something that rattled, so there was not much in the way of audio. Maybe he would get something once they stopped. He watched the arrow move across his screen.

Pseudo smiled in satisfaction at the accuracy of his own instincts. He had decided to keep eyes on Junkman's Daughter after tailing some of the other residents of the Clermont. The cartel tended to be accommodating to them so they would stay happy and working. But as time wore on, many people had either left or overdosed, and the infrastructure that they were supposed to be maintaining was crumbling. The northern side of Atlanta had not had power in months, and the water systems were deteriorating in some of the more densely populated areas.

He checked his screens again. Jinn was in the garage heading his way. He figured she would stop in to see if he had learned anything yet. The truck had not moved for a few minutes, maybe even parked for the night. He considered setting up an alert for when it started moving again. The battery would only last about three days, so hopefully that would give him enough time to learn something useful.

The knock at his door informed him that Jinn was back. He smiled as he stood up. She had taken some hits dealing with the crew at Junkman's, but the way she made out like she was just trying to steal the truck was brilliant. He opened the door to a frazzled, wet, and windblown Jinn.

"How'd I do?" she asked, her green eyes glittering.

"Smooth," he answered truthfully.

"Anyone follow me?"

"I only see what you see, so . . ."

"Should be good then." Jinn sat down heavily on Pseudo's bed. "You like how I launched myself off the side of the truck?"

"Ah, that's what happened," he responded. She was always pumped after a fight, especially when she had won. "I doubt they'll look too hard for you; it was very emasculating."

"Fuckin' hope not," she answered. "Learn anything yet?"

"Not much—couple more distribution centers," he said, looking back at his screen. "Hey, it's moving again." Pseudo sat down and pushed his glasses up on his nose. Jinn stood up and walked over so that she was standing behind him, looking at the moving arrow.

"So, what's up with you and Lucas?" Pseudo asked with a smile. He knew that would make her squirm.

"Something supposed to be up?" she responded flippantly.

"You tell me," he answered, looking up at her. "For such a badass you're kind of a chicken."

"The hell is that supposed to mean?" she asked, pushing his chair against the desk.

"Lucas likes you. Give him a chance," Pseudo said, finding all the right buttons to push to get under her skin.

"Of course he likes me. His other choices are you and Sebastian," Jinn scoffed.

"And Jasmine," Pseudo retorted. He caught the fleeting look of discomfort that passed across Jinn's face. He had to work to keep himself from laughing.

"How's she doing?" Jinn asked, attempting to change the subject.

"Dunno," he answered, shrugging his shoulders. "No news is good news I guess. They're probably just getting to know each oth—ow—" Jinn thumped his ear.

"Watch it, kid," Jinn said smiling.

"You like Lucas," he scoffed, rubbing his ear.

"Yeah, so?" she retorted.

"Y'all complement each other," he said, a rare glimpse of seriousness in his voice. "Don't make him pay for Xandar." Jinn flinched at the statement but shook it off. "Though," he continued, "if you actually become comfortable with the relationship, it'll be harder for me to get under your skin."

"Hmph, I doubt that." Jinn snickered. "I think your truck stopped." Jinn leaned closer to the screen. "Where's that?"

"No . . ." Pseudo said, zooming out of the map.

"No what? What's no?" Jinn asked, looking at him.

"Of course it is . . ." he answered.

"What?" Jinn was becoming exasperated.

"You don't recognize that building?" he answered, the sides of his mouth sliding into a smile. "You've been there."

Jinn cut her eyes over to him, then back to the map. She noted the street names, the area. "Oh my god," she said. "It's so damn obvious." They stared at each other in disbelief before bursting out with laughter. "I can't imagine a better place to grow bacteria than the Centers for Disease Control."

"I thought they'd moved all the equipment out years ago with Exodus," Pseudo mused.

Jinn shrugged. "Probably the lab equipment that was portable, but they wouldn't want to add too much weight on the ships. So, the clean rooms, big equipment, environmental controls . . . It wouldn't be hard to get it back functional." She was kicking herself for not seeing this before.

"Surely they wouldn't have the same security systems as before Exodus," Jinn said, raising her eyebrows hopefully at Pseudo.

"Security systems are easy to restore," he responded, then noted her deflated expression. "But maybe?" he amended.

"I guess we found their base of operations," Jinn said with a smile. "Seems almost too easy."

Pseudo gave her an evil grin. "Looks like we have to figure out how to infiltrate the fucking CDC."

Chapter 33

Choices

Lucas lay casually on one bed next to Sebastian while Jasmine slept on the bed across the room. She seemed to feel much better after the shower but was still exhausted. Lucas had made her a dry sandwich, fearing that her stomach would rebel against her, but she was able to eat and keep it down. She was tired, but otherwise healthy. The first couple of hours were rough, but once that was through, it was just a waiting game to get her energy back. Lucas wasn't sure what exactly Jinn had hoped, but this was a better outcome than he expected.

Jasmine had not bothered to find clothes and was snuggled underneath the blankets, wrapped in the robe and snoring softly. Sebastian was also dozing, and Lucas figured he wouldn't be far behind them. Just as he was drifting off, the door opened, and Jinn stepped through. She had some new bruises on her arms and one on her cheek. She was dirty, but her eyes sparkled.

"Hey," he smiled up at her and then disentangled himself from the snoozing toddler. "You okay?" He gestured to her face and clothes.

"What?" She glanced down at herself then laughed. "Oh yeah, fine. Pseudo found some good info. We're gonna have a big project soon, but we may actually be able to pull this thing off."

"What thing?" He eyed her skeptically.

"Cutting off source," she said and grinned almost maniacally. He found it contagious. She glanced over at Jasmine, who was still sleeping soundly. "How's she doing?"

"Surprisingly well," Lucas said, raising his eyebrows. "Exhausted—here." He reached over and grabbed the notebook, handing it over to her. "I made some notes. I wasn't sure what would be important, and to be fair, I was bored."

Jinn opened the notebook, scanning the pages. After a tense moment, she laughed, and her eyes danced. "Well, you won't be bored for long."

"God, I hope not," Lucas said, rolling his eyes. "I love Sebastian, but I'm about to lose my shit being stuck here all the time."

"You've mentioned that," Jinn said, sidling closer to him.

"Your cheek looks rough. You sure you're not hurt?" Seeing her like this was confusing. He was angry that someone would hurt her, guilty that he was not able to protect her, but impressed and intrigued that she could handle herself.

"I probably need a shower," she said, looking down at herself again. "I could use some company." She lifted her eyebrows, which he found both intimidating and seductive. He grinned and reached for her hand where she led him into the bathroom.

She turned on the shower and stripped off her clothes, trying to be coy, but not quite pulling it off. Lucas averted his eyes, trying to be polite, but found her body enticing. Once she stepped into the steaming water, he stripped off his own clothes and followed her. She winced as the water hit her cheek, and Lucas traced his fingers along the rash going up her arm also. He lifted her arm and allowed the water to wash away any debris left on her skin.

She turned to face him and wrapped the arm he was holding around his neck, pulling him closer. She kissed him, gently at first then with more fervor. The heat from the water was warm and relaxing. She pulled back and smiled at him. He took the soap and very gently washed her injured arm, then worked it through her hair and the rest of her skin, feeling her relax into him. He enjoyed the moment, afraid to read too much into it because she might close up again. Jinn had a lot to deal with, but it was difficult to be so close and yet so distant. In time, hopefully, she would learn to trust him.

Once clean, she pulled him toward her. His fingers traced along her curves and reveled in their sensation. She reached around him and turned off the water. She stepped out of the shower and pulled a robe over herself, not even bothering with a towel. Slipping through the door of her suite, she turned and pierced him with her gaze.

"Coming?" she asked, a devious glint in her eyes. Lucas smiled and almost tripped over himself getting out of the shower. He grabbed a robe and casually snaked his arms through the sleeves, leaving it open. Her eyes flowed over his chest and abs. Lightly brushing fingertips across his collarbone sent shock waves through his body. She put a hand on the back of his neck and pulled him into a deep and hungry kiss. With a grin, she pushed him onto the bed, falling on top of him, her hair dripping down onto the blankets.

There was a knock at the door. Jinn sat up suddenly tense and looked at Lucas. He took a deep breath and sat up.

"Lucas?" Jasmine said through the door.

"Yeah?" he answered. He could feel Jinn's tension feathering through the air around them.

"I'm sorry, but I'm starving," Jasmine said from the other

side of the door.

"There's food in the kitchen. Take whatever you want." Lucas was still holding on to Jinn's hips, though he could feel her retreating. Sebastian started to cry, the noise probably woke him. Lucas let out a breath as Jinn slid off him. She smiled at him, but her eyes were distant. "Be right back," he said to her, smiling.

"I know." Jinn smiled playfully, but Lucas could see that it didn't quite reach her eyes. She rolled over and worked her way underneath the covers, while he stood up and pulled on a pair of sweatpants. He walked over and opened the door. Jasmine stood there; her eyes were glassy, though her cheeks were pink. She might have been embarrassed to have interrupted them.

"I'm sorry, I probably woke him up," she said, her eyes downcast.

"No worries. I'll get him settled and then find you some food," he answered without meeting her eyes.

"Thanks," she said softly, looking up through her lashes at Lucas. He smiled, his protective instincts nagging at him. Her stature was so small, and she reminded him of porcelain. She reached out and touched his arm. Her skin even felt like porcelain, firm and cool. He pushed past her and reached for Sebastian, who was already settling down. It did not take much to get him back to sleep.

When Sebastian was once again snoring, Lucas scrounged up some manufactured sausage and warmed it up on the stove for Jasmine. She stood close to him while he cooked, almost uncomfortably close, especially considering what she had interrupted. In his periphery, he could see her watching him, which made him strangely self-conscious. He shook his head at the thought. There was no reason for him to feel that way. Jasmine was beautiful in her own way; she could appreciate his appearance without it becoming uncomfortable. He found himself rather enjoying the idea. He flexed his arms and liked the way her eyes fluttered slightly.

The door opened behind them, and Jinn walked through wearing shorts and a tank top. Her hair was spiked wildly around her head, and the water had created a dark stain on the back of her red shirt. He smiled despite himself and took the opportunity to show off that much more. Jinn glanced over at Jasmine and narrowed her eyes, but it was only fleeting, then she smiled and turned her attention to the pan.

"Smells delicious," Jinn said, inhaling deeply.

"Doesn't it though," Jasmine said with a disarming smile.

"There's enough for everyone," Lucas said, pulling the rest of the sausage out of the small refrigerator.

"You sure?" Jasmine said. It sounded playful, but Lucas could feel Jinn stiffen next to him. Again, it was only for a moment. "What happened to your face?" Jasmine gasped, finally looking at Jinn.

"A little dust up," Jinn answered, straightening. "I'm fine."

"Can I do anything? Get you some ice or something?" Jasmine asked.

"I am fine, seriously. I think I'll sit down though," Jinn answered, then took the couple of steps over to the couch and sank down, her back unnaturally straight. Something was bothering her, something that she would probably never admit. Lucas rolled his shoulders, trying to shake off his own annoyance.

Chapter 34

Surveillance

Pseudo could not have hoped for better luck with his tracker. At least, once they had it on the truck. He pushed his glasses up on his nose and watched the little arrow move around on his map, grinning as the voice surveillance kicked on. He listened in as the two men discussed where they would be off to next.

"Damn, my jaw hurts," one of them said. The voice was muffled, but it was the same person that Jinn had cracked with her shoulder. There was an unintelligible response, but it sounded like laughter.

"We got any video of 'er?" the voice asked. Obviously, he was in the driver's seat and closer to the tracker. Pseudo listened closely to the response, but it was difficult to understand. His best guess was that he was unsure.

"She looked familiar," the voice said again before starting the ignition. The sound of the engine covered any hope of hearing more of the conversation, so Pseudo went ahead and switched off the sound. He considered the statement that "she" looked familiar. They had to be talking about Jinn. Depending on how close the goons were to Xandar and how long they'd been employed, it was possible they could have met Jinn before. It was unlikely though, and she would be difficult to recognize again anyway.

Jinn had become someone else during that time, someone fake, someone Xandar wanted her to be. Pseudo struggled to understand, but he had watched her gradually change from the headstrong fighter she'd been when they were in college together, into a scared girl who cowered and over-thought her every action.

At first, Pseudo had blamed source, but the more he observed, the more he saw that Xandar was the manipulator. The drug just made it easy. Pseudo knew Jinn realized on some level what was happening, even though she wouldn't admit it. Instead, she'd find any excuse for Xandar's behavior and then suffocate her emotions with a drug-induced haze.

Pseudo had never tried source. He was familiar with addiction, though, and knew there was not much he could do to help until Jinn admitted that she needed it. He had voiced his concern, and it only pushed her away from him. He stayed in the background and waited for her to come around, worried that she never would. Xandar played the part so well that Jinn had fallen hook, line, and sinker for his facade.

In the three years since the first time she was almost killed by Xandar, she had barely ventured outside her circle. Pseudo stood by but allowed her the space to work through what she needed to on her own. He knew she was smart and that she would eventually figure it out. But he also knew what it was like not to trust your own mind.

His foster family had told him repeatedly that his mother was schizophrenic. He had no idea whether it was true. Since he had been sent to the United States at such a young age, he had no memories of his own parents. What little he had learned was that his mother was passionate about many things. Venezuela was under so much pressure at the time there was no way to know if her problems had been within herself or situational. Still, once he started showing such academic promise, he'd been given many different screenings looking for something wrong. It was difficult for anyone to believe he could be brilliant coming from his background. It caused him even to question himself.

Jinn was so confident when they met, but always kind to everyone else. That had drawn him to her. She knew who she was and was sure of herself, especially academically. As they became closer, though, there were some hints at self-doubt, but nothing kept her down. The first time she experimented with source was alongside some classmates. This had not bothered Pseudo, though at the time he didn't realize how easily someone could become addicted.

Then she met Xandar. He'd lavished all his attention and convinced Jinn he thought she was special. He put her on a pedestal. At least, it all appeared that way. Jinn couldn't fathom that he was less than genuine. Once he landed his hooks in her mind, that was it. She no longer trusted her own judgment. It hurt to watch, but she was slowly coming around. Lucas had been a huge boon for that. Pseudo genuinely liked Lucas and hoped that Jinn's insecurities wouldn't push him too far away. But he knew better than to intervene. Despite how smart he was, most people wouldn't take him seriously because of his age. Which was annoying.

Pseudo huffed and focused again on the screen. The truck had returned to the CDC and seemed to be staying this time. He wondered if they still had any functional servers there. If they did, they would most likely be hardwired. Even with all the advances in technology, hacking into a Wi-Fi signal was easy, and surely the CDC would have better security. He had already deduced that their cell phones didn't ping off the towers. They must use a short-range signal that connects the phones to each other rather than a network. Which was smart, Pseudo thought, because that meant people couldn't accidentally listen in to conversations. However, it did make it more difficult when one was *trying* to do that.

A system of security cameras watched the outside of the building, and they were connected to the city's security network. He had simply rerouted the feed from the abandoned police department to the hotel. Pseudo knew his history. He knew that once upon a time the police force had been a service to the community, keeping people safe and protected. But all he had ever known was corruption and apathy. It was a favor when they faded out of existence. Was that where Xandar had gotten the guns? It made sense. A sudden knock at his door startled him so that he almost fell from his chair.

"Yeah?" he called out.

"It's me," Jinn said through the door.

Pseudo made his way across the room and cracked open the door. "What'd you bring me?"

"Nothing," Jinn responded, confused.

"Peace out." Pseudo closed the door, grinning to himself and listening to her footsteps walking away. He waited by the door, trying to contain his giggling. A moment later she knocked again. "Who is it?" he asked, with a theatrical flair added to his words.

"It's me," Jinn answered, her voice colored with irritation. He opened the door to find her holding up a scavenged MRE.

"Nice. Where'd you find it?" Pseudo asked and snatched it from her hands. He read the packaging. It was cheese tortellini and had VEGETARIAN stamped on the front of it.

"I have my ways," Jinn responded, quirking an eyebrow at him. Pseudo tore into the packaging and headed over to the sink for water to activate the flameless ration heater. While he waited, he ripped open the other packages and started munching on the bread and sides. Jinn just shook her head.

"Were there a lot of them?" he asked Jinn.

"Depends on your definition of a lot," she said with a wave.

"There were a few boxes, not exactly what I would call an apocalyptic stockpile."

"Cool," Pseudo said with a mouthful of food. He chewed thoughtfully for a moment and swallowed. "What's up?"

"Nothing really," Jinn answered, looking at the floor. "Just needed to get away for a minute."

"From what?" he asked before stuffing another huge bite into his mouth.

"I wish I knew," Jinn said, taking a deep breath.

"Out with it." Pseudo looked at her over his glasses, raising his eyebrows.

"I think . . ." Jinn said, drawing out each word, "that I . . . might be . . . jealous of Jasmine."

Pseudo furrowed his brow as he opened the next package in the MRE.

"Every time she went near Lucas, I was all prickly. I know you think it's stupid," Jinn continued.

"I think most things are stupid. Doesn't mean they aren't real," Pseudo said in between bites.

"Why am I jealous, though?" Jinn responded, exasperated. "I mean, I know how dumb jealousy is. I also *know* it doesn't serve any purpose and will just push him away. What the hell is wrong with me?" She hung her head.

"Where does jealousy come from?" Pseudo asked without looking up at her.

"What? I . . ." Jinn stared at him.

"You know the answer," Pseudo said as though he were talking to a child.

"Of course I know the answer. That's the problem—I know better."

"You still haven't answered the question," Pseudo said with a slight smile.

"I . . . uh . . ."

"Having trouble admitting it?" Pseudo grinned at her.

"Insecurity," Jinn finally answered. "Insecurity and self-doubt."

"Yes, jealousy is toxic to a relationship, but it isn't useless," Pseudo said. "It's a visceral reaction that lets you know that there's something you need to work on."

"Why do you always make sense. You are like half my age," Jinn rolled her eyes. "You strip everything down to bones, and as much as I want to argue, you're usually right."

"Occam's razor," Pseudo chided.

"Yeah, yeah, 'Plurality should not be posited without necessity.'" Jinn snorted. "How the hell am I supposed to know when it's necessary?"

"Always assume it's not," Pseudo said with a mischievous grin. "Question," he said, changing the subject. "Those guys you tied up with yesterday—did you recognize any of them?"

Jinn considered for a moment, her mouth half open from the abrupt shift in conversation. "No? I don't think so. Should I have?"

"I don't know," Pseudo answered. "The one you hit in the face said he thought you were familiar."

"I don't remember," Jinn said, trying to picture the man. "I don't think so, but anyone I met before is likely to have been erased, or I purposefully avoided contact."

"Purposefully avoided?" Pseudo asked, scraping the last of the tortellini sauce out of the bag.

"Yeah, Xandar would lose his shit if I acknowledged anyone else, especially men," she answered. "It was easier if I didn't see them in the first place, not that it mattered."

"Ah," Pseudo answered, pulling out the cookies, the last morsel of his meal.

"Have you learned anything new?" Jinn asked, looking over at Pseudo's screens, desperately trying to change the subject again.

"Learned? No," he answered. "Confirmed some theories, though."

"Good. So now what?"

"Let's figure out how to take these bastards down," Pseudo said, his eyes sparkling with excitement. Jinn grinned, a spark flaring momentarily behind her eyes, but Pseudo watched as the spark faded. "I can't fathom the idea that I would think like Xandar," Jinn said, looking down.

"You don't. It's not the same," Pseudo said.

"Jealousy is jealousy," Jinn retorted.

"No, jealousy is insecurity rearing its nasty head. Xandar was after control. You know it's different," Pseudo answered, looking directly at her. "Regardless, do you think it is possible that the goon recognized who you really were? Should we be on alert?"

"I really want to say no, but . . ."

Chapter 35

Planning

Jinn made her way upstairs, both annoyed and excited after her conversation with Pseudo. The sound of Lucas's laughter snapped her from her thoughts. A sting of jealousy clouded her mind, and she pushed it down. This was her issue, not something that needed to be projected onto Lucas or Jasmine. Sebastian squealed with happiness, and then both Lucas and Jasmine laughed out loud again. Sebastian must be showing off. Jinn smiled at the thought. He was such a little ham when he wanted to be. The door was open as Jinn approached, and she poked her head inside to find Lucas and Jasmine seated on the couch while Sebastian was posing with his arms held close to him and growling like a dinosaur.

"Hey Jinn," Lucas acknowledged, standing up a little too quickly.

"Hey," Jinn forced herself to smile, looking back and forth between Lucas and Jasmine. Jasmine gave Jinn a smile but would not look directly at her. Sebastian continued to growl and ran toward Jinn. She gave a dramatic scream and held her arms out to stop the vicious dinosaur. He giggled and squealed before taking off down the hall.

"What's up?" Lucas asked, stepping closer to her.

"Not a lot," Jinn answered. "Pseudo's gonna come up in a bit to talk about our next moves."

"Yeah?" Lucas said raising his eyebrows. "Find out anything new?"

"Confirmation, to use Pseudo's words," Jinn answered as Lucas leaned over and kissed her cheek.

"Good," Lucas said, squeezing her hand.

"Confirmation of what?" Jasmine asked, still seated on the couch.

"Some research that we've been doing," Jinn deflected. She still wasn't sure how much to disclose to Jasmine. Jinn had hardly spent any time with her, but she figured that if Lucas found any reason to be suspicious, he would let her know.

"I forgot," Jasmine said with a pout, "I'm the outsider."

"No," Lucas said taking a seat next to her again, "it's just complicated."

Jinn fought the urge to sit next to him and proverbially mark her territory, but when Lucas squeezed Jasmine's shoulders she had to look away. Jasmine leaned into Lucas, testing Jinn's resolve. "Hey, can we talk?" Jinn asked him, gesturing to the adjoining room.

"Sure," he responded, furrowing his eyebrows.

"Hey, when you're done, we should head down to the gym," Jasmine said, her hand trailing along his back as he stood up. "You could use a workout." She winked at him, then looked pointedly at Jinn.

"Okay," Lucas said over his shoulder. Lucas focused on Jinn, and his eyes tightened. A wave of prickly discomfort washed over her. She struggled to keep her face neutral. She couldn't figure out if Jasmine was intentionally pressing her buttons, or if she was just reading too much into it all.

"Know what? It can wait; you go. Pseudo should be up here by the time you get back. I'll keep an eye on Sebastian," Jinn gushed, fighting to keep her emotions in check.

"You sure?" Lucas asked.

"Yeah," Jasmine answered, causing Jinn to clench her teeth. "You need a break."

"From what?" Lucas asked incredulously.

Jasmine just shrugged her shoulders, giving him a playful smile.

"Seriously, I've got this. Go," Jinn said, corralling them toward the door. "I need to think about some things anyway."

"Um," Lucas hesitated, pressing his lips. "Okay."

"Sebastian? Want a snack?" Jinn called down the hallway.

"Yeah!" he called back and came running toward her.

Lucas let Jasmine get a few steps away before looking at Jinn. "You okay?" he asked.

"Of course," Jinn said trying to project indifference. Lucas narrowed his eyes but didn't press the issue.

"Jinn, I can have these?" Sebastian asked, holding the refrigerator open and pointing to some frozen yogurt.

"Sure, buddy," she answered, turning away from Lucas. His eyes trailed after her, then he shook his head and turned to follow Jasmine down the hallway.

Jinn sat down heavily on the couch. She was uncomfortable around Jasmine, but it was probably just her own projected insecurities. Jasmine had spent a solid twenty-four hours with Lucas and Sebastian, which was bothersome but not unexpected. Jinn expected her to disappear to find more source as soon as she was up to it. Though Jinn had hoped that Jasmine would stick around so that she could evaluate how Jasmine recovered after the antibiotic, considering it only treated the physical withdrawal, not whatever caused the addiction in the first place. She had to admit that Jasmine's recovery was going better than expected, but she also didn't expect how she would feel about Jasmine quickly becoming so close to Lucas.

There was Sebastian to think about as well. They had a lot to talk about, and she had to stay out of her own head before she messed it up. Jinn knew that she needed to discuss this with Lucas. Communication was the only way to ease her mind and get to the bottom of the matter. She didn't know why she was having such a hard time talking about it. Lucas cared about her, and he cared about Sebastian. And in a strange way he cared about Jasmine, too. Jinn knew logically that this was not a bad thing.

Jinn turned her mind toward the antibiotic. Jasmine had handled the side effects well, though just one test subject was hardly thorough. Based on Jasmine, the antibiotic did cause some increase in the withdrawal symptoms, but they were cleared up in a fraction of the time. Jasmine had said it had been almost a week since she blitzed, but there was only so far that she could trust that assessment. Assuming Jasmine was telling the truth, there was still a risk of overloading a person's system with the toxin dump if they had blitzed more recently. She really needed more people willing to test. That would be on the agenda to discuss with Pseudo.

Then there was Xandar. If he found out that Jinn was still alive after his second attempt to murder her, there was no telling how far he would be willing to go to make sure she didn't survive a third time.

Chapter 36

It's Complicated

Lucas followed Jasmine down the stairs, headed for the hotel's gym. A strange feeling he could not quite place settled uncomfortably in his mind. Jinn had been guarding her reactions when she had come up the stairs, but he wanted to give her space to handle her feelings. It was frustrating that she couldn't just tell him what was going on in her mind. How quickly his feelings had developed for her had surprised him. He knew that she felt similarly toward him, but she struggled to sort out her issues.

Jasmine turned and smiled over her shoulder. She truly was beautiful. She had an ethereal quality about her. Between her translucent skin and hair and waiflike form, she seemed fragile. This triggered a certain protective instinct in him, though he worried that she had more in mind. He was also aware that Jinn was feeling threatened by her. Even though he hadn't known Jinn for very long, he was certain she would never be willing to admit it. Frustrating as it was, that was one of the things he admired about Jinn. She was strong, intelligent, and beautiful in her own warrior-like demeanor. His mind drifted back to the night before. He didn't know what Xandar had done to chip away at her psyche, but when she was comfortable, she was amazing. He'd become so lost in his thoughts that he barely noticed they were in the gym.

"You okay?" Jasmine asked, her face angelic.

"Yeah," he answered, returning to the present. "Yeah, I'm good, just stuck in my head, I guess." He chuckled at himself.

"What're you thinking?" she asked him.

"Dunno," Lucas shook his head. "Everything's been so crazy lately. I think I'm losing my grip."

"What d'you mean by that?" she asked as they headed toward the free weights.

Lucas grabbed a couple of barbells from the rack and sat down on a bench. "I just, I feel content, almost happy, which doesn't make sense because I also feel trapped."

"Why would you feel trapped?" she asked, tilting her head as she stretched out on the bench next to him.

"Ah . . ." Lucas's thoughts scrambled for purchase. He shouldn't tell her that they were running from Xandar or the truth about Sebastian. He still knew next to nothing about Jasmine. "I just . . . I don't feel like I've a lot of options for keeping Sebastian safe outside of the Clermont . . . It's uh, it's complicated."

Jasmine eyed Lucas carefully. She wasn't stupid. She had to know that he was hiding things from her, but that should be expected given the circumstance.

"Speaking of complicated," Jasmine said, thankfully turning the conversation. "Are you and Jinn, like, together?"

"I . . . uh . . ." Lucas stammered.

"It's complicated?" Jasmine supplied, feigning insult.

"Yeah, I guess so," Lucas laughed, trying to defuse the situation. "Really, it's just . . . It's new, I guess, so I don't really know what we are." Lucas took a breath and then continued. "I like her, but . . ."

"I get that," Jasmine answered flippantly, though Lucas saw the fleeting look of disappointment as it crossed her face. "I just hope she feels the same about you."

"What do you mean?" Lucas asked, intrigue getting the better of him.

"Well, she's, she's barely been here at all since I got here and seems very distracted and distant when she is around," Jasmine said, watching him from the corner of her eyes.

Lucas flexed with the weights. He was starting to work up a sweat, and he caught Jasmine watching him. He knew it was vain, but he enjoyed it. "It's not like that," he said, coming to Jinn's defense. "Like I said, the situation is just complicated."

"Why don't you take Sebastian and join up with NOMAD?" Jasmine asked.

"We just left there," Lucas sighed. Responding that it's complicated was only going to get him by for so long. Jasmine turned to him, confusion written on her face.

"Sebastian is not my biological son," Lucas said against his better judgment.

"I kind of figured that," Jasmine said, giving him a half-smile. "I'm guessing that's also why you feel trapped?"

"Yeah," Lucas let out his breath before heading over to the rowing machine. Jasmine trailed behind. She had lifted a couple of small free weights, but clearly this was more about her trying to spend time with him than working out.

"So, are you gonna let me in on the big secret?" Jasmine asked. "You're too nice to have kidnapped him."

"I shouldn't. I don't think you'll want to be involved," Lucas said, trying to shut down the questioning.

"You can't answer with some bullshit like that and expect me to drop it," Jasmine said with a wry smile.

Lucas pumped a few more strokes on the rower before leaning back and looking over at her. She hadn't even broken a sweat, which he found annoying. "Please," he said, looking directly into her eyes. "I don't know what the plan is or if there even is one, but we have some dangerous enemies. You don't want to be involved." His eyes searched hers.

"Lucas," she responded, putting her hand to his face. His eyes tightened at the gesture, but he didn't pull back. "Trust me, maybe I can help."

"Fine." He pulled away from her touch then told her the truth. Jinn finding Sebastian and taking him to NOMAD, unaware of who his father was. How NOMAD had disavowed them as soon as it came to light, and that they were trying to keep him hidden until Xandar was dealt with. When Lucas was finished, Jasmine had a strange sparkle in her eyes. Lucas couldn't decide if he should be worried, and Jinn would probably be annoyed. Something else he would have to deal with later.

"Look," Jasmine said, focusing on Lucas. "Thanks to source, I've nowhere to go, no family or friends left, nothing. I will stay. Let me help." Jasmine smiled. "I know you don't know me, but I'm asking. Please don't shut me out." Jasmine's large pale eyes were swimming, creating an innocence that Lucas found hard to resist. Without thinking he put his arms around her shoulders, pulling her into a protective hug.

"We won't shut you out," Lucas said with a smile.

"Thanks," Jasmine said, her watery eyes misting over. "I don't wanna be alone anymore." She buried her face in his chest.

"Don't worry," Lucas said, looking down at her, "you have friends here." She smiled as he squeezed her one more time before breaking the embrace. "Let's get back upstairs. Jinn's probably waiting." Lucas spotted a fleeting hint of anxiety at the mention of Jinn. The urge to comfort her pressed on him, but he hesitated.

Chapter 37

Broken Walls and Rolling Out

The sound of the door jolted Jinn from a doze she'd unknowingly slipped into. Lucas walked in, his shirt damp and sticking to his broad shoulders, followed by Jasmine. Jinn blinked a couple of times and extricated herself from the sleeping toddler next to her. Little Sebastian stirred when she moved, but he quickly went back to sleep.

"Hey," Lucas said softly, smiling at them both.

"Hey," Jinn responded, followed by an enormous yawn.

"Have a good nap?" Lucas asked, his eyes twinkling.

"Wasn't long enough," Jinn chided.

"Pseudo made it up yet?"

"If he did, he didn't stick around," Jinn answered, looking around the room.

"Good, I'm gonna get a shower," Lucas said. Leaning over her, he brushed Jinn's forehead with his lips.

"Okay." Jinn stood up and stretched. Lucas watched her.

She gave him a coy smile, and he smiled and shook his head. Lucas headed into the bathroom and closed the door.

"Want something to drink?" Jinn asked Jasmine as she walked over to the small refrigerator.

"Um, sure, some water?" Jasmine answered, sitting on the couch.

Jinn pulled out two charcoal-filtered water bottles from Pseudo's collection. They were slow to fill, but they were reusable and they worked. She handed one to Jasmine and sat down next to her on the couch. She took a breath, trying to ignore the uncomfortable silence.

"Get a good workout?" Jinn asked.

"Yeah," Jasmine answered, nodding her head.

"I haven't been down to the gym," Jinn said, trying to fill the space with chatter.

"It's pretty busted," Jasmine admitted. "There's some weights and a couple of the machines are functional."

"Better than nothing, I guess," Jinn said. "I need to check it out."

They sat for a few more moments in silence. Jinn took a deep breath and turned toward Jasmine. "You have any family or friends around here?"

Jasmine eyed Jinn for a moment. "Not really. Do I need to leave?"

"No—no, I was just curious," Jinn said, feeling a little flustered.

"Sorry," Jasmine said, her face turning pink. "I am probably paranoid, but I feel like you don't like me much."

"Sorry if I made you feel that way," Jinn said quickly. She hesitated, wondering how much she should tell Jasmine. She was compelled to admit that she felt insecure and threatened, but she didn't want to reveal that vulnerability to Jasmine any more than she wanted to show Lucas.

"It's fine, it's just . . . hard to be confident after struggling for so long." Jasmine's eyes started to cloud over. Jinn knew that feeling all too well.

"I get that," Jinn said. Maybe it was because Jasmine was so small and waiflike, but Jinn wanted to protect her. "We've all had our struggles. It makes it hard to trust anyone."

"I know," Jasmine answered, "but I wish you would trust me. I understand why, but I just . . . I wish I belonged like you do."

Jinn laughed heartily at that, drawing a surprised look from Jasmine and causing Sebastian to stir. She stifled herself before responding to Jasmine's confusion. "I don't think any of us *belong* here," she said, wiping her eyes. "We were thrown together by random-ass ridiculousness, so I can tell you with certainty that you belong here as much as any of us." Jasmine smiled, her eyes lighting up, making Jinn feel warm. "Truth?" Jinn continued, "I'm so insecure I can hardly function, and you are very pretty. Lucas and I just started doing . . . whatever it is we are doing, and if I try to think any further ahead than tomorrow, I have a panic attack." Jinn was giggling again. She was starting to feel just a bit unhinged.

"That's exactly how I feel," Jasmine said, joining in the laughter. "I've tried to think further than where I am going to sleep tonight, and it's overwhelming." The women's laughter was starting to reach a fevered pitch. The weight of everything seemed to have cracked them both. The next thing they knew, Sebastian had woken up and joined in the laughter, although he had no idea what was funny. He ran over and threw himself on the couch between them, and they both turned and tickled him until he started squealing.

Their eyes lifted to the bathroom door as Lucas stepped out wearing jeans and a dark T-shirt that was just a bit too tight, and both Jinn and Jasmine started trying to quell their giggles. Lucas glanced back and forth between the two of them with a confused and somewhat scared expression. They both looked up at him and smiled before Sebastian jumped up and attacked him. Before they knew what was happening, all four of them were laughing uncontrollably, with Sebastian squealing and screaming, fully believing that he was the reason for the frivolity. They turned as the door opened and a very confused Pseudo peeked into the room.

"What is happening?" he asked tentatively.

"I think we've cracked," Jinn said right before Sebastian gave his best dinosaur roar and went after Pseudo, attempting to bring him into the fray. Pseudo growled back and tickled him while everyone tried to calm down.

"It's not like you had far to go," Pseudo said, picking up Sebastian and tossing him onto the couch in a squirming, giggling heap.

"I know," Jinn said between breaths. "I dunno about y'all, but I needed that."

"We all did," Lucas agreed.

"Who's hungry?" Jasmine asked, heading over to the kitchen area.

"Can I have nuggets?" Sebastian asked, vying for his favorite meal.

"Of course you can," Jasmine answered, then glanced at the others.

"Lemme help," Jinn said getting to her feet. Jasmine smiled at her, and Jinn acknowledged that a wall had been broken down. It felt good.

After consuming some rather plain sandwiches, the four of them were finally able to get down to business. Pseudo had given Sebastian a tablet to play with to keep him occupied, and they were seated in the small common area.

"So, the antibiotic works?" Pseudo asked, looking over at Jasmine.

"Antibiotic?" Jasmine asked.

"It's what I gave you," Jinn supplied. "Source is bacteria."

"How does that work?" Jasmine asked incredulously.

"I'll explain later," Jinn responded.

Jasmine nodded before answering Pseudo's initial question.

"I feel great," Jasmine said. "It was rough but worth it, so I'd say it works."

"I don't know," Jinn said. "It is possible that we were lucky; all the variables happened to align. I really need to run more tests."

"You've been making more?" Lucas asked.

"Yeah, I've got about twenty doses so far, and I'm getting faster. I could have a few dozen by next week," Jinn answered.

"What do we know about Xandar?" Lucas asked Pseudo.

"Most of my theories have been proven," Pseudo said. "Source is manufactured at the CDC. Now I'm trying to see exactly how big the network is."

"You've been following Xandar?" Jasmine's jaw dropped.

"Not physically," Lucas answered for him. "His operation."

"Oh," Jasmine said, still not fully understanding. Pseudo looked back and forth between Jasmine and Jinn, raising his eyebrows slightly. Jinn gave a quick nod, signaling to Pseudo that it was safe to talk in front of Jasmine. It was probably risky to trust her, but she had proven herself so far.

"So, we ready to move on the CDC?" Jinn asked.

"Not yet. I want more information," Pseudo said. "I am not sure about the logistics of the campus yet. I've been trying to get into their cell network, but they're not pinging off any towers."

"What does that mean?" Jinn asked.

"I believe their network is just phone to phone, more like radios than cell phones, so they won't have as much range as we do with Roxanne," Pseudo supplied. "But it makes it harder to eavesdrop."

"Roxanne?" Jasmine furrowed her brows at Lucas, who shrugged.

"Roxanne is the radio tower on the roof," Jinn answered, rolling her eyes. "She's how Pseudo has kept cell service."

"You can do that?" Jasmine asked. Pseudo nodded, trying to look nonchalant, but failing.

"Can they listen to us?" Lucas asked.

"Possible, but unlikely," Pseudo said. "Most of their people are just trying to keep things running. They don't have time for espionage."

"Well," Lucas said, "what's our next step?"

"We should roll out the antibiotic," Jinn said. "That'll get some people on our side while Pseudo finds the CDC's weak point."

"How do you propose we do that?" Pseudo asked.

"Well, I, uhhh . . ." Jinn said. "I have no idea."

Everyone sat in silence for a minute, considering.

"You know Dr. Brinson?" Jasmine asked, pulling all eyes toward her.

"Roland Brinson?" Pseudo asked.

"Yeah, you know him?" Jasmine said, looking hopeful.

"I know of him," Pseudo said. "His name's come up in the online rooms."

"What's an online room?" Jasmine queried.

"Don't ask; you don't wanna know," Jinn responded, causing Jasmine to raise her eyebrows.

"You make it sound weirder than it is," Pseudo said, shooting a glare over at Jinn. "It's just a communication platform, like social media of last generation."

"If I remember my history, social media did get weird," Jinn responded.

"Not. The. Point. Jinn." Pseudo said, daring Jinn to antagonize him further. "Anyway," he continued, "Brinson's been mentioned in connection with source rehab, but I don't really know anything else." Pseudo paused. "Well, that and he's mean."

"Mean?" Jinn lifted her eyebrows.

"He is mean," Jasmine offered, "but, yeah, he has a small . . . practice? I guess that's what you would call it, where he takes in people who are wanting to dry out. He doesn't have a high success rate. I was one of his patients. I could take you to him."

Chapter 38

The Doctor

Everyone turned toward Jasmine, this waif they had known for barely a day. The doctor could be the connection they needed, but Jinn was still not sold on the idea of trusting her. She considered it, turning over in her mind how Jasmine could hurt them or turn on them if they let her in on this.

"Definitely a start," Jinn said, once she came up with nothing. "Hopefully, he's willing to take some risk."

"Risk won't be the problem," Jasmine supplied.

"You don't think he would work with us?" Lucas asked, touching her hand. Jinn's eyes tightened.

"He's . . . jaded," Jasmine said, looking at Jinn and pulling her hand away from Lucas's.

"Jaded?" Jinn asked, raising an eyebrow.

"I dunno how much of it is true, but supposedly he was rejected from Exodus at the last minute because of a heart condition, so he decided that he would clean up what's left of the city. But he's tired of fighting a losing battle."

—

The crumbling walls of the old apartment buildings surrounded Jinn. Their weight pressed in on her. The power supply hadn't reached this far south for a long time. The whine of mobile generators reverberated from several different locations, signaling that there were at least a few people still around. She glanced over at Jasmine, who had uncharacteristically kept her eyes down since they parked Pseudo's roadster in a dilapidated garage about a block over. The buildings had originally been apartments, but most of the windows were boarded up and the shrubbery was completely overgrown.

"You sure we're in the right place?" Jinn asked.

"Yeah," Jasmine answered, looking furtively from side to side. "I was here the day before Lucas found me, but Dr. Brinson wouldn't let me stay."

Jinn furrowed her brow at the statement.

"Here it is," Jasmine said, gesturing toward a boarded-up door attached to a smaller building sandwiched between the apartment complexes.

"We just go in?" Jinn asked, reaching for the door.

"Not exactly," Jasmine said and approached. She knocked loudly three times and then stepped back. They waited until Jinn started to wonder if the building was abandoned.

The door pushed open a crack and a raspy voice called out, "Yeah?"

"Dr. Brinson, we need to talk to you," Jasmine responded, looking at the ground.

"Jasmine?" the voice responded.

"Yes, we have a proposition," she said quickly.

"No." The door slammed in her face. Jasmine glanced over at Jinn, her pale eyes tearing up.

"Knock again," Jinn said, rolling her eyes. Jasmine proceeded to knock three times again.

"I said no!" he shouted from behind the door.

"Dr. Brinson, my name's Jinn, and I have something you'll be interested in—at least if you're the Dr. Brinson Pseudo told me about," Jinn shouted.

"Pseudo?" The door cracked open again.

"You know him?" Jinn asked, positioning herself in front of the door.

"No," Dr. Brinson said, "but he has a reputation for being unreasonably smart. And weird."

"That's him," Jinn said. "Listen, I have something for you, but I don't want to shout it through the door."

He pushed the door a bit wider and squinted out at Jinn. He was roughly middle-aged with salt and pepper hair and lazy stubble shadowing his face. "What're you doing with *her*?" he asked, jutting his chin toward Jasmine.

"She recommended you," Jinn answered.

"And?"

"I'm a microbiologist," Jinn stated, straightening her shoulders. "I have something to help source withdrawal."

"Why would I care?" Dr. Brinson said, the lines on his face growing hard.

"Can we come in?" Jinn asked, losing her patience with the situation. "If you're not interested, say so. I'll find another doctor."

"Fine," he responded, pushing the door open and allowing them in. "Don't touch anything," he snapped pointedly at Jasmine, which Jinn found curious.

"She tell you about the last time she needed *help*?" Dr. Brinson said, not even attempting to mask his dislike for Jasmine.

"No," Jinn said, attempting to shut down the conversation. "But she was my first test subject."

"Test subject, eh?" he said with a malicious laugh. "I guess that was after you left with half my equipment."

Jinn raised her eyebrows at Jasmine. "She didn't mention

it." Jinn answered flatly.

"I'm hoping to repay you for that. That's why I brought Jinn," Jasmine said without looking at either of them.

"Alright, what d'you have?" Dr. Brinson asked, directing them toward some chairs that had seen better days. At that moment, a loud groan emanated from the room behind Dr. Brinson. Jinn glanced at Jasmine with concern, but Brinson didn't even flinch. He continued to look at Jinn with his eyebrows raised expectantly.

"I've been researching source and learned that it's not a chemical, but bacteria," Jinn began. "It is a mutation of a staphylococcal strain that causes—"

"Get to the point," Brinson cut her off.

"Uh . . . okay. I made an antibiotic that will kill it," Jinn finished.

"And you tested it on her?"

"Yeah."

"It worked?" Brinson eyed Jasmine suspiciously.

"Yeah, but there were side effects," Jinn said. "She said she hadn't blitzed in a week before the injection . . ."

"A week?" Brinson raised an eyebrow at Jasmine.

Jasmine nodded quickly.

"A week?" Brinson repeated, dropping his voice.

"Three days give or take . . ." Jasmine murmured, her cheeks flushed.

"Take . . ." Brinson said.

Jinn furrowed her brow at Jasmine.

"I tried to sell his equipment," Jasmine said, tears sliding down her cheeks while she continued to look at the floor. "I'd found some buyers, but when we met up at the Clermont, they offered to blitz. Then they took everything and locked me in the gym."

Brinson laughed uproariously. Jinn stared at him in shock. It took several minutes for the laughter to subside, with Brinson wiping tears from his eyes. "You can't be serious," he said between chuckles.

Jasmine just nodded.

"Well, that's actually good news," Jinn said, trying to defuse the situation. "The antibiotic exacerbated the symptoms for a few hours, but then they were gone, other than weakness and fatigue."

"Why's that good news?" Brinson asked.

"I was worried the toxin dump could be lethal if there was more source in her system," Jinn responded.

"But it works?" Brinson asked.

"Did for her," Jinn responded. Another loud moan sounded from behind Brinson. Jinn raised her eyebrows in question, but he, again, didn't respond.

"You have it with you?" Brinson asked instead.

"I have about five injections, yeah," Jinn said, reaching into her backpack and pulling out a handful of syringes.

"What d'you want for it?" Brinson asked.

"Test subjects and syringes if you have them," she answered.

"And?" Brinson raised an eyebrow.

Jinn glanced over at Jasmine, who was still unwilling to meet anyone's gaze.

"That's . . . That's it," Jinn said. "We're trying to help people."

Brinson chuckled, his humor dark. "You can't break addiction by treating symptoms. Trust me."

"I know," Jinn answered, meeting his eyes with determination. "But this will give them a fighting chance."

"Ahh . . . I remember being optimistic," Brinson said. He rolled his head toward the ceiling as though lost in nostalgia.

"Will you help or not?" Jinn asked.

"Come with me," Brinson said, turning toward the door behind him. Jinn and Jasmine followed him through into a room with broken-down beds lining the walls. Most of them were empty, but three were occupied, the patients appearing tortured and on the verge of death.

"Jasmine?" a pale and lethargic man said, barely above a whisper.

"Shawn?" Jasmine said, rushing over to the bed. "How long've you been here?" She put her hand gently on his.

"'Bout a week," he whispered. His skin was pale and green, but he shared some similar features with Jasmine. Perhaps they were related. Jinn's attention was pulled away by Brinson.

"These people," he says, not trying to hide his contempt, "don't wanna break the addiction. They just want to feel better. That's what causes the addiction in the first place. No injection will fix that."

"Trust me, I know," Jinn answered. "I'm intimately familiar with addiction."

"Shawn's been in here three times," Brinson said pointing over at Jasmine and the man in the bed. "Alicia, four," he gestured to an unconscious woman writhing in the bed nearest them. "Scott here," he pointed over at a tall man who looked to be in his thirties currently hanging over the edge of his bed and vomiting into a bucket. "His fifth trip, and his last."

"Last?" Jinn asked.

"Yeah," Brinson said, his jaw tightening. "I've given him five chances to kick the habit. When they leave here, they're completely detoxed, but they always come back, I have had to start turning them away. Turns out they usually can't pay anymore after about five."

"What?" Jinn asked, thoroughly confused.

"I don't run a charity," he said. "Tried that. I'd help and they'd promise to pay me once they're clean and productive, but they never do. I've learned relying on an addict to get better just leaves you destitute. So, they pay up front. Credits, service, trade—doesn't matter, but they pay before treatment."

"Why do you do it then?" Jinn asked.

"I'm a surgeon," was Brinson's unhelpful answer.

Jinn raised an eyebrow waiting for him to elaborate.

Brinson sucked in a deep breath and rolled his shoulders. "I went to med school for general surgery. I was supposed to leave on Exodus, but an undiagnosed heart murmur prevented that." He sighed. "I tried to run a practice, but there's not a huge demand for surgeons in this post-apocalyptic hellscape."

"That's a bit hyperbolic," Jinn said.

"Is it?" he responded while sardonically gesturing around him.

Jinn opened her mouth to respond, but simply closed it again.

"I'll try your drug," Brinson said. "But I'm fresh outta optimism."

"I don't need optimism. I need test subjects," Jinn said and handed over the syringes.

Brinson took them and walked over to a cabinet on the far wall. He took out a box and handed it over. "You've an autoclave?"

"Yeah," Jinn responded, pulling back a flap on the box.

"You don't wanna touch those," he said. Jinn's nostrils flared at the syringes. They were all used, and quite dirty. She flinched and quickly closed the box.

"I'll get these sterilized and bring more in a few days," she said as he went back to the cabinet and pulled on some gloves.

"May as well not waste any time," he said taking a syringe over to the unconscious woman.

"You're not gonna wait 'til she's awake?" Jinn asked.

"Why? She's probably going to die either way," Brinson said.

Jinn turned away, her skin crawling. She needed test subjects, but this was wrong. Brinson straightened up, noting her discomfort. "I'll see you in a few days then," he said and nodded toward the door.

"Jas?" Jinn called as she turned toward the door.

"I'll be back, promise," Jasmine whispered to Shawn, who was barely conscious. She stood and followed Jinn out the door.

They left the building and walked back to the roadster in silence. Once they were in the car and the doors were shut, Jinn put her face in her hands and took a breath.

"You hate me now?" Jasmine asked quietly.

"Who's Shawn?" Jinn deflected.

"My brother," she answered. "Haven't seen him in a long time."

"Ah," Jinn said, straightening up and starting the roadster.

"You didn't answer the question," Jasmine stated.

"I don't care what you did. I care what you do," Jinn said as they sped back toward the Clermont.

Chapter 39

Unforeseen Circumstance

Two weeks later Jinn was back at Dr. Brinson's run-down clinic. She was bringing him more of the antibiotics and getting an update. She was still uncomfortable with his methods, but she couldn't argue with the results. They had gone through over one hundred doses of the antibiotic, mostly successful. So far, only two people had died after receiving the antibiotic, but Brinson was certain that they would not have survived the night, regardless. The other patients recovered from the withdrawal symptoms within a day or two. Despite this, Brinson was in a foul mood.

Jinn walked into the room, where there were now somewhere between fifteen to twenty patients in different stages of recovery. He had also hired a couple of younger-looking people to serve as nurses, helping to clean and keep up with the patients as they went through the more intense, shorter withdrawal. The medical equipment looked better, too. Or perhaps his employees were just taking better care of things than Brinson had ever done.

"More wasted time?" he asked, his face set in grim lines.

"What's that now?" she responded.

"Now there's a *cure*, I'm getting repeat customers," he griped. "Most everyone here's already had a dose and swore they would 'do better this time.'" His voice dripped with contempt.

"You expected that," Jinn countered.

"Not this fast," he said, pursing his lips.

"Turn them away—you haven't had a problem with that before."

"They're paying," he responded as though that was the answer for everything.

Jinn rolled her eyes. Dr. Brinson was a genuine pain in the ass. They exchanged boxes—Jinn's holding syringes filled with the antibiotic, Brinson's full of used syringes. She didn't want to think too hard about how he was able to run a clinic without an autoclave.

"Careful though," he said, his voice tinged with warning. "Word's getting out that there's something that helps. *People* are starting to notice."

"You haven't told anyone where you're getting it, have you?"

"Not specifically, no."

"Keep it that way."

"I will 'til someone asks too hard," he said, raising his eyebrows knowingly.

Jinn huffed in response.

"See ya in a couple of days," he said, waving her away.

"Yep, see ya." She headed for the door, carrying her box of dirty needles.

Brinson just grunted.

She walked out and scanned her surroundings. The air was strange—her hair lifted from her scalp and her skin tingled. The storm season was mostly over, but a lingering possibility always existed that one waited on the outskirts. She called Pseudo.

"What's up?" Pseudo's face popped up on her screen.

"You check the weather?" she asked, glancing up at the sky. It was clear, but the few wispy clouds that she could see were moving fast.

"Yeah, this morning—looked clear. I'll look again." Jinn could see him glancing toward his computer screen.

"Hmm . . . we do have cell development. Don't think it'll get too close, but you might want to hurry back," he said, his eyes darting away from the phone.

"Alright."

"You have your AR?" Pseudo asked, referring to her glasses that would send signals to him.

"Yeah, battery's low though," she said, reaching into the bag attached to the back of her bike.

"Wear 'em," he said.

"Should I be worried?" Jinn asked.

"Nah. There's some sketchy stuff to the north, but probably it'll blow itself out. Just pay attention. And hurry up." He ended the call while Jinn activated her AR glasses. The battery was low but should last long enough for her to get back to the Clermont.

As she cleared the apartment buildings, an ominous line of clouds pushed down from the north. She increased the throttle and picked up speed, turning toward the interstate. Pavement sped beneath her, but the line of clouds started to curl inward. It wasn't good. Her heart pounded. She needed to get to the other side before it turned into a funnel. Pushing her bike to the limit and heading straight for the hook in the clouds, she mentally kicked herself for forgetting to put in the earpiece that accompanied the glasses. Pseudo could see what she was looking at, but he could not hear or speak to her.

"Shit, I'm not gonna make it," she said to no one and watched a funnel start to take shape. This was going to be a big one. An overpass approached, forcing a snap decision. The bike slid out from under her as she jumped off and scrambled up the sloped concrete. The clouds' slow rotation gained speed and spiraled toward her. Tucking herself tightly into the topmost corner, she closed her eyes and prayed to anyone listening that the structure would hold.

Jinn could no longer see the impending tornado, but the noise it created was deafening. The wind pulled at her hiding place as the storm competed with gravity for its hold on her. She tucked her face underneath her arm and held on as the wind tore all around her and the bridge groaned under the pressure. Her body was curled as tightly as possible against the girder. Screams ripped from her throat as the structure screamed in reply.

Searing pain flooded through her as the girder broke free from the structure. It wedged itself in her hold, likely protecting her from flying debris. But all she could focus on was the pain from her arm that was now being crushed under the beam. After an eternity of deafening noise and blinding pain, the wind began to calm around her. The tornado moved past and turned west. She attempted to pull her arm free, but this proved impossible and caused more blinding flashes of pain. Trapped. Jinn looked around frantically trying to keep her senses, but the pain began to distort her vision and pull at her consciousness.

She twisted her body to pull her phone from her jacket pocket with her free hand, but couldn't hold it steady. She tapped the screen, and Pseudo's name was the first to come up. The edges of her vision darkened as she tapped it again.

"Jinn!" Pseudo shouted before the phone even rang.

"I'm trapped," Jinn said through clenched teeth.

"I know where you are—hang on," Pseudo said. The world started spinning around her. "Jinn stay with me." She could hear his footsteps pounding as he ran for . . . something. Her mind was slipping. "Jinn, you there? Jinn—"

Chapter 40

Recovery

Lucas was in the kitchen warming up some food as he stole a glance over at Jasmine. She was looking down at Sebastian with fondness. They had spent a lot of time together lately; Sebastian had really taken to Jasmine. Lucas felt a little remorse at pulling back from him, but they were content to just be around each other. Lucas remembered Jasmine telling him about losing her child. He wondered if she was finding some sort of solace in Sebastian. She gave Sebastian a little squeeze then turned toward the door with an interesting expression that combined guilt and fear.

"What's up?" he asked her.

"Nothin'. Bored," she answered, her face breaking into a smile. Whatever had been on her mind quickly vanished.

"Sorry, life's not very exciting right now," he answered. "Why don't you get out, go do something. You don't have to be trapped here." He took a seat on the couch next to her.

"There's nowhere I'd rather be," she answered, gazing down at Sebastian. "I know you're bored too, especially with all Jinn's extra hours lately."

"I dunno what to tell you," Lucas said with a laugh. "Jinn has some books in her room. They're pretty old, but they're interesting."

"I'm not as into sci-fi as she is," Jasmine said.

Suddenly, there was frantic pounding on the door. Lucas shot up from the couch, almost knocking over Jasmine in the process.

"Lucas!" Pseudo shouted as he yanked open the door.

"What's going on?" Lucas asked, noticing the frantic look in Pseudo's eyes.

"Jinn's hurt. We gotta go," Pseudo practically shouted, pulling him toward the door.

"What do you mean? Go where?" Lucas asked, turning back inside.

"Come on—" Pseudo shouted, looking panicked.

"Okay. Jas, can you stay with Sebastian?" Lucas asked, reaching out and snatching his phone from the countertop.

"Yeah," she answered.

Lucas and Pseudo were running down the hall before the door closed.

"There was a tornado. Jinn's trapped," Pseudo huffed between breaths as they reached the stairwell.

"Tornado?"

"She was on the way back," Pseudo said.

"You know where she is?" Lucas asked.

"Pretty close."

They raced into the garage and jumped into Pseudo's roadster. Pseudo put on a pair of glasses, tapped the side, and Jinn's location popped into the AR with an estimated distance. He launched the car in drive and raced out of the garage.

"How'd you . . .?" Lucas asked. He could see the little point of light on Pseudo's glasses.

"The glasses are connected to Roxanne. It'll give me her location."

"Does she know this?" Lucas asked, wondering how else Pseudo tracks everything that happens around him. Lucas couldn't figure out how Pseudo knew everything going on without ever being present.

"Yes? Maybe? She doesn't really ask," Pseudo said, shrugging his shoulders.

Lucas shook his head. He had a lot more questions, but he figured they could wait until they made sure that Jinn was safe. He looked out the rounded windows. Already, he could see the destruction where the tornado had touched down. The path showed that the tornado had not stayed on the ground for long, but where it did, it was destroyed. He could see the steel from the overpasses strewn around on the roads. Pseudo dodged the debris with expert precision. They came up to the broken remains of a particularly large overpass, and Lucas spotted Jinn's bike within the rubble.

"There—" he shouted, and Pseudo skidded the roadster to a halt. Lucas jumped out and yelled for Jinn. There was no response. Everything was eerily silent, especially considering that it had only been a few minutes since the event that had caused the surrounding destruction.

Pseudo took off toward the side of the road and Lucas followed close behind. Pseudo started to pull debris away from where the overpass had crumbled onto the interstate, and Lucas quickly scanned the area before joining him.

"Shit. Shit. Lucas!" Pseudo shouted. Lucas jumped over to him and had to pause to register what he was looking at. Jinn was unconscious, half buried in concrete. There was blood smeared on her cheek. Lucas reached out and felt for a pulse.

"She's alive, she's breathing," Lucas said and set to removing the debris surrounding her. He pulled away most of the steel and concrete that had closed in on her legs when Pseudo spoke again.

"Lucas, this's gonna be a problem," Pseudo said. His voice was quiet, frightened. Lucas swung over to position himself next to Pseudo. Jinn's left arm was completely crushed underneath a square of concrete and steel that had shifted when the overpass collapsed. "Even if we could move this, she'd bleed out as soon as we did." Pseudo's voice was strained, like he was teetering on the edge of panic.

"I'll tourniquet," Lucas said quickly. "Call Brinson."

Pseudo nodded, his eyes glazed over.

"Pseudo, I need you here," Lucas said, shaking him by his shoulders. Pseudo nodded briskly. "Call Brinson. I'm going to tourniquet the arm. See if Brinson wants to come here or if we should take her there."

"Okay," Pseudo said, still nodding. He jogged back to the roadster to get his phone. Lucas immediately set to tearing his shirt and using a busted piece of rebar to twist into a tourniquet for Jinn's arm. She started to stir as he was tightening it.

"Lucas," she whispered, a smile on her face despite the pain.

"Shh," Lucas intoned. "We're gonna get you out of here, promise."

"Thank you," she whispered before losing consciousness again.

Lucas closed his eyes as tears threatened to fall. He had managed to distance himself from the situation, but that slight smile had caught him off guard. He had to focus. He couldn't lose her.

"He said tourniquet and take her to the clinic," Pseudo shouted from the roadster.

"I need help moving the block," Lucas shouted back.

Pseudo ran back to Lucas's side, and together they were able to lift the block enough to pull Jinn's mangled arm from beneath it. Pseudo's eyes went straight up as Lucas pulled her free.

"Pseudo, you good?" Lucas asked, noticing how pale Pseudo had become.

"Ya," he answered.

Lucas gathered Jinn up in his arms, praying there weren't other injuries that he was exacerbating with the movement. Pseudo ran with him, not looking at Jinn or the blood seeping from her shoulder. Lucas prayed again that the tourniquet would hold as Pseudo sped off toward the clinic.

Chapter 41

Now We Wait

It was raining again when Lucas returned to the Clermont. He stepped, exhausted and dirty, into the suite. His clothes were covered with Jinn's blood, dirt, and debris from the afternoon. Jasmine's eyes went wide as he pushed through the door. Sebastian was asleep, so she gently nudged him over before rushing to Lucas's side.

"You okay?" she asked, her watery eyes shining with worry.

"Yeah," Lucas answered as he pushed toward the bathroom. "Jinn's in pretty bad shape though."

"Where is she?" Jasmine asked.

"With Brinson. He's keeping her sedated overnight. He's hoping that'll help prevent shock when she does wake up."

"How bad is it?" Jasmine asked, her voice tight.

"She lost her left arm just past the shoulder," Lucas answered without looking at her.

Jasmine recoiled with a gasp.

"She also has some busted ribs, a broken ankle, and some internal injuries, but those should heal fine." He ran his hand over his face.

"He amputated her arm?" Jasmine's eyes went wide.

"He didn't have a choice. It was completely crushed. That's why she was stuck," Lucas said, stepping into the bathroom. He turned and glanced at Jasmine before lowering his gaze. "Thanks for watching Sebastian."

"Of course," she answered quickly, looking over at the child.

Lucas nodded and softly closed the bathroom door. He studied himself in the mirror. His face was drawn, his eyes dull. He was so tired. Everything had been weighing on him, especially being trapped in this hotel. His heart broke for Sebastian. It was such a struggle to keep him here, and Lucas knew that this would not last long. For now, Sebastian was small, and the top floor of the Clermont was enough space for him to exist safely. But he was growing fast. Something would have to change, and soon.

Lucas wiped a hand over his face in frustration. He didn't have the ability to think about the future when he was having to take on survival. It seemed like every time they started to move forward, something catastrophic happened. Now it was Jinn who was just barely hanging on to life. Lucas had exaggerated her stability to Jasmine, but he had to come back for Sebastian. Brinson didn't believe Jinn would last through the night. There was nothing left that could be done for her. Brinson had amputated the arm and cauterized it. He had also inflated her collapsed lung and quelled some other internal injuries. If she did make it through the night, she would have to have her pain managed for a while yet.

He could leave. The thought entered Lucas's mind uninvited, but he considered it anyway. It would require leaving Jinn behind. Jasmine would be more than willing to go with them, probably, and they could find somewhere else. Jinn's soft smile when she saw him hovered in his mind, and Sebastian's reaction every time Jinn came around. He turned the water on in the shower and peeled off his soiled clothes. The warm water slid over his skin, washing away the dirt and grime. The water turned a dark rust color as it circled the drain.

After scrubbing and toweling off, he returned to the room to check on Sebastian, who was still sleeping soundly and likely would until morning. Jasmine was lying in the opposite bed, reading a book. She sat up and regarded Lucas as he stood looking over the child.

"What's on your mind?" Jasmine asked, pulling him from his stupor.

"Nothing. Everything," Lucas said, then sat on the edge of Jasmine's bed.

"Sounds complicated," Jasmine said, sitting up fully and allowing him space. "Worried about Jinn?"

"Yeah," he answered honestly, looking at the floor.

"You really care for her," Jasmine said in a small voice.

Lucas didn't answer right away. He continued staring at the floor, trying to work out the answer before turning to look at Jasmine. Her eyes were shining through her translucent hair, her expression soft and expectant.

"Why are you afraid to answer?" she asked softly, putting a hand on his shoulder.

Lucas released a small chuckle. "I'm not afraid," he said, but then still hesitated.

"Well?" Jasmine prodded.

"Course, I care about her," Lucas said, taking a breath. "I just wish I knew what comes next, y'know?"

"Don't we all?" Jasmine responded with a slight smile.

"I dunno how much longer I can stay here," Lucas said, wiping his face with his hand.

"What do you mean?"

"Something's gonna have to happen so we can feel safe leaving the building. I can't stay trapped here."

"But?" Jasmine pushed.

"But I don't want to leave Jinn," Lucas finished with a sigh.

"Of course you don't," Jasmine responded after a breath. "So . . . what?"

"I think . . ." Lucas paused. "I think that as soon as Jinn recovers, we need to figure out what we have to do to get out of here."

"What if she don't want to?" Jasmine asked.

"Well . . . I guess." Lucas paused again. "We'll just . . . I dunno. It won't matter if she doesn't survive the night, anyway."

Jasmine's eyes widened a bit, but she just moved a hand over to Lucas's shoulder and squeezed softly.

"I need to sleep," Lucas said and stood up and crossed over to where Sebastian was asleep. His eyes trailed toward the door to the adjoining room before thinking better of it and just curling up in the bed next to Sebastian, who immediately snuggled into his arms without waking up. Lucas smiled at the child and closed his eyes.

"G'night," Jasmine said and turned off the light. She was answered by Lucas's soft snoring.

Chapter 42

Pain

Gasping machines and the constant drip of IV fluid penetrated Jinn's ears as her eyes fluttered open. She was quickly blinded by the searing pain in her left arm. She tried to move but her entire left side was broken and bruised, and there was a pinch in the top of her chest. She slowly angled her head to look down at herself. She was completely naked except for a scraggly blanket that had been haphazardly thrown over her. She used her right arm to push it down to take in just how bad the damage truly was. She found a small tube running into her chest just below her left collarbone. There was also a small incision that had been stitched just underneath her rib cage. The focal point of the pain was still in her left arm. She moved the blanket again and lifted her arm. Her eyes failed to focus on the cauterized stump that ended just below her shoulder.

She started to sweat as the realization she was no longer whole settled around her. She was missing her entire fucking arm. The memory started to flood back to her—the tornado, the climb to what should have been safety, the column shifting and crushing her. Calling Pseudo, losing consciousness. *Lucas.* She attempted to take a deep breath but couldn't. Her heartbeat sped up until the machine next to her began to beep in protest. She reached over with her right arm and knocked it to the floor, startling Pseudo who had been dozing on a nearby bed.

"Jinn, you're awake." Pseudo rushed across the room to her bed where she was still trying to process the pain and missing limb.

"Yeah, not sure I wanna be," she answered through clenched teeth.

"Who's fucking up my equipment? Shit's hard to come by," Dr. Brinson complained as he entered the room and took in the knocked over heart monitor. "Oh, it's you." He pressed his lips into a thin line and looked down at Jinn.

"What happened?" Jinn said slowly trying to bite through the pain.

"Remember the tornado?" Brinson asked as he pulled out a syringe and gauged the dosage before sticking it into the tubing connected to her IV.

Jinn was finally able to breathe as the pain dulled. "What'd you give me?" she asked.

"Acetaminophen."

"Acetaminophen doesn't block pain like this," Jinn countered.

"Mine does," Brinson responded with finality.

"I remember, sort of, but what's wrong with me?" Jinn asked again, her words slurring slightly as the pain medication worked its magic.

"Well, collapsed lung, broken ribs, busted ankle, internal bleeding, and, well . . . that." He gestured toward her missing arm.

"Did you even try to save it?" Jinn accused.

"No," he responded. "There was no point."

212 | J. D. MARCEY

"Why would that be the first choice y—" Jinn started before Pseudo put a hand on her shoulder.

"You would have died if I hadn't handled the other stuff first." Brinson rolled his eyes.

"The arm was toast, Jinn," Pseudo said trying to calm her down. Brinson was picking up the monitor that was still screaming its protests at Jinn's elevated heart rate and blood pressure. "Besides, I'll make you a new one."

"I—You—What?" Jinn spluttered. She glanced back and forth between Pseudo and Brinson, who just shrugged.

"He said he could do it," Brinson said without looking at her.

"It's going to be awesome. I can even figure out how to equip the taser." Pseudo was smiling.

Jinn just stared at him, her mouth agape. She eyed Brinson for confirmation that Pseudo was being irrational.

"He said he could do it," Brinson repeated with a shrug.

"I'm not a fucking avatar," Jinn shouted at them both. "You don't get to *equip* me with shit."

"So . . . no taser?" Pseudo said before Jinn threw some medical instrument at his head. She had no idea what it was, just that it was within reach. Brinson growled at her.

"Where's Lucas?" Jinn snapped.

"I told him I'd call as soon as you woke up," Pseudo said, pulling out his phone.

"How long've I been asleep?" she asked as Pseudo tapped the screen to open the call.

"Three days," Brinson said. "You were in and out for a while until I got the pain controlled."

Jinn sat back and tried to cross her arms, which sent a jolt of pain as well as a spike of rage. Of course Pseudo would miss the obvious struggle and consider her pain as a challenge to build something better and more effective.

"Lucas's on his way," Pseudo said, stepping up to her bedside again.

Jinn's relief at the statement was quickly overtaken by

apprehension. "Is he bringing Sebastian?"

"Doubt it," Pseudo answered. "Jasmine's there."

Jinn looked down at herself. She was still naked, and her skin was mottled with bruises and welts from her injuries, not to mention the stitches from her surgeries. Her eyes moved over to the missing arm. The end was covered in bandages, though they were discolored and dirty. Brinson moved over and began to unwind them. She could see the purpling near the end of the stump and had to close her eyes. Brinson continued until she could feel the cool air around the end. It felt wrong, like her brain couldn't process where the nerve endings had been severed. She forced her eyes open to see the dark purple cauterization. Her eyes started stinging with tears. Brinson sprayed a foul-smelling solution all over her arm, turning the skin a strange shade of yellow, and then wrapped the end again. He never met her eyes through it all.

"Given the shit condition you were brought to me in, I did a great job patching you up," Brinson said with a matter-of-fact tone, still without looking at her.

"Nothing else that could've saved the arm?" Jinn whispered, tears threatened to fall at any moment.

"No," Brinson answered, finally meeting her eyes. "But if you need someone to blame, go ahead and put it on me. Sometimes it makes it easier to get through."

Jinn furrowed her brow. She understood his words, but she couldn't figure out why he said it. It was like he was being nice, but that couldn't be right.

"Besides, we've already designed the prosthesis, and you are gonna be happy with it." Brinson smirked, and Jinn had to stop herself from slapping him.

"Y'all are so sure that I'll be just fine without my fucking arm as long as I get some sort of mechanical upgrade?" Jinn said through a clenched jaw.

"We know you will," Brinson said, pursing his lips.

Jinn's nostrils flared and she growled, as no words fit the

response.

"The fact is that you no longer have a *fucking arm*, and you don't have a choice but to be fine without it," Brinson said, a smirk playing at his mouth. "Or you can be fine with a prosthesis. Either way you're going to survive, and you're too pig-headed to wallow in self-pity."

"Wellll . . ." Pseudo countered.

"You seem awfully sure of that," Jinn retorted.

"I am sure of that, Jinn," he said, turning away from her to throw away the used bandages. "Despite what you think, I notice things."

"Can I at least have my clothes?" she grumbled, unable to argue.

"Got 'em," Pseudo said, handing her the usual leggings and black shirt. Dr. Brinson had to assist her with putting them on, but once she was dressed, she felt a little better. Though the smallest things were a challenge when she only had the use of one arm.

Lucas's voice carried into the room just before he stepped through the door. The tears that had been threatening finally came full force when she laid eyes on him. He crossed the room but didn't say anything, just stroked her hair and smiled. Using his thumb, he tenderly wiped the tears from her cheeks.

"Hi," she finally said.

"Hey," he responded, his own eyes wet with tears. "I thought I'd lost you."

"You should know better," Jinn said, attempting to lighten the situation.

"I should've," he answered, then leaned down and kissed her deeply. He pulled back when she grimaced, her sutures pulling uncomfortably.

Pseudo was watching their interaction and smiling slightly.

"What?" she asked, frowning.

"It's the first time you've expressed affection in front of me," Pseudo said. "It's cute."

Jinn found another medical implement to throw at him before he ducked out of the room.

"Jinn," Lucas started then took a deep breath.

"What is it?" she asked, suddenly nervous. She spiraled through all the things that he could possibly say—it was too much, he was too attached, he couldn't be with an amputee, he was unhappy.

"Never mind, focus on recovery," he said.

"You can't do that to me," Jinn chided, masking her fear. "Whatever I think for you is going to be worse."

"It's not important," Lucas answered, stroking her hair. "Just worried about our future."

"What about it?" Jinn pressed.

"I heard Pseudo's already building a prosthesis for you."

Jinn snorted as her panic quelled at the distraction. "Yeah, the little asshole is enjoying my lost arm. He's probably disappointed it wasn't a leg."

Awkward silence stretched over them before Jinn finally prodded. "Lucas, what are you worried about? I want a better future, too."

"We can't hide in the Clermont forever," Lucas said, averting his gaze. "But we can figure it out later."

"What'd you have in mind?" Jinn asked.

"That's the problem, I've no idea," Lucas said, taking Jinn's hand. "Like I said, we will figure it out." He paused, then locked onto Jinn's eyes. "I just . . . I love you."

The breath stilled in her lungs. She knew that she felt the same way, but for some reason the words stuck in her throat. She started to fight for air, her eyes spilling over again.

"You don't have to say it, Jinn," Lucas said, offering her a reassuring smile. He squeezed her hand.

"But?" Jinn pushed.

"But I want a future, and I want Sebastian to have a future."

"Okay," Jinn said, "but you want it to be *our* future?"

Chapter 43

Recovery

Jinn groaned as her phone buzzed next to her. She eyed it warily. Pseudo had spent two weeks repairing it after the tornado, but in the few days she'd had it back, it still acted possessed from time to time. To be fair to Pseudo, he expended most of his energy on the prosthesis. She had not seen it yet, but she could tell he was excited about it. Despite the situation, Jinn was always amazed at Pseudo's abilities. She picked up the phone and was surprised to see Juniper on the other end of the call.

"Hey Jun," Jinn answered, Juniper's face popping up on the screen. "How are things?"

"That's a loaded question," she responded. Juniper appeared tired, even beyond her advanced years.

"Everything okay?" Jinn asked.

"Not really," Juniper answered. "Do you know where Sebastian is?"

The air went still around her. She had not heard from Lucas since he had left the night before. Pseudo was supposed to be coming this morning, but she had not heard from him yet either. She suddenly became very apprehensive. "Not specifically, no. What's up?"

"Did you know Xandar was offering a reward?" Juniper asked.

"What?" Jinn asked, thoroughly confused at this point.

"I don't know all the details, but NOMAD has been targeted a lot lately by random groups who were supposedly looking for Sebastian. The garrison has managed to thwart most of them, but they just keep coming," Juniper answered, her voice filled with annoyance and a hint of satisfaction.

"What do you mean?"

"They keep trying to sneak past the boundary. There have been about seven attempts so far. Two of them almost tricked the council into letting them in, and the others tried to slip past the borders unnoticed. Nothing has worked yet," Juniper responded.

"Damn," Jinn said. "Something you need from us?"

"I tried calling Lucas, but I couldn't get through," Juniper said. "The last group who tried to get in suddenly called the whole operation off, claiming that Sebastian had been found."

"When?" Jinn asked.

"Yesterday."

"I'll try to make some calls," Jinn said. "I've been out of the loop for a while."

"Are you not staying with Lucas?" Juniper's brows furrowed.

"Ah, yeah but there was a . . . an accident." Jinn held the phone further away so that Juniper could see her missing arm.

"Oh my god, Jinn. Are you okay?" Juniper's face contorted between shock, sympathy, and guilt, which forced Jinn to stifle a giggle.

"I'm good, Jun," she answered, chuckling. "Well, I mean,

considering."

"Shit, Jinn, I'm sorry," Juniper said, shaking her head. "What happened?"

"I was trapped under an overpass when a tornado came through," Jinn answered, trying to sound flippant. "Pseudo and Lucas got me out, and thanks to a new doctor fr—er . . . acquaintance, they saved my life." She lifted her eyes as the door opened, and Pseudo came through holding what appeared to be an iridescent metal arm and a slight smile. "Pseudo's here." Jinn glanced up and spoke to Pseudo. "It's Juniper."

Pseudo's face broke into a grin. "Hey Juniper," he said, leaning over the bed and into the camera's view. "Check it out." Jinn suddenly saw Pseudo as a small child showing off his artwork to a doting grandmother.

"Is that for Jinn?" she asked.

"Yeah, how cool is it?" Pseudo was obviously quite proud of his work, much to Jinn's annoyance. She wished he could be a little more sympathetic to the fact that she had to lose an arm to provide him with the opportunity.

"You will both have to come by and show me once all this mess is sorted out," Juniper said in typical grandmother fashion. "Do you know where Sebastian is?" she asked Pseudo.

"Right behind me," Pseudo answered. Jinn lifted her eyes to find Lucas and Sebastian coming into the room.

"Oh good," Juniper said. "Keep a close eye on him for me."

"We will make sure to," Jinn answered.

"Well, I will let you get back to recovering. Call me if you need anything," Juniper said.

"Hi!" Sebastian called when he recognized who was on the screen.

"Hey bug," Juniper answered.

"You wanna speak with Lucas?" Jinn asked.

"Sure, real quick," Juniper answered.

Jinn handed her phone over to Lucas, and they exchanged pleasantries. Juniper explained what she had been told about

Sebastian, and he took the call to another room while Pseudo and Brinson examined the prosthesis.

After a few minutes Lucas returned looking worried, but he quickly dismissed it as Pseudo showed off his handiwork. The piece was a work of art. It gleamed like titanium, and each mechanism served a distinct purpose. Aside from the material, it was anatomically similar to a human arm, with each socket, joint and muscle meticulously placed.

"It's made from the titanium alloy that was used on Exodus," Pseudo said proudly. "It'll work with your shoulder to maneuver like a physical arm, but check this out." Pseudo pushed aside a small pad that served as the bottom of the palm. "I modified your taser to fit here. You'll be able to shoot plasma blasts like Iron Man."

"Iron Man?" Lucas asked.

"You don't know Iron Man?" Pseudo lifted an incredulous eyebrow.

"I guess not," Lucas said squeezing the bridge of his nose. "Is that one of the sci-fi people that you're always on about?"

"One of 'em, yes," Jinn answered. "You should really read my books."

"Trust me, I'm trying." Lucas chuckled. "You have a lot." Lucas glanced over at Jinn, hoping she would appreciate it as much as Pseudo.

"True," Pseudo said. "Still, he's awesome." He was positively giddy. "It's close to impossible to break, but it is light and flexible." He pointed to the shoulder cap. "This'll go on over your shoulder almost to your collarbone, but you'll be able to move easily once you get the hang of it. It responds to touch and pressure. Once you get it, you'll be more capable of delicate surgery than Dr. Brinson."

"How long will it take to learn?" Lucas asked Pseudo.

"I haven't the slightest idea," he answered. "Depends on how bad she wants it and how much she practices."

"Uh, hello? She's right here," Jinn said with irritation.

"Right, sorry. I haven't the slightest idea. It really depends on how bad you want it and how much you practice," Pseudo said, a smile playing at the corners of his mouth.

"Really?" Jinn raised an eyebrow. "How long is this going to take?" Jinn implored with annoyance.

"It'll only take a minute to show you how it works, but I dunno how long it'll take to get the hang of it. I've tried to mimic the major muscle groups so that it will feel natural, but the more delicate movements will take a lot of practice."

"Put it on me," she directed as Brinson walked in.

"Wo-ow," Brinson said, eyeing the metal arm. Pseudo immediately launched into all the work that he had put into it. Jinn did her best to ignore them as Brinson removed the bandages and then covered the stump with a protective layer of latex. Brinson and Pseudo worked together to maneuver the prosthesis into place, and Jinn jerked in discomfort as it clamped down onto her shoulder and around what was left of her arm. It wasn't painful, but it was wrong. She took a couple of deep breaths and fought the creeping irritation that threatened to make her lash out at them—that made her want to take it off and throw it. She had to adapt. She had to get through it.

Once it was in place, Jinn began to work through the movements. The basics—up, down, left, right—were simple enough and responded easily to her cues. But things like opening and closing her hand or stopping movements before going too far were difficult. She completely knocked over the table next to her bed while trying to reach down and to the left. Brinson's laughter didn't help.

"Be patient with yourself," Lucas said, putting a hand on her right shoulder. "You've got this."

"I know." Jinn took a breath and tried again, this time without knocking anything over.

The noise had gotten Sebastian's attention, and he watched Jinn with enormous eyes. She smiled at his innocence. She found herself thinking that maybe this wouldn't be so bad, but she knew it was going to be a long road ahead.

Chapter 44

Outside

Lucas was lying on the bed listening as Sebastian struggled to get a bag of cookies opened. Lucas gritted his teeth in frustration. Jasmine had gone down to the gym, and Jinn was back at Dr. Brinson's working on physical therapy. They'd left him alone with Sebastian, as usual. The toddler was letting out little grunts of frustration as he fought with the stubborn bag. Lucas kept his eyes closed. Eventually Sebastian's grunts turned into yells, and Lucas finally rolled over and snatched the bag from Sebastian.

"Here," he snapped as he handed the bag back to Sebastian. The child's eyes turned watery, and his lip started to protrude, and Lucas immediately regretted his actions. Sebastian was just a toddler after all. "I'm sorry, buddy," Lucas said softly, picking Sebastian up and setting him down on the bed next to him. He put his arm around Sebastian in a comforting gesture, and Sebastian calmed. He snuggled into Lucas's side and started munching on his cookies.

Lucas's eyes swept around the room. His frustration had been growing in the last couple of weeks. Jinn was doing well learning how to use her new prosthesis, but ever since he told her that he loved her, she had only reinforced her walls. When he'd first said it, he was certain he could be patient with her. After all the trauma she had been through, it only made sense that she'd be hesitant. But at what point did patience become enabling?

He stroked Sebastian's curls, then the boy got up and threw his now empty bag into the trash can. He smiled back at Lucas, proud of his accomplishment. Lucas smiled reassuringly at him and took a deep breath. He loved Jinn; he knew that, but he was ready to climb the walls of this place. He just wasn't sure if his patience was going to hold out much longer. He couldn't spend his life hiding from Xandar, and it was no way for a child to live, either.

There were voices out in the hallway. He recognized one as Jasmine's, but he wasn't sure about the other. He tried to make out what they were saying, but it was unintelligible. Then to complicate things further, Sebastian started singing along with whatever game he was playing on Pseudo's old tablet. Lucas got up and walked to the door, straining to hear what was on the other side, when the handle turned, and Jasmine came into the room.

"Jazz!" Sebastian yelled and ran to her, wrapping his little arms around her legs. She squeezed him before kneeling at his level.

"How are you, Sebastian?" Jasmine asked with enthusiasm.

"I had cookies," he smiled and then pointed at the trash can. "And threw all my trash away." He beamed with pride.

"Nice job!" Jasmine responded, giving him a high five.

Lucas watched their interaction with a slight smile. Jasmine and Sebastian had become close. She spent as much time with him as Lucas, if not more. Lucas considered this for a moment before asking her, "Who were you talking to?"

"My brother," Jasmine answered, standing up and patting Sebastian on the back. "Don't worry, he don't know about Sebastian." She smiled at Lucas. Her hair was damp with sweat, and her skin was glistening. Her pale eyes were misty, but she had been gaining weight and strength since Jinn had given her the antibiotic. She was still small and seemed fragile, but not nearly as much now. Her skin had gained a beautiful golden glow, and her ash-blond hair was now brilliant, almost iridescent. As she smiled, Lucas realized that she was very beautiful, in a sweet, sort of angelic way. He smiled back.

"Loud as he was singing, he was probably hard to miss," Lucas said, teasing.

"True," Jasmine reached down and ruffled Sebastian's hair. "Your turn?" she asked, indicating the door.

"Yes, I need it," Lucas said and pulled on his sneakers. Jasmine plopped down on the bed next to Sebastian and started asking him about the game he was playing on the tablet. Lucas closed the door behind him and headed to the gym.

When Lucas returned an hour later, he found Jasmine and Sebastian still snuggled together on the couch playing with the tablet. Jasmine was natural in this maternal role, which piqued Lucas's curiosity. She barely knew the boy, yet she had already developed a closer bond with him than Lucas or Jinn. Jasmine glanced up at Lucas and smiled.

"Have a good workout?" she asked.

"Yeah," he answered. Sebastian started trying to draw Jasmine's attention back to the screen.

"Just a minute, buddy," Jasmine said, extricating herself from the couch. "You okay?" she asked Lucas.

"Yeah," he answered. "Thinking."

"About what?"

"I don't wanna stay here," Lucas said slowly, as though the words were difficult to get out.

"What do you have in mind? Jasmine asked, directing his

gaze from the floor to her.

"Dunno," he responded. "I'm climbing the walls. I don't know the last time Sebastian went downstairs, much less outside. I'm not serving a purpose other than Jinn likes having me around, and I'm not even sure how true that is."

"I get that," Jasmine said, putting a hand on his shoulder. "But Jinn cares about you a lot; she's just . . . I dunno . . . tough?"

"Tough fits," Lucas said with a huff.

"She needs time," Jasmine said.

"Why are you defending her?" Lucas asked, furrowing his brows at Jasmine.

"I don't know," Jasmine said with a shrug. "I get it, I guess—that inability to open up out of fear. She's been through a lot."

"Didn't think you were that close," Lucas said.

"I mean, we're not, but she accepts me warts and all," Jasmine said with a slight smile.

"Not sure what you mean, but okay," Lucas responded.

"Most people would've taken one look at an addict like me and sent me packing, understandably so. We are notoriously unstable." She cocked an eyebrow, seeing if Lucas would object. "It was probably curiosity initially, and then I helped connect her with Brinson. Even though that almost went sideways, she still let me stay. I've grown very fond of Sebastian. I dunno how I would handle it if I were to be put out now. It's a constant fear. But Jinn's never treated me as less than trustworthy. I appreciate that."

"Have I made you feel otherwise?" Lucas asked.

"Course not, but we're talking about Jinn right now. You, Jinn, Pseudo, I'm lucky to've found my way to you, even though the road was rough."

Lucas smiled slightly and dropped his gaze. "I worried there was gonna be drama between you two."

Jasmine chuckled at that. "The potential was there," she said. "But that's why we work. We both see our own insecurities for what they are, and we don't blame each other for them."

"That sounds very mature of you," Lucas said with a grin. "But doesn't solve my problem. I'm trapped, and who knows how long before Jinn and Pseudo are going to be able to actually do anything about Xandar. If it's even possible."

"Fair," Jasmine said. "But what's the alternative?"

"Well, we could leave," Lucas said with a shrug. "We could start over somewhere else, hopefully somewhere source doesn't have a mortal hold."

"I don't think Jinn and Pseudo would be up for leaving," Jasmine answered.

"They were ready to join NOMAD."

"That makes sense, though. They know NOMAD. Life would be better there." Jasmine paused. "Just to up and leave though? There's no guarantee that we would survive the trip, much less another city. Birmingham's a war zone, and Nashville has been taken over by the Numerians and their fanaticism. Women aren't allowed to walk down the street without a chaperone. I guess we could go west, but none of us have any idea what life is like in that direction."

"Jinn and Pseudo don't have to come," Lucas said, dropping his gaze to the floor.

"So just you, me, and Sebastian, a happy little nuclear family?" Jasmine asked with a little more sarcasm than she had intended.

"Well . . . I, I mean . . ."

"Listen," Jasmine said, sitting him down on the couch and taking a seat on the other side of the toddler, who immediately snuggled deeper between the two of them, his eyes never leaving the tablet. "I can't pretend it doesn't sound tempting." She gazed down at Sebastian, and her eyes went misty. "But what I know is that things are never that easy. Despite my um . . . apprehension . . . about being second choice to Jinn, where would we go? What would we do? How would we even get there?"

"I have the bike," Lucas offered, knowing how ridiculous it

sounded. Jasmine just lifted her eyebrows at him.

"You're getting cabin fever. I get it," Jasmine said. "But storm season is mostly past, and there's a park about two blocks over. I've never seen anyone there, so it should be safe. What do you think? Wanna go on a field trip? Clear our heads?"

"Sounds great," Lucas said, then pulled in a deep breath.

"Sebastian, wanna go outside?" Jasmine asked. His eyes finally lifted from the tablet screen, and he squealed before tossing the tablet to the side and starting to jump up and down.

Chapter 45

Close Call

They made the short walk in silence. The mostly abandoned buildings loomed over them like ancient sentries. The air hummed with the distant buzzing of generators in the few occupied rooms nearby. Jasmine and Lucas were hyper aware of their surroundings, constantly watching and listening for potential dangers. Sebastian was his usual chatterbox self, ready for the next adventure. Lucas met Jasmine's eyes and smiled softly. She had changed from her workout clothes to a pair of jeans and one of Jinn's T-shirts. The shirt was big on her, but it only added to her ethereal quality. Jasmine smiled back and turned her focus forward as the playground came into view.

Sebastian immediately became excited, tugging Jasmine's hand to hurry her forward. The playground was old but still in fair shape, though the bright colors had faded and most of the sign's lettering was worn away. Despite Sebastian's protests, Jasmine made him wait while Lucas checked the ground and equipment for anything that could harm the boy. Finding the equipment sturdy enough, he signaled Jasmine to let Sebastian run free. The child immediately took off toward a pirate ship with a slide down one side.

Lucas stepped back over to where Jasmine stood watching Sebastian squeal and struggle his way along a rope bridge.

"Well?" Jasmine asked, looking up at Lucas.

"We needed this," Lucas responded. "All of us."

Jasmine smiled, but their gaze didn't hold for long before their eyes began moving again, constantly searching for danger. After a few minutes, they started to relax. There was a small bench nearby, and Lucas indicated to Jasmine, silently asking if she wanted to sit. Sebastian started calling for her before she made it.

"Be right back," she chuckled, turning back toward the playground while Lucas settled onto the seat. The open air was heavy with moisture, but a slight breeze kept it from feeling stagnant. At least there was no rain. Lucas pulled a deep breath into his lungs and allowed himself to relax just a little more. He watched Jasmine and Sebastian happily playing on a climbing wall.

A flicker of movement caught Lucas's eye, and his heartbeat quickened. Scanning the area, he instinctively got up and moved closer to Jasmine and Sebastian. As Lucas watched the space between two buildings bordering the playground, a man stumbled out onto the street, his skin a greenish color from withdrawal. His wild glassy eyes rolled around and settled on Jasmine and Sebastian. Lucas edged a little closer before the man took a few stumbling steps toward them. Jasmine turned as Lucas quickened his pace.

"Hey, kid," the man slurred as he approached. His eyes met Lucas's briefly, and he rushed toward Sebastian, reaching out with shaky hands. Lucas broke into a sprint, but in the few seconds it took him to close the distance, Jasmine had pulled Jinn's dagger from underneath her shirt and stabbed the addict from behind. Lucas watched, stunned, as she twisted the blade, and the man dropped in a confused heap. When the man started to moan, Lucas grabbed Sebastian, Jasmine returned the dagger to the sheath around her rib cage, and they jogged back to the Clermont.

The elevator ride to the top floor was tense and quiet. Jasmine and Lucas were both trying to process what had happened, and Lucas still held the boy against his hip. When they arrived, they found Jinn waiting for them, looking particularly peeved.

"Where've you been?" she demanded.

"We took Sebastian to the playground," Jasmine replied, lifting her chin slightly.

"Why would you do that?" Jinn asked, looking back and forth between them. Then she saw the blood on Jasmine's clothes. "What happened?"

"We needed to get out for a while," Lucas answered, stepping between Jasmine and Jinn. "So we took Sebastian—"

"Addicts and thugs are all over looking for him," Jinn snapped, cutting him off. "You know that Xandar put a price on his head."

"Yeah, but—" Lucas began.

"But nothing—" Jinn snapped, then pulled herself back. She took a deep breath. "I'm sorry," she said in a softer tone. She put her hand on Lucas's arm and sighed. "I've been waiting, losing my mind because I had no idea if you were lost or kidnapped or killed. You scared me. Then you come back with Jasmine covered in blood. Are you hurt?" She finally turned her attention to Jasmine.

"We know," Jasmine said from behind Lucas. "We realize how stupid and dangerous it was, but it's all fine now."

"Anyone see you?" Jinn asked, looking up at Lucas.

"Well, yeah," Lucas answered, gesturing toward Jasmine. "She killed him though."

"You killed him?" Jinn's eyes flew wide.

"He was coming after Sebastian," she answered, then pulled the bloody knife from her waistband and handed it over to Jinn.

Jinn eyed the knife with a slight smirk of appreciation. "I guess I underestimated you." She gave Jasmine a genuine smile. "You sure you're okay?"

"Yeah, but I really need a shower," she answered, then stepped into the bathroom.

"I . . . I'm sorry," Jinn said, taking the dagger over to the sink.

"You think we can't function without you," Lucas accused.

"No, I just . . . I'm sorry. I'm more worried about you than I thought," she said, lowering her eyes. "What happened?"

Lucas answered honestly, quickly explaining everything. Jasmine reemerged from the bathroom a few minutes later and sat down next to Sebastian on the bed. He turned and leaned into her, the only indication that anything had gone wrong that day.

"I wanted to see if you would help me get the next batch of antibiotics to Brinson," Jinn said, turning toward Lucas. "I'm getting the hang of this arm, but . . ." she trailed off as she glared down at her titanium arm and flexed the fingers.

"You mind going with her?" Lucas said to Jasmine. "I wanna catch a nap."

Jinn nodded her head once and went to pull Lucas closer, but he resisted. Jinn blinked a couple of times before dropping her hand. She looked at him, but he wouldn't meet her eyes.

"I . . . yeah, of course," Jasmine answered. She shared a look with Jinn. He knew they could sense his unease, but he really needed space to think right now.

Jinn turned to Lucas and put her hand on his chest. "Are you okay?" she asked him, searching his eyes.

"I'm fine," Lucas answered, looking away. "Just frustrated."

"I understand," Jinn said. "It won't be forever, I promise. I'm sorry for being such a bitch." She lifted herself onto her toes to give a quick kiss to Lucas, but he turned, and it landed on his cheek. Jinn's eyes tightened, but she pulled away.

"It's okay," Lucas mumbled. "Just need to think."

"Um . . . alright," Jinn answered, then turned to Jasmine. "Ready?"

"Yeah," Jasmine answered squinting between both Lucas and Jinn.

"Be back soon," Jinn promised, and they turned toward the door.

Lucas sat down heavily once the door was closed behind them. Sebastian scooted himself up on the couch next to Lucas, leaning into his side. Lucas put an arm around the small child and looked down at him. His little eyes were bright and glassy. Even though it was a short excursion, it had apparently been good exercise for the boy, despite how it ended. As if in response, Sebastian let out a huge yawn, and his eyes started drifting closed. *This isn't fair to him*, Lucas thought, looking down at the boy. He had to do something. Anything. This was no life for a child.

Chapter 46

Gone

Jasmine felt tired, but good. Jinn had clearly been surprised by what happened at the playground, but it almost seemed that she was impressed. Jinn was doing well, considering. And the prosthesis that Pseudo made was amazing. Jinn had gained a lot of maneuverability with it already. She only needed minimal help getting the antibiotics sorted into doses and delivered to Brinson. Jasmine had come back while Jinn stayed behind to work on her physical therapy, which was hell according to Dr. Brinson. Jasmine's eyes tightened thinking about him. He was still hostile to her, but to be fair he was that way toward everyone. Jinn managed to face off with him regularly, but neither of them backed down. Jasmine considered that for a moment. She couldn't help wondering why Jinn was so hesitant toward Lucas.

Jasmine took stock of her situation. She was able to see Sebastian as much as she wanted. Even though she still didn't know Jinn very well, she trusted her. And Lucas was clearly bothered by their situation, but was otherwise a genuinely good man. These were people that she had not encountered often in her life. The most amazing thing about all of them is that they were willing to accept her, even after learning all the reasons why they shouldn't. A smile played at her lips as the elevator counted up the floors.

Jasmine couldn't believe her luck. She'd spent her life running. Both her parents had been killed by a roving gang when she was eleven. They were wearing watches. Addicts had killed her parents over *watches*. She'd been forced out on the streets with her brother, but Shawn quickly found himself ensconced in source. At first she avoided it and instead spent her time learning to defend herself. She was small and not particularly strong, so she became quick and lethal. People tended to underestimate her, which she also used to her advantage. The man in the park was far from the first person she had killed, but that was not who Jasmine wanted to be anymore.

At first, it was self-defense. The guilt would drown her, even though she would have been dead otherwise. After a few years, she became bolder, braver. Whether she took a life was no longer a question of survival, but of opportunity. It made her feel powerful, powerful enough that she could use source without consequence. That was a lie she told herself, but it only made her more vicious.

When she found herself pregnant, she changed. She didn't want to be heartless anymore—she wanted to matter. Fighting her addiction and making a life for herself, however meager. Whoever the father was didn't matter. Jasmine was going to make it on her own. Then two days after birth, no reason that could be found, her beautiful, perfect son died in his sleep. Within days she was an even worse monster than she had been before. That is, until she met Lucas.

It was darker than usual when the doors opened on the

top floor. The electricity might have shorted out. Even if it had, they could always move floors. It was very quiet. Jasmine paused after stepping off the elevator. It was *really* quiet. Admittedly, it was late, but something was wrong.

Her skin tingled as she slowly approached their suite. The door was slightly ajar, and her adrenaline spiked. She pushed the door open the rest of the way and found the suite completely empty. Lucas's things, Sebastian's toys, everything was gone. A notebook sat on the counter in the kitchen, open to a quickly scrawled note.

Jas,

Sorry, but I can't continue to keep Sebastian (and myself) captive in this hotel any longer. If we step out the door, we immediately become targets, and there is no telling how long it will take Jinn and Pseudo to fix the situation if they can even do it. I'm taking Sebastian to Nashville. I wish you would have come with me.

-L

Her eyes scanned the note again, and then again. She set the notebook down, and her eyes searched the empty room. This couldn't be real. She picked it up and read it again, then threw the notebook across the room and sprinted toward the elevator. Smashing the button repeatedly, she couldn't stand there and wait, so she darted toward the stairwell. The door clanged so loudly that it popped her ears as she shoved her way through it and started taking the stairs at a perilous speed. Blood pounded in her ears. Sebastian was gone. *Gone.* Even if she tried to follow them to Nashville, it was incredibly unlikely that she would ever be able to find them. She cursed Lucas. He knew how much she cared for Sebastian, and how much Sebastian had come to care about her. *How could he just leave?*

She sped down the stairs to Pseudo's room and pounded on the door. When there was no response, she pounded again, shouting Pseudo's name. After a second, she heard movement, and Pseudo pulled open the door slightly.

"They're gone," Jasmine shouted, pushing the door open and shoving past Pseudo to pace around the room. She panted after her sprint down the stairs. Her blond hair fell around her face in knots, and her eyes were wild and watery.

"What? Who's gone?" Pseudo said, visibly shaken at the sight of her.

"Sebastian and Lucas," she shouted, before grabbing the edge of Pseudo's desk and straining to control her emotions.

"Where?" Pseudo asked.

"There's a stupid note saying Nashville," she said, closing her eyes. "How could he do that? Why would he take Sebastian from me?" She sat down heavily on Pseudo's bed and put her face in her hands. Her shoulders started hitching with sobs.

"So, what do you wanna do?" Pseudo asked, eyeing her warily.

"I want Sebastian back!" Jasmine shouted, piercing Pseudo with her blue eyes.

"Okay," Pseudo said and moved over in front of his computer and started typing.

"Okay? What do you mean okay?" Jasmine asked, breathless.

"I have a tracker on Sebastian," Pseudo said calmly, his fingers flying across the keyboard.

"You have a tracker on . . . wait . . . When did you put a tracker on Sebastian?"

"When we first got here," Pseudo said. "I figured there's a good chance that he could be taken or wander off, so I put one behind his ear."

Jasmine blinked in surprise. "Do I have one?" she asked absently, touching the skin behind her ear.

Pseudo turned and raised an eyebrow.

"You know what, never mind. Where's Sebastian?" Jasmine said, leaning over and looking at Pseudo's monitor.

"Still with Lucas," Pseudo answered. "Looks like they're

moving fast."

"Can we go after them?" Jasmine asked. "How do you know he's with Lucas?"

Pseudo raised an eyebrow again.

"Okay," Jasmine responded to his implication. "Where?"

"Best bet is to wait until they stop. They've got a head start already, but if we lose track or connection, we'd have both of you lost," Pseudo offered.

"I can't just sit here," Jasmine said, tears forming in her eyes.

"Okay, take these," Pseudo handed Jasmine his AR glasses and a small device that reminded her of a simpler version of their phones. "They're connected to Roxanne, so they'll update the coordinates periodically, but they're not reliable. If we lose signal . . ."

"I'm willing to risk it," Jasmine said with conviction.

"I'll program it to follow them," Pseudo showed Jasmine how to activate the device and turn on the geolocator. He typed in the coordinates, and the dot popped up in Jasmine's field of view with a number indicating how far they were. Then, he connected an earpiece to her phone.

"Wait," Pseudo said, looking at his computer screen. His voice had a faint echo as it came through the earpiece.

"What is it?" Jasmine asked.

"They've separated," Pseudo said, making Jasmine's heart drop. Sebastian was alone now. There was only one reason why Lucas would leave him. Jasmine knew that much.

"On it," Jasmine said and headed for the door.

"Take the roadster," Pseudo said, tossing his keys. Jasmine snatched them out of the air and rushed out the door. She headed for the garage, where the roadster was parked, and jumped inside. She took in all the specially modified controls on the dash and was momentarily overwhelmed.

"Pseudo, how do I drive this thing?" she called out, hoping their communication link was open.

"Big button on your right, push it," he responded in her earpiece. She pressed the button, and the familiar vibration of the engine pulsed to life.

"Okay," she said. "Now what?"

"The lever next to you, switch it to forward," Pseudo coached. "Keep your foot on the brake."

"Okay, I'm good," Jasmine said, taking the steering wheel.

"Go get the youngling," Pseudo said.

Chapter 47

What Have You Done?

Jasmine approached the location where Lucas's tracker had last pinged, looking for any sign of him. She pulled the roadster to the side of the street and climbed out, checking her phone. She had not received anything from Pseudo, so Lucas should still be in the area. There were mostly broken-down buildings surrounding her. This part of Atlanta had been abandoned for decades. The nearby university was once a hub for scholars leaving on Exodus, but even the last of their faculty had left several years before.

She could just see the tops of the CDC buildings to the north, and steam was spouting from one of them. Jinn had mentioned that Xandar was using them for source production, and it certainly looked as though they were active, unlike the rest of the area.

Jasmine followed the flashing green dot in her view. It read that she was only a meter away. Then she saw him. He lay in a crumpled heap against the wall of a dilapidated storefront, his clothes disheveled, and his hair was tangled and matted with blood. She rushed over to him, fell to her knees, and felt for a pulse but found nothing. She attempted to see if he was breathing, but again nothing.

"Pseudo, what do I do?" Jasmine practically screamed into the air.

"Nothing. He's dead," Pseudo responded.

"You sure?" Jasmine said, her voice hitching. She was beyond angry at Lucas for taking Sebastian away from her, but she knew that he did not deserve this. He was only doing what he thought was best for the child.

"Trust me, Jas," Pseudo said softly.

"Shit, no. No!" Jasmine yelled and attempted to shake Lucas's lifeless body.

"He was shot, Jas," Pseudo said. "See the hole in his temple?"

Jasmine glanced down. Seeing what Pseudo was talking about, she started to sob. "He didn't deserve this."

"I know," Pseudo said softly.

"What're we gonna tell Jinn?" Jasmine asked, stroking Lucas's matted hair away from his face.

"I don't know," Pseudo said, "but we've got to find Sebastian."

Feeling numb, Jasmine made her way back to the roadster, this time heading toward Sebastian's tracker. As she approached the location, the phone vibrated next to her. She picked it up, swiping quickly to answer.

"Hey." Pseudo's face popped up on the screen, but the image was choppy, and the sound was cutting in and out.

"You have an update on Sebastian?" Jasmine asked.

"Sort of, you should—near—" Pseudo's image froze. "I lost his—I think there is some interference coming from the C—"

"Pseudo, you're very choppy," Jasmine said squinting at the phone as though that would clear up the connection. "Sebastian is at the CDC?"

"Yeah, last—I had—nal," Pseudo answered, his face distorted. "I can't get any signal once h—there, I doubt the phones wi—either." His face froze completely.

"Pseudo?" Jasmine shook her phone as though that would unfreeze Pseudo's face on her screen. "Pseudo—" she shouted again as the screen went dark. "Damn it," she muttered to herself. She shoved the phone in her pocket and looked around. She could see the curved buildings of the CDC rising at the end of the road, but she had no idea how to get in there or where she should even look.

Jasmine glanced back at the roadster and began to walk. The buildings loomed over her. Cables from enormous generators snaked into the sides of several buildings, but none of them were running. The sign at the entrance appeared clean and maintained, a stark contrast to the surrounding areas. The curved glass buildings intimidated her. There was no way that she would be able to find Sebastian in this labyrinth.

Fighting the panic in her chest, she worked her way around to the back of the buildings and found clean but mostly empty parking structures. Footsteps echoed around her, amplified by the concrete. She ducked behind a barrier then recognized the figure walking toward her.

"Shawn?" Jasmine said, emerging from her hiding place.

".Jasmine," Shawn responded, his eyes darting all around him. He was blitzed. Disappointment weighed heavily on her.

"You seen Sebastian?" Jasmine asked, latching on to her brother's arm.

Shawn started backing up toward the building. "I don't . . . I dunno what you're talking about," he stammered. Jasmine's blood ran cold.

"What've you done?" she asked, tears welling in her eyes.

"I got the reward; you can't take it," words spilled from Shawn's mouth as he tried to pull away from her.

"You think I give a shit about a reward?" Jasmine hissed.

"Where's Sebastian?" She shoved him to the ground, surprising herself with the violence.

"Took 'im to Xandar. I got the reward—" Shawn shouted, cowering on the pavement. His recent blitz effectively clouded his mind.

"Where. Are. They?" Jasmine shouted again, putting her hands on Shawn's shoulders.

"Main building," Shawn whimpered, pointing toward the central structure in the compound.

She shoved him to the ground, disgusted. She hated him in that moment and recognized the reflection of herself, or who she used to be. This only furthered her resolve. She would find Sebastian and make sure that Xandar and all his sycophants were punished.

A key-card lock sealed the entrance. Forced to look for another way in, she finally noticed a small open window on the third floor. The face of the building was sheer, but she knew she could shimmy up along the corner and then probably reach the window. A deep breath settled her nerves, and she prayed no one was in that room. Gripping the tiny lip of rubber molding, she pulled herself upward. Slowly, she used the protruding edges of the windows to inch her way up until she could see into the exposed room. It was empty, but there was a strange smell— a heavy chemical odor, like bleach and something else.

Her toes barely gripped the edge of the window frame, and she stretched her arm toward the opening. It was just beyond the tips of her fingers, so she braced her knee against the building and leaned further, still not quite reaching it. She returned to her position at the corner and reevaluated. Reaching up, she found a ledge just wide enough for her to hook the tips of her fingers. She swung her leg over and knocked the pane askew, which allowed more space for her to squeeze through. She edged over, put her leg in the window, and shifted her weight. Closing her eyes, she let go. As she tumbled through, a sharp burst of pain shot through her arm, and she landed heavily on the floor.

A small trickle of blood ran down her hand where she had scraped her arm on the corner of the window. Her eyes followed the trail of blood that dripped onto a floor already covered in it. Panic flooded her, but the blood wasn't hers; it was dried out and tacky. It dawned on her what the scent was that lingered beneath the heavy cleaning chemicals. Decay. From what she could gather of the floor, and the smell, something—or more likely someone—had died violently in there and was left for who knows how long before anyone came along to clean it up. Her heart started pounding, and bile rose in her throat. She needed to get out before she retched.

A door on the opposite side of the room opened out onto a railed walkway that wrapped around the inside of the building. The rooms and offices sat on the outer perimeter, leaving the inside open down to the lobby. The place was clean, and there was electricity running throughout, but she did not see any signs of life. There had to be someone there somewhere, however. An elevator dinged to a stop across the walkway, and her breath froze in her lungs. Without thinking, she ducked into a restroom.

It was clean, and the lights bright and steady. The floors were pristine as well. Jasmine couldn't remember ever having been in a building this well-maintained. Footsteps echoed outside the door, but faded into the distance. Apparently, whoever it was did not need the facilities. Her attention turned toward an enormous mirror hanging behind the sinks. It was also pristine; age and decay had not managed to creep into this one's reflective ability.

As the footsteps retreated, she peeked out the door to find the corridor empty once again. She kept her body pressed against the wall and tiptoed down the corridor until she reached a door marking the stairwell. The door creaked as she slipped through and climbed to the next floor. It was clear, so she continued her ascent. Her blood froze when she spotted a person in the corridor of the fifth floor, talking into a cell phone. She tried to slip past him, but he entered the stairwell just as she made it to the door. He simply gave her a curt nod before scuttling down the stairs. A sigh of relief escaped her as she pushed upward to the next floor.

The door to the stairwell was yanked open, and her eyes widened in both shock and relief when a small familiar voice cried, "Jazz!" Before she could process what was happening, Sebastian's small arms wrapped around her legs. Jasmine scooped him up and gasped as she came face to face with Xandar, followed by two extremely large bald men.

"Hello Jasmine," Xandar said coolly. "I was not expecting you."

"You know me?" Jasmine pulled Sebastian protectively to her side, placing her own body in between that of Xandar and Sebastian.

"I know who you are. Your brother told me all about you."

Jasmine took a step back and curled herself around Sebastian as though she was preparing for a fight.

"Stop stressing. I'm not gonna hurt the kid," Xandar said with a flippant wave of his hand.

"What do you want then?" Jasmine asked, fighting to keep her expression neutral.

"I don't really care what happens to the kid, but I can't let it get out that he's been found," Xandar said.

"What are you talking about?" Jasmine asked, her muscles tensed and prepared to run.

"Ugh, I don't have the patience for babies," Xandar continued. "He seems to like you—so whatever. You can stay."

"Stay?" Jasmine spat.

"He *is* my son," Xandar said, tension building in his voice.

"You don't care," Jasmine retorted.

"You're right, but he serves a purpose," Xandar said with a smirk.

"What purpose?"

"Wouldn't you like to know?" Xandar said with a laugh. "Take them to the basement. Don't worry, it's not permanent. Just 'til I'm done with NOMAD."

Sebastian clung tightly to Jasmine as they were herded toward the elevators by the enormous men. Even if they weren't armed, there was no way Jasmine could overpower them, especially with Sebastian. She begrudgingly acquiesced to their prodding and stepped onto the elevator.

"Smart girl," Xandar said as the two giants stepped onto the elevator behind her. They turned and pressed a button labeled B2 before swiping a key card, and the doors closed, leaving Xandar behind. Jasmine watched the man slip the key card into his back pocket. The top of a similar card poked out from the back pocket of the other man. She closed her eyes and silently apologized, then pinched Sebastian's little leg.

"Ow!" the child cried and started squirming.

"What happened?" Jasmine asked innocently, allowing Sebastian to slide down to the ground and bump into the man in front of him. Sebastian started squirming and prodding at his leg where Jasmine had pinched him, while she slipped the card from the man's pocket and palmed it before picking Sebastian up again. When they reached the basement, Sebastian and Jasmine were pushed off the elevator and left. Jasmine put Sebastian on the floor and studied the walls around the elevator doors, noticing with dismay there were no buttons to call it back down. The floor was entirely square, with a small restroom on one side, a couple of cots, and no stairs. The floor was metallic and shiny, and the ceiling was solid. Jasmine guessed that it used to be some sort of clean room, especially considering the multi-stage ventilation system that went out through the walls.

They were trapped.

Chapter 48

Necessity

"Fuck," Jinn growled as she dropped the pencil yet again. Dr. Brinson rolled his eyes then stared at her.

"Just concentrate," Brinson said, bored.

"I am," Jinn said through clenched teeth. Again, she reached for the pencil with her new prosthesis. She managed to pick it up, but then it snapped in half. "Damn it." A knock sounded at the door, drawing both of their attention.

"Who the hell's that?" Brinson sighed.

"Probably Jasmine bringing my bike back," Jinn answered as Brinson walked out of the room. She reached into the tray again and picked up one-half of the broken pencil. She raised it to eye level and smiled, then it fell from her fingers. She clenched her metal fist, noticing that she would be able to crush just about anything with the new arm. "Goddammit."

"Y'know, cussing and shouting isn't helpful," Brinson called out as though he was chastising a toddler. He came back with a worried Pseudo trailing behind him.

"It makes me feel better," Jinn snapped.

"I'm sure," Brinson answered with another roll of his eyes. "I think we are done for the day."

"I've almost got it," Jinn said, looking at the broken pencil in the tray.

"Whatever, don't take the medical expert's advice. Do what you want, just don't be mad when you die," Brinson said with a huff.

"I definitely won't be mad if I'm dead," Jinn said, standing up from the bed. She went to stretch and accidentally hit herself on the forehead with the prosthetic arm. She had to fight not to respond to the snickers coming from Brinson and Pseudo.

"You are both assholes," Jinn said.

"Don't care," they responded in unison and then grinned at each other like fools.

"Look, you've got the major movements down. The rest takes practice," Brinson said in the most supportive tone he could muster. Which wasn't much.

"I know," Jinn answered, attempting to pick up one of the pencil's pieces between her metal thumb and index finger.

"Sit," Pseudo said quickly. He would not meet her eyes.

"What happened?" she asked.

"Just sit," Pseudo responded. His voice was firm, the jovial connection with Brinson evaporating.

Jinn flared her nostrils while Pseudo silently battled against her defiance. Finally, she perched on the edge of the hospital bed.

Pseudo took a deep breath and tried to make eye contact but could only manage a moment before looking down at the floor again. "Lucas is . . ." Pseudo began before taking another shaky breath. Jinn leaned in toward him, her heart racing. "Lucas is gone." Pseudo said with finality.

"What d'you mean?" Jinn asked. "He left?"

"He tried, but he didn't make it very far. Someone got to

him." Pseudo finally met Jinn's eyes. "They shot him and took Sebastian."

The room tilted around her. It couldn't be real. Surely Pseudo was mistaken. There was some other explanation. Lucas couldn't just be gone. The frustration of her physical therapy was instantly washed away, replaced with fear and dread. "What . . . what happened?" Jinn managed through tight vocal cords.

Pseudo relayed what he knew, and she stared at him for a minute, trying to grasp the situation. Brinson was helpfully silent. Jinn's throat closed and her chest tightened. "Have you heard from Jasmine since?" she finally managed.

"No, I lost all signal once she went into the CDC complex."

"You're sure this is Xandar?" The edges of Jinn's vision were turning red.

"You have a better theory?" Pseudo asked. He was finally able to meet her eyes, holding her gaze for a few tense seconds.

"Okay, we go get them," Jinn said through clenched teeth.

"You don't need to go anywhere," Brinson said, looking at her arm.

"Yeah, I do," Jinn responded. "I'm not gonna sit here while they're in danger."

EXODUS MISSED | 249

Chapter 49

Source Lab

"Why're you insisting on tagging along?" Jinn asked Pseudo as they approached the main curved buildings of the Centers for Disease Control.

"'Cause I can't get a signal, you're almost dead, and you're still learning your prosthesis. You need a babysitter," he responded coolly. Jinn rolled her eyes in response before he continued. "It's not safe if you're recognized. Xandar's not going to fail to kill you again."

"You're not exactly on their friends list," Jinn chided.

"Yeah, but they don't know what I look like," he responded.

"Xandar does," Jinn scoffed, but he was right.

"You know what these buildings were before Exodus?" Jinn asked.

"Not really," he answered honestly. "Once upon a time they each had a specific purpose, but when people started leaving, they consolidated and rearranged almost yearly."

"Do you know their layout?"

"No."

"Really?" Jinn's brows lifted in surprise. He would generally have the whole place mapped out and a plan of action already formed and in mind.

"It's been empty for a while. At least that's what everyone thought," Pseudo said.

Silence weighed heavily as the curved glass buildings loomed over them. They tried to appear casual with quick, confident strides while scanning their surroundings. Pseudo nudged Jinn and gestured toward some large box trucks as they pulled through an alleyway a couple of buildings over.

"Should we check it out?" Jinn asked raising her eyebrows. Pseudo just shrugged.

The pounding thrum of enormous ventilation fans was deafening as they worked their way around to the back and found the truck bays. Jinn put her hand out to stop Pseudo when voices echoed off the embedded concrete.

She knelt low to the ground and peered over into the sunken bays. Two men stood just outside one of the roll-up doors that was still slightly open at the bottom, both men holding vaporizers and talking. One of them complained about leaving the door open before they both ducked through and closed it behind them.

After a moment's hesitation, Jinn tried to slip over the edge to drop the few feet into the recessed bay, but her grip on the edge didn't hold and she fell awkwardly, landing with a thud. She quickly ducked behind some stacked pallets, holding her breath to keep from cursing at her bruised hip, and pride. Pseudo slid down behind her, checking to see if she was hurt.

The metallic rasp of an opening bay door caused both of them to freeze where they crouched. They watched one of the box trucks pull through the door before it started to lower again. Jinn gave Pseudo a knowing look. He shook his head fervently, but she bolted anyway, darting under the falling door. Pseudo was close behind her, and as the door slammed shut, they found themselves standing in a large warehouse, squinting through the dim lighting. The ventilation fans vibrated the entire building, and Jinn strained to hear anything above the noise.

Sliding along the wall, they worked their way around the warehouse until they found a set of double doors. They peered through the glass, the windows brightly lit compared to everything else, but their view was obstructed by thin plastic sheeting. Jinn tried the door and found it unlocked. She carefully pushed the sheeting aside, pushing her head and shoulders through. She immediately pulled her head back out and closed the door, turning to Pseudo with wide eyes.

"What? What is it?" Pseudo whispered.

"Could you kill the power to this building?" she whispered urgently.

"Probably. Why?" Pseudo's brows furrowed.

Jinn's mind raced. She had seen about six people, all in full Mission Oriented Protective Posture gear. Every inch of them was covered in white plastic material, complete with helmets, masks, and air tanks. The enormous ventilation, the lack of outer lights, the extreme gear, she was certain of it.

"This is where they farm source. It has to be. If we kill the power, then we kill the environmental control, and we kill source," Jinn said.

Pseudo's face broke into a grin. "Yeah, I can do that."

"They aren't here," Jinn said, adrenaline pumping. She knew Jasmine and Sebastian would not be in this building. "We need to find them and then shut this bitch down."

At that moment, the door swung open in between them, and two men in MOPP suits pushed through. Pseudo's eyes went wide before one shouted, "Who are you?" with a voice muffled by the hood.

"Shit," Jinn said then bolted back toward the bay doors with Pseudo close behind her. She was annoyed that—thanks to her injuries—Pseudo was keeping up.

The men were shouting behind her, their words garbled by the hoods, but they were not able to move quickly in the bulky suits. Pseudo and Jinn covered the distance to the bay doors and found a button on the wall. Holding her breath, she reached out to hit it with her left hand. Her mouth dropped open when the arm went completely through the box that housed the button, but her surprise was quickly quelled when the doors did not open.

"Hit it," Pseudo hissed at her.

"Hit what?" she shouted back.

"Hit the damn door," Pseudo said and hit the flimsy garage door with his fist, causing it to wobble.

Jinn glanced back and forth between Pseudo and the door before putting all her strength into her new arm and slamming her fist into the metal. Her eyes burned as the door tore completely off the rollers and afternoon sunlight poured in.

"Holy shit, Pseudo! What'd you do?" Jinn shouted as they both took off through the bay area and disappeared in between the buildings.

"Told you you'd like it," he shouted back breathlessly and smiled. The smile melted from his face when sirens blared from overhead.

"I think they noticed us."

"Yeah, I'd say so." Pseudo nodded toward a group of men with large muscles and vacant faces sauntering toward them from the main building.

"Get behind me," Jinn ordered Pseudo, who didn't hesitate. Jinn stormed forward with Pseudo in close pursuit. She tightened her metal fist as she approached the first of the security detail. A rush went through her; they were holding batons and not guns. The lead guard swung his baton high, and Jinn caught it with her metal arm before shoving him backward into the rest of the group. He flew with enough force to knock over several of the men. As they scrambled to get up, another of the men attempted to rush her, but a punch sent him flying into the building several feet away. Jinn grinned as the rest of the men started to circle around them, but none were willing to approach. She glanced at Pseudo, who was holding her old modified taser.

"Couldn't let you have all the fun," he said with a wink.

"Course not," Jinn responded. Pseudo should be scared, at least that is what Jinn believed, but she could never tell with him. The maniacal grin on his face implied that he was having a great time. She had only a moment to think about it before the security went for the attack. Pseudo tagged one with the taser, leaving him convulsing on the ground while Jinn launched another with a quick uppercut. The two of them remained back-to-back while dodging batons and sending security guards flying. Jinn hit one in the ribs, and the crunch turned her stomach, but he went down. Even though the taser still required time to recharge, Pseudo managed to hit at least one other guard with it. Soon, Pseudo and Jinn were breathless and surrounded by the bodies of eight security guards in various states of injury.

Pseudo directed Jinn's attention to the main building, where they were now close enough to see the staircase through the glass walls.

"What?" Jinn asked, trying to figure out what Pseudo was getting at.

"Look—" he shouted, pointing. The frenzied thumping of someone pounding on the glass drew her eyes toward the two figures in the stairwell.

Chapter 50

Run

Jasmine sat next to Sebastian on the rickety cot and scanned the room around them for the thousandth time. She had searched the place thoroughly, and the only possible escape that she could fathom was through the ventilation. But without knowing where the shafts led, she was hesitant to take Sebastian through them. Little Sebastian knew that things were bleak. He wasn't able to smile and be his usual happy self, and had taken to clinging to Jasmine as much as possible. He was sleeping at the moment, but Jasmine knew that as soon as she attempted to stand, the toddler would wake up terrified. Anger flashed through her, and she took a breath to cool herself. She had to think.

The elevator doors opened to reveal one of Xandar's bodyguards coming in with a covered tray of what she assumed was food. Sebastian pulled closer to Jasmine and buried his face in her leg. The man grunted at them and walked past to place the tray on the small table and turned back around.

"Where's the key?" he asked Jasmine, his voice like rocks scraping against each other.

"I dunno what you're talking about," she said through her teeth. She stood, angling herself between the thug and Sebastian.

"You took it. Where is it?" the man repeated, stepping closer to her.

Jasmine squared her shoulders. "I don't know what you're talking about," she repeated. The man towered over Jasmine, trying to intimidate her. Jasmine's heart pounded furiously. She scrambled around for anything she could use as a weapon.

Suddenly, an alarm started resounding through the room, eliciting a strangled cry from Sebastian, who stood up on the cot and wrapped himself around Jasmine. The man's eyes lifted to the ceiling as though he could see the cause before turning toward the elevator.

Jasmine pushed Sebastian from her, much to the dismay of the child, and quickly snatched the plate from the table. She rushed toward the monster, shattering the plate across the back of his head. This stunned him momentarily but did not incapacitate him. Jasmine used the shard left in her hand and jabbed it into the side of his neck. The guard slapped a hand to his wound. Jasmine watched, horrified, as blood began pouring through his meaty fingers. With his other arm he reached toward her, breaking her out of her shock. She knocked his hand away quickly, grabbing Sebastian, and ran into the elevator. She hit the button to close the door as the man attempted to push himself off the ground. He stumbled toward them, gaining momentum. Jasmine pushed Sebastian behind her and closed her eyes. As the doors sealed, the enormous man thudded against them.

Jasmine's vision swam as the elevator began to rise. She could feel Sebastian pulling on her hand. He was saying something, but she couldn't bring herself to focus. She finally forced her gaze downward onto Sebastian's worried expression.

"Jazz, are you hurt?" he asked in a tiny voice.

Jasmine blinked a couple of times. Her eyes slowly trailed down to the hand that was holding on to Sebastian's and saw blood trickling down. She picked up her arm and stared at it, though it took a moment before she could comprehend what she was seeing.

"Jazz?" Sebastian's tiny voice pulled her back. She kneeled to look Sebastian in the eyes.

"No, baby, I'm not hurt," she said, fighting to keep her voice steady. "You're safe with me." Sebastian put his arms around her neck and whimpered softly. Jasmine pulled him into a deep hug as the elevator doors opened to the ground floor.

Sebastian slapped his hands to his ears as the alarm's pitch reached piercing levels. Jasmine picked him up and headed for the door. She tried to push it open, but it wouldn't budge. She swiped the card, but the reader did not respond. She guessed that the alarm must have locked everything down.

Jasmine's mind started to clear. She needed to find a way out. She tucked Sebastian into her side and went for the room with the open window. Hopefully, no one had thought to close it. She raced up the stairs, and as she turned the corner, movement outside caught her attention. She stopped, sliding Sebastian down to the floor, her arm trembling from carrying his weight. Through squinted eyes she could see a group of people, though she couldn't tell who or what was going on. Her eyes went wide as she watched a body launch through the air, but Sebastian was the first to recognize what was happening.

"Jinn!" Sebastian yelled, pointing through the glass.

Holy shit, that is Jinn, Jasmine thought. Pseudo was running next to her.

"Sebastian, bang on the glass," Jasmine said, pounding with her fist and leaving red smears of blood.

"It'll break," Sebastian whimpered.

"That's okay. We want it to break so we can get to Jinn," she said quickly, then continued pounding on the glass and shouting at the top of her voice. Sebastian added to the mayhem, and it was just enough to catch the attention of Pseudo, who pointed, causing Jinn to stop in her tracks. They both altered course and headed to the building. Jasmine scooped up Sebastian and ran back to the bottom floor.

The four of them reached the doors simultaneously, and Jinn started trying to pull them open.

"It's locked down," Jasmine shouted, unsure if they would be able to hear her over the alarms.

Jinn reached back and hit the glass as hard as she could, causing it to reverberate but not crack. Jasmine pushed Sebastian behind her, stunned by the amount of force Jinn was able to put behind the punch. Jinn was preparing to try again when the alarm suddenly went silent. Pseudo touched her shoulder as the four of them looked around warily.

Jasmine tapped the key card to the pad, and the light flashed green, allowing her to open the door. Sebastian rushed out, openly crying, and wrapped around Jinn's legs.

"Hello *again*, Jinn," Xandar's voice carried from behind Jasmine. She watched as the color drained from Jinn's face. "Your new addition works for you," Xandar said, gesturing to her arm.

"Get 'im out of here," Jinn hissed and pushed around Jasmine, forcing them both out the door.

Jasmine hesitated, looking back and forth between Jinn and Xandar.

"Go ahead. I need him to disappear anyway," Xandar said, dismissing Jasmine and Sebastian with a flip of his hand. "Pseudo stays."

"Get him somewhere safe," Jinn murmured to Jasmine, blocking the door.

"I'll be back," Jasmine said, determination turning her blue eyes to ice.

"I know," Jinn said, smiling at her.

"How touching," Xandar said, rolling his eyes. "But I'm starting to get impatient." He pulled a silver revolver from beneath his jacket and turned it on Jinn. She immediately shut Jasmine and Sebastian outside and turned toward him, her metal arm glistening, but it was not moving as smoothly as it should have been.

"Damn it," Pseudo's voice barely carried through the glass. "You must have busted some hydraulics."

"We're going upstairs. I've a proposition for you," Xandar said, waving the revolver. "You can come willingly, or I can put the gun in your back." Xandar glanced at Jinn's determined expression. "Or I can just shoot *him*," he said, glancing over at Pseudo.

Jasmine's breath caught in her throat as she watched Jinn and Pseudo begrudgingly walk toward the elevator. Pseudo was nodding reassuringly at Jinn, and he smiled when Jinn furrowed her brows. *That's weird*, Jasmine thought, then she turned, picked up Sebastian, and headed back to the roadster.

Chapter 51

Proposition

Jinn and Pseudo stepped onto the elevator followed by Xandar, still brandishing his revolver.

"Where'd you get that?" Pseudo asked Xandar, indicating the weapon.

"Museum in Germany," Xandar said, his voice arrogant and prideful. "Jinn, you were with me when I bought them, remember?"

"They still work?" Pseudo continued as Xandar pressed the button for the top floor.

"They were decommissioned a long time ago, but I was able to restore them," he said. "Well, have them restored."

"They reliable?"

"Quite," Xandar answered with a smile.

"How many do you have?" Pseudo continued.

"More than you," Xandar answered, shutting down the conversation.

The elevator arrived at the top floor, and the doors slid open to reveal a long hallway with offices set up on each side. They followed Xandar down the hall to the far wall, which was floor-to-ceiling glass. Xandar paused and gazed out the window over the campus. He turned, opened the door, and gestured for Pseudo and Jinn to enter the room.

Once inside, they found themselves surrounded by monitors, each recording a different part of the campus. Jinn recognized the lobby area they had just left. The monitors on the far wall were recording the warehouse where she and Pseudo had discovered the source operation.

"Paranoid?" Jinn chided as she glanced from monitor to monitor.

"Nah, addicts are quite predictable," Xandar said with an air of authority that made her skin crawl. She shuddered.

"So, what do you want?" Jinn asked. "You've tried to kill me twice, so I can't imagine it's the pleasure of my company."

"You're right, but I'm impressed by your . . . resilience," Xandar said with a slimy smile. "You've proven to be clever and formidable, and I need your expertise."

Jinn furrowed her brows, unsure where this was leading.

"I've heard that you've been busy creating a counter medication for source," Xandar said, turning to face her directly.

"And?" Jinn asked, figuring there was no point in trying to deny it.

"This could be profitable," Xandar said, "and helpful for convincing NOMAD to reestablish trade with us."

"What're you talking about?" Jinn asked, growing impatient.

"I've been trying to get NOMAD to reopen trade, but they are terrified of source. We need their food production, but they refuse to even talk. If they see that I am making a concerted effort to *fix* the problem, then maybe they'll listen. I admit they're tougher than I'd assumed," Xandar explained as though this was all common sense.

"You've no intention of fixing anything," Jinn said dully.

"Course not. If people wanna melt their brains, who am I to say no? Turns an excellent profit, but money isn't useful when there's no food. I need resources, so I need NOMAD. I offered the reward for Sebastian with the sob story of how he was kidnapped, so people would attempt to rescue him, and I could see how NOMAD's defenses stacked up. I've been paying everyone who tries, even though they weren't successful. Who knew NOMAD would actually throw him out?" He rubbed his eyes in a mock-crying gesture.

"That's why you needed Sebastian gone," Jinn said, anger heating her cheeks. "You never wanted him back. You just wanted an excuse to attack NOMAD."

"Honestly, I'd assumed that he was dead a while ago, but then we saw you when we went to clean out Maddie's place," Xandar said.

"You're a monster. How can you do that to a child?"

"There's abandoned kids everywhere. What's one more?" Xandar said dismissively.

"He didn't have to be one of them," Jinn shouted, her body trembling with rage. She grabbed the edge of the desk where Xandar was sitting and launched it into several of the monitors. She lunged at him, but her mechanical arm struggled to obey her commands and threw her slightly off balance.

"No, no, no," Xandar said with a placating voice and tilted the revolver toward Jinn's face. "I need you, though. You found a way to farm source in your own lab. We can't move it from the biocenter." Jinn assumed that was the label for the warehouse building.

"Why would I help you?" Jinn hissed.

"Freedom," Xandar said, a smile playing at the corners of his mouth. "NOMAD rejected you, and you'll forever be looking over your shoulder should you stay. You know as well as I that the rest of this god-forsaken country is in even worse shape. If we come to an agreement, then I'll guarantee your safety. I will even include Jasmine and Sebastian." He turned his attention from Jinn. "I could use your help with infrastructure." Xandar's expression shifted. "Where the fuck is Pseudo?"

Jinn scanned the room. Pseudo was no longer in there with them. She grinned. *That bastard*, she thought to herself. "You obviously underestimated him." Jinn began to laugh; she couldn't help herself. Within a few seconds she was laughing uproariously and holding her sides while tears were streaming down her cheeks.

"What the fuck," Xandar said through clenched teeth. He turned to the monitors, searching frantically from one to the next for any sign of the ghost. He grabbed a two-way radio and started shouting into it. The next thing Jinn knew, the alarms were blaring and everything was once again locked down. Jinn laughed that much harder.

"He's gone, Xandar," Jinn chided, attempting to catch her breath. "You won't find him." She began to laugh again.

"I should have known," Xandar turned the gun on Jinn. "Get him back."

"I don't know where he is," Jinn answered, giggling. She pushed the gun barrel away from her. "Good luck."

Xandar grunted and tucked the gun back into the holster underneath his jacket. He picked up the radio again and started barking orders, which were met with affirmations from the other side. Jinn sat down on the floor while Xandar tried to regain control of the situation. With each minute that passed, she could see Xandar becoming more agitated. She started to move toward the door.

"Don't even think about it," he shouted at her.

"You're not going to find him," Jinn said.

"Yes, I will," Xandar growled. "You'd better hope that I do, or you will be the one paying for it."

"Why is Pseudo so important to you?"

"He can keep our power grid up," Xandar said without

looking away from the monitors. "He has to be here somewhere."

"Yeah, I guess source is quite finicky about its environment," Jinn chuckled. "And no one's better than Pseudo at figuring out stuff like that."

"Shut up," Xandar shouted at her, which only caused her to laugh harder.

He continued watching the monitors, looking for any sign of him. "Fuck it. He'll come back for you. I can just wait him out."

"No, he won't," Jinn said rolling her eyes. "He might do something to make it easier for me to escape, but he's not going to put himself in physical danger. You obviously don't know him very well."

"He's come for you before," Xandar spat, his tone accusatory.

"Yeah, not the same. He came *after* you thought I was dead. Trust me, in a physical fight he's less than useless."

"Fuck. Fuck. Fuck!" Xandar shouted as he slowly came to the realization that he was not going to subdue the slippery Pseudo so easily. "Goddamn it—" he shouted then rounded on Jinn who was still sitting on the floor, fidgeting with something on the bottom of her boot.

She grinned at him.

"You know what, you're definitely not worth this much trouble," he pulled the hammer back on the revolver and held it to her face. Jinn blinked, and everything went dark.

Chapter 52

Bring on the Darkness

Pseudo could hear Jinn's raucous laughter coming from the floor above him. They must have realized he was not there anymore. *Xandar should really learn to keep better tabs on his surroundings.* Pseudo chuckled at the irony of Xandar not noticing something in a room designed to keep watch over the entire campus. The elevator shaft yawned beneath him as his weight pulled him downward along the cables. The use of the cables was archaic, but he was glad the building had not been updated in the last few decades. The elevator doors were heavy, but Pseudo was able to pry them apart just enough to slip through to the quiet lobby. He sprinted to the glass doors that led outside the building, and pushed through them just as the alarms began to blare around him. He saw no one rushing toward him, so he stumbled forward and almost tripped when he ran headlong into Jasmine and Sebastian.

"Pseudo?" Jasmine hissed, barely above a whisper.

EXODUS MISSED | 265

"Hey," Pseudo said as he recovered, a smile breaking out on his face. Sebastian was crouched down messing with the grass in between Jasmine's knees. "You were supposed to be getting somewhere safe."

"There were a bunch of goons running around. I figured it'd be safer to hide."

"Ah," Pseudo said, then scanned the area. "You know how to disable a generator?"

"I could figure it out, why?" she asked.

"I need you to bust the generator on that building," Pseudo said, pointing across the lawn.

"Why? Jinn's in *there*," she said, tilting her head.

"Jinn'll be fine," Pseudo said.

Jasmine pressed her lips together but did not respond.

"I am going to knock out the campus power station, but all the buildings have generators," Pseudo explained. "That building," he indicated the building he had mentioned, "is where they're producing source. Knocking out the power could take down the whole operation, or at least cause some massive problems for them."

"Really?" Jasmine asked. Pseudo nodded. "What about . . ." she asked, tilting her head downward at Sebastian.

"He can come with me," Pseudo said. "I'm gonna hit the solar complex across the street. Hopefully, they don't still have ties to any of the older stations."

"Okay, be careful," Jasmine said. "Meet back at the roadster?"

"Yep," Pseudo answered, then turned his eyes down toward Sebastian. "Wanna piggyback ride?"

"Yeah!" Sebastian squealed excitedly. Pseudo turned around and kneeled so that Sebastian could scramble up onto his back. Pseudo winked at Jasmine. The look on her face told him she found the colloquial gesture strange.

Jasmine took off toward the other lab building. Pseudo watched her disappear around the corner and then turned back to his goal of the solar complex.

"Ready?" Pseudo asked, turning his head toward the child on his back.

"Uh-huh," Sebastian answered. Pseudo couldn't help but smile. He bolted in the direction opposite Jasmine, keeping to the side of the buildings to stay out of sight.

He approached the solar complex, which sat surrounded on three sides by buildings with reflective surfaces on the inner walls. Pseudo could feel the heat radiating from the basin that was dug slightly into the ground. The mirrors worked to concentrate the light and beam it into the basin surrounded by insulation and fencing. He set Sebastian on the ground and instructed him to stay put while he searched the area for the outbound current.

With the solar complexes, the transformers were mostly located underground, but because of the massive amount of heat generated by the mirrors, the distribution control center was located far enough from the site so as not to be damaged. It didn't take Pseudo long to find it. With quick action, he reprogrammed his phone to piggyback off the signal that controlled the distribution center remotely. He hacked in and reprogrammed the signal receiver so that it could no longer be controlled by the on-campus energy director and then sent the command for it to shut down.

Everything suddenly went quiet. Pseudo listened for the mechanical humming of the mirrors inverting themselves so they would not overheat while the distribution control was down. Once the mirrors were inverted, the back-up generators started to kick on, trying to maintain the environmental controls of the labs.

Pseudo knew it wouldn't take long for someone to come and reprogram the distribution center, if they knew what they were looking for. But he hoped his obscure frequency would buy him enough time to damage the biolab beyond repair.

"One more ride?" Pseudo asked Sebastian. He kneeled again

and allowed Sebastian to climb up.

Sebastian's head bobbed up and down with a smile, and Pseudo chuckled.

"Let's go," Pseudo said, then started jogging into the heart of the neighboring university campus where Jasmine had left the roadster. There was not much else he could do, and he needed to get Sebastian safe. A reverberating thunk-thunk-thunk, which he hoped was a very large generator fan being stopped suddenly and violently, echoed from the distance. Pseudo smiled. He had no idea if any of what they were doing was going to have a long-term impact, but it was so much fun to be a thorn in Xandar's side.

Chapter 53

Disengage

Jinn held her breath, anticipating the gunshot that would end her life. She heard a click. Then Xandar started cursing. She opened her eyes to see that the power had shut off to the entire room, leaving it almost pitch dark. Something crashed and clattered to the floor. As her eyes adjusted, she grinned. Xandar's revolver had malfunctioned, and he had thrown it into one of the monitors. Keeping herself low to the ground, she scurried to the other end of the room, putting as much distance between her and Xandar as possible. He was cursing into the two-way radio again, seemingly unable to get through to anyone.

"What've you done?" Xandar accused, striding over to where Jinn had backed against the wall. He towered over her as she shrank back. "Fix it," he roared down at her.

She straightened her shoulders and glared up at him. "No."

"No?" Xandar repeated. "No? You can't tell me no." Xandar

leaned toward her, trying to intimidate her with his physical presence. "You *will* fix this. Call Pseudo off or whatever, but get the fucking power back."

"No," Jinn said again, this time with more strength in her voice. "I was here." She stood up, keeping her back to the wall for support. Her chest tightened in panic, fighting the compulsion to defend herself and make Xandar understand. She was terrified, but she was not going to let Xandar know.

Xandar reached his hand back, threatening to strike her. "Do it."

"No."

Xandar's hand came toward her cheek with surprising speed and force. She moved her arm to block it, causing the back of his hand to clash loudly with the titanium. She could hear the small bones breaking against the metal. She smiled. Pseudo was right. As much as she hated to admit it, she liked her new arm.

As Xandar crumpled to the floor in pain, Jinn started to laugh again.

"Why?" he asked her while cradling his broken hand. "Why are you trying to hurt me?" The pain in his voice was genuine. Jinn was amazed he could possibly believe he was the victim in the scenario. That everything he had done to lead up to this point had been innocent, and Jinn was somehow being unnecessarily mean.

"Are you serious?" Jinn asked. "You tried to kill me. Twice!" she shouted at him.

"You didn't give me a choice," Xandar said, his voice full of remorse as though he believed his own words. Jinn just stared at him with her mouth open. Suddenly she found herself frozen. She was completely perplexed. How do you explain something to someone who dismisses reality when it doesn't fit their narrative? How could she possibly get him to understand?

Abruptly, he launched himself from the floor with a feral yell. She tried to block him, but his momentum bowled her over, cracking her skull against the wall and causing her vision to swim with flashes of light. She pulled her arm out from under her and threw all her weight into it, smashing it across his face. Her control was slipping, and it was only slightly more than a glancing blow, but it was still enough to send him flailing backward. He hit the ground, catching himself slightly, and then stumbled forward, putting his hand to his nose as blood began pouring from it. Then he fell forward, landing face-first on the ground and unmoving.

A loud thunk-thunk-thunk had her reaching out to hold on to something, but the sound was not connected to the main building. Jinn took off down the stairs, and as she rounded the corner of the staircase, saw dark smoke pouring from the biolab. She eyed the glass, then put her fist through it. Luckily the glass shattered, though she was losing more and more range of motion in her prosthesis. She ran toward the biolab and almost tripped over a small person covered in soot and grease, lying in a crumpled heap on the ground.

"I did it," the figure strained to say, waving her hand and forcing a smile.

"What the hell, Jasmine?" Jinn responded, rolling her over and scanning for injuries.

"Pseudo said to disable the generator, so I did," Jasmine whispered. She grunted as Jinn pulled her upright and slung Jasmine's left arm over her shoulder.

"Now what?" Jinn asked, looking around. They could hear the confusion in the lab, people moving things around and trucks being loaded.

"Where's Xandar?" Jasmine asked.

"There," Jinn responded, tilting her head back toward the main building.

"Let's take him out," Jasmine said with a sadistic grin.

"How?" Jinn asked, leaning toward her.

"We'll figure it out," Jasmine said, ducking from underneath Jinn's arm and walking toward the front of the building. Jinn shook her head, unsure if it was a wise idea, but Jasmine was emboldened. Jinn's eyes widened as they trailed up the massive generator housed on the side of the building behind them. There was a lot of smoke and twisted metal surrounding the housing for the turbines.

"How'd you disable the generator?" Jinn asked as they approached the corner of the building.

"I took a piece of railing and threw it in the turbine," Jasmine answered with a smile.

"Wow," Jinn said.

"Yeah, probably not the safest strategy but effective," Jasmine said with a grin and leaned around the corner.

"You sure you're alright?" Jinn asked as she winced when straightening back up. "Should we go back to the Clermont and regroup?"

"Hell no," Jasmine said. "Let's get this over with."

Jinn was suddenly nervous. She was not sure if Jasmine was thinking clearly. Before Jinn could voice her concern, Jasmine darted from the corner and made her way around to the front of the building.

"Wait," Jinn called and hurried to catch up. "Let's take out the lab first."

Jasmine's watery eyes met Jinn's, registering what Jinn was saying. She nodded her assent and then followed Jinn as they hurried back toward the bays beneath the biolab. Chaotic noise surrounded them as they approached. The sound carried through the bay door Jinn had wrecked earlier. They took stock of their surroundings and slipped into the lab.

There were probably forty people decked out in full personal protective gear. While some were frantically loading boxes into trucks, others were attempting to stop them. Suddenly, Jinn spotted Xandar at the far end of the room. He was shaking and out of breath. He was shouting and gesticulating wildly at two other people. Xandar stood out as the only person in the room without the white MOPP gear.

"Xandar!" Jasmine bellowed. Jinn's eyes widened in shock. She had never heard Jasmine raise her voice before, not even with Sebastian. The force of her yell reverberated through the room. Everyone paused, but when they realized she was focused on Xandar, they resumed their own scuffles.

Xandar raised his revolver and pulled the trigger. The shot went wide as the two people close to him attempted to stop him from using the weapon inside the lab and causing even more damage. Xandar pulled away from the others and took off toward Jasmine and Jinn, his eyes wild with anger. They ran to meet him, closing the distance in the room quickly. Xandar raised his gun again, firing off more shots erratically . At this point, most of the others in the room had ducked out of the way, though they were still trying to keep their hands on the crates full of source. Jinn quickly figured out that they were just trying to get as much as possible and run with it. Loyalty was never something that Xandar could command for long. It was every drug dealer for themself.

"What?" Xandar shouted, throwing his hands into the air. He still held his revolver, though it was empty.

"That a new one?" Jinn asked sardonically, indicating the revolver.

"Fuck you," Xandar spat at her, pointing the weapon. Jinn rolled her eyes because she knew it was harmless.

"You're done, Xandar," Jasmine said. She walked toward him with her hands in a placating gesture. "Just stop."

"Who the fuck do you think you are?" Xandar spat as Jasmine approached. "Why do you think you can talk to me like that? I. Have. The. Gun."

"You have a paperweight that smells like gunpowder," Jinn chided.

Xandar started pointing the weapon again, switching back and forth between Jinn and Jasmine, who was still steadily approaching.

"You need me," Xandar shouted.

"If that's how you see it," Jasmine responded. "Either way, you're done. Stop. Stop coming after Jinn. Stop brutalizing anyone who doesn't wanna do shit your way. *We* can negotiate with NOMAD. *We* can do this without having to control everyone with drugs."

"I'm not controlling anyone," Xandar retorted. "They choose source. All I do is provide it. It's not my fault they're hooked."

"If that's how you see it," Jasmine repeated.

Suddenly things crystallized for Jinn. Jasmine was not bothered by Xandar's misrepresentation of reality. Jinn snorted in annoyance that she hadn't figured this out a long time ago. There was never a point in trying to convince Xandar to see reason. He would never understand. He could never see things her way, from her perspective, no matter how right she was. Xandar was blind to everyone and everything that didn't fit his version of reality.

Xandar reached out to strike Jasmine with the gun, but she easily ducked out of the way. She shoved Xandar forward, and he toppled over, landing heavily on his side. Jinn laughed. She couldn't help it. Xandar pushed himself off the ground and turned his attention to Jinn, lurching toward her. She quickly threw up her arm and knocked him backward. He fell hard onto his ass, growing more and more frustrated. He stood and attempted to backtrack to the people he believed were loyal to him.

"Hey, watch this," Jinn said, throwing a wink at Jasmine. She touched a spot in the middle of the palm on her prosthetic hand, causing a small click. She then straightened her arm and raised her fingers so that her hand opened out. Three short bursts of plasma shot from her arm, hitting Xandar and knocking him to the floor, convulsing.

"Fucking awesome," Jasmine shouted, radiating a momentary beam of joy, quite out of place for the situation.

"Don't tell Pseudo how much I'm enjoying this," Jinn said

274 | J. D. MARCEY

with a grin.

Jinn's and Jasmine's eyes wandered around the room while Xandar convulsed violently on the floor. Most everyone had cleared out, but the two who had been arguing with Xandar were still huddled in the corner. Jasmine walked over to them, her shoulders straight and ready for an attack. They both raised their arms in surrender, though their posture was straight and self-assured.

"What do you want from us?" the first one said, addressing Jasmine.

"Nothing," she answered. "We're shutting it down. All you gotta do is leave."

"What about Xandar?" the other asked.

"He's done," Jasmine answered, looking at Jinn, who had taken her dagger out of its sheath and was standing over Xandar. "Go."

Jasmine walked over and placed a hand on Jinn's trembling shoulder.

"Can't do it," Jinn whispered, clearly struggling.

"You want him to live?" Jasmine asked softly.

"No," Jinn said. "I just don't wanna be responsible for it."

"You—don't—ha—have the—balls," Xandar stammered through his convulsions. Jasmine kicked him.

"I don't have the desire," Jinn corrected. "I'm not afraid of you anymore. Why should I stain my conscience?" She turned away from him and started to put away her dagger.

"Can I see that?" Jasmine asked casually, holding out her hand.

"Huh?" Jinn said, looking down at the dagger. "Yeah," and handed it over.

Jasmine turned it over in her hands for a second, admiring its black and red coloring.

Jinn's eyes widened, and time slowed as she watched Jasmine lean over Xandar, and with a quick, precise motion, slit his throat. Ruby blood poured out, covering the top of Xandar's light-colored shirt and absorbing its way down. Eventually it flowed to the floor and started to pool as his convulsions subsided into stillness. Life left his eyes, and they glazed over, staring into nothing.

"That's for Sebastian," Jasmine said, standing up. She grimaced at a patch of blood on her knee and started to wipe it, but thought better of the action.

Jinn's mind swam. She gaped at how anticlimactic the whole scene played out. Xandar was dead, but all her emotions were still swirling—fear, anxiety, defeat. She was momentarily disappointed in herself for not being able to end it, but she pushed that feeling aside. It no longer mattered. Relief washed over her. She no longer had to live in fear. Sebastian would be safe. It was over.

"My conscience is fine," Jasmine said.

"I . . . Uh," Jinn opened and closed her mouth a couple of times, trying to find words to express her turbulent emotions. After a moment, her breath hitched, and she collapsed into heaving sobs. Jasmine knelt next to her, rubbing her back and stroking her hair.

They stayed in this position for several minutes before Jinn's sobs finally subsided.

Jasmine stood up, one of her knees popping loudly, and pulled Jinn to her feet. "Ready?" she asked softly.

"Yeah," Jinn answered. "Let's go home."

Chapter 54

End of an Era

Jinn was lying on her bed in the Clermont waiting for Pseudo to return from repairing her prosthesis. Her heart was heavy as she looked around at some of the things Lucas had left behind. He hadn't even finished reading her prized copy of *The Time Machine*; the dog-eared page irked her. Emotions battled in her mind—grief, hurt, anger. If he was so unhappy, why didn't he tell her? Her own faults weighed on her. She had not been the most receptive of partners. Her thoughts were interrupted when Pseudo arrived carrying her newly repaired arm. Jasmine and Sebastian popped over from their adjoining room when he arrived.

"I have a question, Pseudo," Jasmine began as they reattached the arm to Jinn's shoulder.

"Yeah?"

"You have a tracker on me?" Jasmine attempted to penetrate Pseudo's confidence with a stare. It didn't work.

"Yep," he responded, finishing up the attachments. Jinn started moving the arm around. She still needed to work on gaining agility in her fingers, but most of the movement was natural now.

"When? How?" Jasmine sputtered.

"It's his way of showing that he cares," Jinn answered for Pseudo. "He doesn't follow you around or anything creepy."

"It's still weird," Jasmine protested. "Where is it?"

"Your shoe," Pseudo responded, looking down at the shoes that Jasmine had left next to the door.

"Bumped her up to shoe already? Nice," Jinn chided, nudging Pseudo.

"What does that mean?" Jasmine asked.

"Shoe is like the top tier of friendship for Pseudo, just short of an implant," Jinn chided.

"Shut up," Pseudo said, pushing Jinn to the side and looking at Jasmine.

"I put trackers on people when I worry I might need to find them. Jinn's had one since college. Sebastian got his when we got here. It's so I can help if anything happens," Pseudo said, trying to play it off like it was nothing. "It came in handy, didn't it?"

Jasmine couldn't argue that point. Without Pseudo's tracker on Sebastian, it was likely that she never would have found him.

"You're okay with this?" Jasmine turned toward Jinn.

"Yep," she answered, pulling her earlobe out to reveal the sub-dermal locater that had been placed there. "You have no idea how many times it saved me."

"Maybe stop doing dumb shit," Jasmine grumbled, realizing she was not going to win this argument.

"Pass," Jinn said and started trying to pick up the book with her prosthetic hand.

"I'm surrounded by crazy people," Jasmine said to no one in particular.

"We can smell our own," Jinn chided, and Pseudo laughed.

Jinn forced a smile as her thoughts returned to Lucas.

"Did you get Lucas?" Jinn asked Pseudo, the air in the room taking on a new thickness. Even little Sebastian stared at the floor.

"Yeah, he's at the crematorium," Pseudo responded, avoiding eye contact. "You should be able to pick him up this afternoon."

"Thanks," Jinn said softly.

"Yeah," was Pseudo's curt reply.

—

Jinn leaned against the railing on the roof of the Clermont, watching the sun set over the city, a plain box filled with ashes sitting by her side. She had spent the last few hours mourning Lucas. Earlier in the evening, the others had come up to say their goodbyes, but now only Jinn remained. Her eyes were red and swollen, and she was exhausted. But she couldn't bring herself to scatter the ashes and go to sleep. She couldn't believe this was all that was left of the man she had begun to love. She couldn't believe he had been willing to leave her behind. She couldn't believe she would never see him again.

Jinn reached over and touched the rough edges of the cardboard. "What the hell, Lucas?" she muttered, her throat thick and heavy. "I was so scared to trust you that I let you slip away. Sorry." A new wave of sobs broke out, and she doubled over.

"Don't be sad, Jinn," a tiny voice said a few feet from her. Jinn opened her eyes to find Jasmine, Pseudo, and Sebastian standing in front of her.

"This wasn't your fault," Pseudo said. "Don't take it on."

"He cared about you so much," Jasmine continued. "He was afraid of messing it up."

Sebastian ran over and wrapped his little arms around Jinn's shoulders. "Don't cry. It's okay." His face was pressed into Jinn's shirt, muffling his voice. Jinn smiled. She couldn't help it.

"Thanks," she said and hugged him back. Sebastian stepped back and latched onto Jasmine's hand. Pseudo picked up the box containing all that was left of Lucas and handed it to Jinn. She moved to the edge of the roof. Roxanne towered above her. Jinn opened the edge of the box and allowed the ashes to slowly drift downward. She watched as they caught on the wind and were carried away. Jasmine came up beside her and slipped an arm around her waist, resting her head on Jinn's shoulder. Pseudo stood close by, keeping Sebastian entertained. Finally, with an aching slowness, Jinn and Jasmine turned from the edge and went back to their rooms. Jasmine offered her something to eat, but Jinn refused. She fell onto her bed fully clothed and was almost instantly asleep.

Epilogue

Rebuilding

"About damn time you showed up," Dr. Brinson barked as Jinn walked through the door carrying a new batch of the antibiotic.

"Show some gratitude, sir," Jinn said with a laugh.

"For what? You working my ass to death? Or not getting me the meds I need?" he quipped, taking the box from her and handing her a box of used needles.

"How 'bout a fancy new fucking facility?" Jinn said, with a snarky raise of her chin.

"How long are you going to remind me of this?"

"'Til you stop using it," Jinn chided.

"Fine, I quit," Brinson said, setting the box down.

"No, you don't," she retorted.

"Damn it," he responded, taking the box and pushing through the double doors into the hospital area. In the three weeks since they'd taken out the biolab, Dr. Brinson had been inundated with people who were looking for anything to quell the withdrawal from source. There was still some of the drug floating around, but it was much more difficult to find. Jinn hoped no one would realize that to make the antibiotic, she had to manufacture it herself.

With Xandar gone, there had been something of a power vacuum within the city, but Jasmine had stepped up to try to maintain order. It had not taken long for people to fall in line behind the woman who had killed Xandar. But Jinn worried what kind of loyalty that really elicited.

The new hospital unit was repurposed from one of the unused CDC medical buildings. This gave Brinson all the medical equipment he could possibly need and access to the tools and machines that he would use for general purposes. Though the main purpose for now was walking the masses through withdrawal.

With the dissolution of the source manufacture, there were some perks. Many people who had taken to living underground, or at least out of sight of Xandar and his cartel, were slowly coming back to the surface. They found people to employ as nurses and security as well as lab assistants. Pseudo had a team working for him to keep the infrastructure running. They had grown the cellular network to cover most of Atlanta with mostly reliable service, and they were able to revive several of the solar complexes so that more of the buildings could have power without having to rely on generators.

They were, however, struggling with resources. The new citizens were reliant on them to provide their basic needs. Jinn had set up a massive lab for producing manufactured proteins, but the process was slow and didn't provide complete nutritional value. Jasmine had taken Sebastian along to help start several rooftop gardens, which would be helpful in the long run. But they were still struggling. With the influx of roving bands of source abusers, it was difficult to keep everyone safe.

After Jinn made her rounds of the labs, she headed back to

the Clermont. Pseudo was waiting for her as she pulled her bike into the garage. He was less pale, and the newfound leadership role he had taken was starting to impress upon his personality. He was standing straighter and had a new air of confidence about him.

"Hey," he called as she swung her leg over the bike and walked toward him.

"Hey what's up?"

"You have company," Pseudo said with a slight smile.

"Who?" Jinn cocked an eyebrow at him. There was still a residual coldness that accompanied the unexpected, but Pseudo gave no indication that she should be worried.

"NOMAD," Pseudo grinned stupidly.

Jinn flexed the fingers in her prosthetic arm and rolled her eyes. "What the hell . . ." she muttered.

It took a while to get into the building. Not long after the group's assault on the CDC, everyone who'd been dependent on the cartel became desperate, and the Clermont had been hit with several attempts at burglary and vandalism. Pseudo installed new security using the hotel's old systems and reinforced the doors with the same titanium alloy as Jinn's prosthesis.

Finally, they made it to the top floor. Pseudo followed close behind Jinn and probably hoped for fireworks. They were greeted by Juniper; her face glowing with a wan smile as she glanced over her shoulder at the three council members seated on Jinn's small couch.

"Can I help you?" Jinn said, straightening her shoulders as she walked past Juniper. She clenched her teeth to keep from saying something she would later regret.

The three council members took in Jinn's appearance, their eyes lingering on her prosthetic arm. Jinn attempted to show off by running her metallic fingers through her hair but ended up pulling it more than she had intended. Pseudo snorted behind her, but she kept her face impassive and hoped the council didn't notice. He shook his head, but, realizing that there were no impending explosions, he drifted back down the hallway.

"We want to extend a truce to the city of Atlanta," Adams said, standing and extending her hand. "We have heard about the progress you are making and would like to open communication between our societies."

Jinn shook the council member's hand, but the expression on her face was puzzlement. "I don't understand why you're talking to me about this," Jinn responded.

"We would like you to be the liaison," Adams said in response.

"Liaison?"

"We would like to negotiate trade, and you would be our point of contact," Adams explained.

"What do you need from us?" Jinn asked, suddenly suspicious.

"Security," Juniper answered for them, a slight smirk on her face. "There have been a lot more people looking to NOMAD for a safe haven, and it is becoming difficult to vet everyone that comes through. We are running into problems that we are unaccustomed to handling."

"Okay. How's it work?" Jinn asked, still standing.

"We will set up a meeting where we will present things that we need, and you can do the same. We will have representatives from the different parts of our society, both the ones that need help and the ones that we believe may be beneficial to you. Hopefully, we can share our ideas and come up with a trade system," Adams explained. The other council members nodded behind her. Juniper waggled her eyebrows—obviously this had been her suggestion.

"Why would I help you?" Jinn asked, finally acknowledging the elephant in the room.

"Because it will be beneficial to everyone, past circumstances notwithstanding," Adams said, obviously struggling to maintain eye contact.

Jinn shook off her annoyance and rolled her shoulders. "Okay," she finally acquiesced. "When?"

"Two weeks. You can decide the location," Adams said.

"Might I make a suggestion?" Juniper intervened. Everyone's eyes turned toward her. "What about the old landing site? That is where we held our meetings fifty years ago. The building is still in good shape as far as I am aware, and it is already set up for us."

"I like that," Jinn responded. The landing site was on the outskirts of the city, connected to the old airport that had stood empty since NOMAD stopped trade with Atlanta.

Juniper smiled and nodded. "It would allow us to use the dirigible again."

Jinn grinned. "Great. Two weeks old landing site?"

"We can all agree to this," Adams said, the others nodding their approval. "Thank you for agreeing and respecting our past choices."

"Didn't say I respected anything. This could be mutually beneficial. If it isn't, then we're done," Jinn answered, her voice cool and confident.

"We will leave you now," Adams said, and Jinn saw Juniper suppress a chuckle.

Jinn tilted her head in parting, and they walked out the door. She saw Jasmine coming down the hall with Sebastian in tow, both covered in dirt. She let out a small chuckle at the sight of them.

"Look!" Sebastian shouted, just a bit too loud, showing Jinn a rock of some sort.

"Cool," she responded with appropriate enthusiasm for a toddler.

"What was that?" Jasmine asked, glancing at the retreating council members.

"NOMAD. They want to open trade," Jinn answered and lifted her eyebrows in a smirk.

"Interesting," she said. "You can explain when we get clean."

"Want me to make some dinner?" Jinn asked.

"God, yes," Jasmine responded with something akin to desperation in her eyes.

"Jinn!" Suddenly Pseudo was behind them. Jasmine chuckled and turned toward the bathroom, waving Sebastian over to get him into a bath.

"What?" Jinn asked, the frantic look on Pseudo's face causing her anxiety to spike.

"My room, now." Pseudo's grin was unsettling. Jinn truly couldn't tell if he was happy or terrified. They raced down the stairs.

She burst into the room, immediately recognizing the Exodus logo on Pseudo's computer screen. Her breath caught in her throat. Her wide eyes swept between Pseudo and the screen and back again. "Is it . . . is it them?"

About the Author

J.D. Marcey (she/her) holds an M.A. in English, an M.F.A in Creative Writing, and is an active member of the Atlanta Writers' Club.

She finds storytelling an immersive method for contemplating the big questions of our shared human experience and is fascinated by the endless possibilities of imagination.

She resides in the wetlands of South Georgia with her husband and three beautiful boys, while a piece of her heart remains firmly in the Pacific Northwest. When she is not writing, you will find her (or not find her) exploring new places or deep within her own comfortable ones.

Author Website: https://www.jdmarcey.com

Facebook: https://www.facebook.com/jennie.d.marcey
LinkedIn: https://www.linkedin.com/in/jennie-marcey-311386143